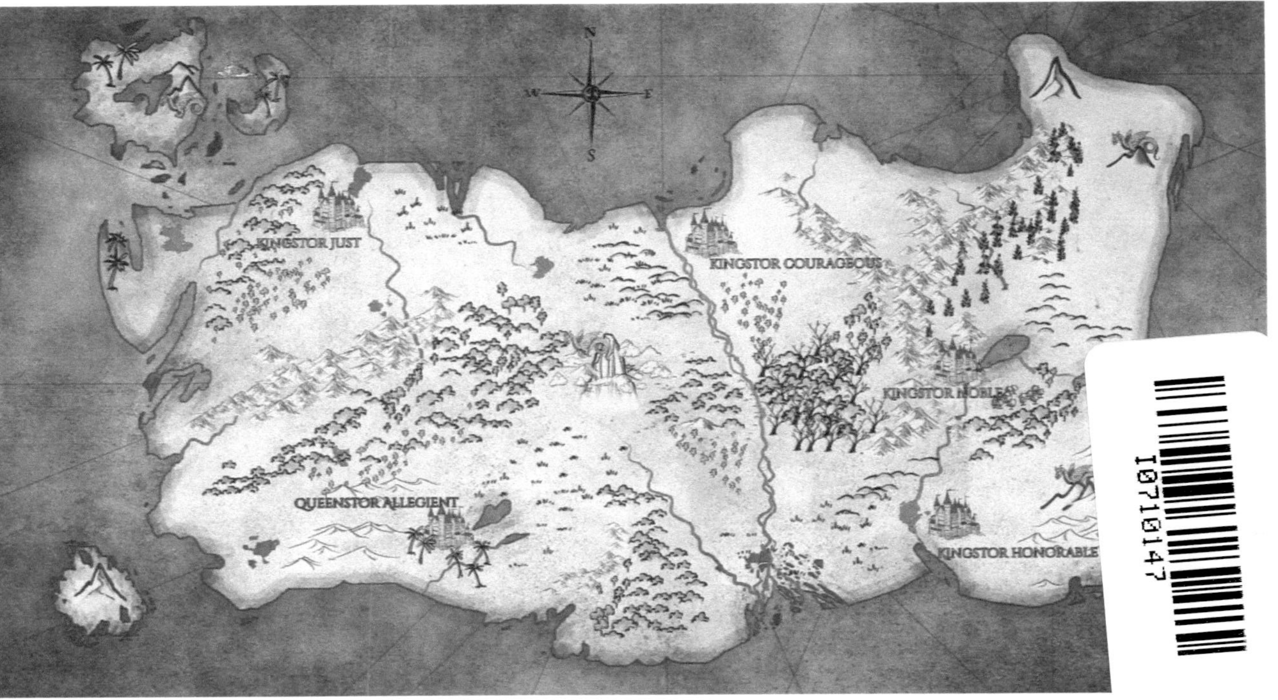

N
W E
S
KINGSTOR JUST
KINGSTOR COURAGEOUS
KINGSTOR NOBLE
QUEENSTOR ALLEGIENT
KINGSTOR HONORABLE
I0710147

THE KRUSIBLE OF AVONOA

THE KRUSIBLE OF AVONOA

HRB COLLOTZI

AVONOA SERIES BOOK FIVE

This book is dedicated to my three F's!
Fans!
Friends!
Family!
To everyone who has stuck with me through this entire
adventure,
Thank you and I hope you've had as much fun as I have!
I love and appreciate all of you!

CONTENTS

PROLOGUE

Like most tragic stories, it all began with two sisters falling in love with one man.

He was an apprentice, training alongside his best friend, to the shaman of the faerie council. While most faeries practiced majik in one form or another, the shaman to the faerie council was the most accomplished of faeries in order to attain the position. To apprentice with him was a great honor.

Two daughters of another council member both fell in love with the young faerieman. The elder sister loved to star gaze – finding peace in the stars, but also glimpses into the future. Using her limited understanding of majik, she found a spell that would enhance her eyes to see the stars better, growing them to twice the size of other faeries'. The younger sister was vain. She only used the most reliable spells to make her hair softer, her lips fuller, her wings shimmer more and other common beauty enhancements.

The young apprentice soon revealed that he was in love with the elder sister and not the younger. Upon learning this, the younger sister sought revenge against her elder sister. So, through deceit and trickery she turned her elder sister into a centaur. Thus, the first centaur was created.

However, the elder sister accepted the change gracefully, glad for the chance to be different from her sister. The apprentice only loved the eldest more for her forgiving nature. The younger sister also selfishly made her own dream possible to take her mother's place on the faerie council, seeing as her elder sister was no longer a faerie. But neither of these circumstances could stave off the younger's desire for revenge, and instead she only became further enraged.

In this season of the faeries, the race actively sought to breed dragons. Since dans, the brown and gray male dragons, had only one heart to break, they often sired only one or two offspring with one of the bright and multi-colored dames. Many faeries experimented through majikal means to replenish the species. But unbeknownst to the faeries, the multitude of spells they created released unbridled majik into the world, the results of which could not be predicted.

One common practice was to separate the dans and dames and only allow mating through controlled and majikal environments. Many dragons, male and female, were adopted by faeries and kept as pets. Because of her mother's high position, the eldest daughter kept a female pet dragon, one often sought after to breed with through majikal means.

Seeing the eldest sister's kind and compassionate heart, despite finding herself a centaur, the young apprentice made a spell to give her pet dragon the gift of speech. Finding her voice, the dragon begged for a specific mate and for her mate to be able to speak as well.

When the two dragons were finally brought together, they expressed their love for each other and produced an egg. When the egg hatched, it was discovered that their precious new daughter could also speak. The gift had been passed along in the species, altering the course of their future.

Ever spiteful, the younger faerie sister discovered the frivolous use of majik and revealed the culprits to the council. Immediately, the council imprisoned the apprentice until they could undo the majik of the dragons' speech. The elder sister learned of the imprisonment and begged the council to free the young faerieman.

However, the council members, including the most accomplished shaman, were not able to reverse the spell entirely. They could reverse the original spell and quell the parents' speech, but not remove the daughter's gift. Finally, the council deemed that the young faerieman must die for the spell to end.

Meanwhile, the humans lived a barbaric life. They fought amongst themselves for land and took each other as slaves. They attempted to force faeries to give over their majikal secrets to use as advantages against other humans, and they often hunted dragons for sport, as a symbol of power. Faeries avoided humans at all costs.

Since the spell of the dragons' speech was so unintentionally powerful and implicated the faeries' ruinous lack of regulations over the use of majik, the council decided to use the young apprentice's death to enact a great spell that would ensure a harsh lesson learned: the spell would confer immediate death on any faerie who spread the truth of the dragons' speech and intelligence to the vile humans. Sacrificing one or more of their own species to ensure no human would ever learn the truth came at an even greater cost: the council would also take a second faerie's life during the process of making the spell. Thus, it was decided that the apprentice must die to reverse the power of his transgression, and the eldest daughter must die to ensure the potency of the great spell.

The mother of the two daughters was a council member but could not agree to her daughter's death, therefore she secretly informed her eldest daughter about the council's decision and helped her escape. She herself then left to warn the humans of the dragons' intelligence and the impending alteration of the species.

She knew she must find a human king she could suffer before she was prevented from speaking the words she wanted to share. Upon entering the kingdom and insisting upon seeing the king on urgent business, she felt the great spell take effect before she could warn them. To cover her real reason for being there, she thought of a ruse and decided she would instead make a grand gesture with an unexpected and powerful gift. She would use the opportunity to help the humans overcome their barbaric ways by announcing the faeries' gift to the humans of the majikal Five Swords of Avonoa.

Then, having no council, family or home to return to because of her presumptuous betrayal, the faerie mother changed her name and lived out her life in solitude as a simple shaman named Shampy.

In the meantime, while hiding from the council's threat to kill her, the elder sister spread the news of the impending great spell among the faeries before it was performed. As word traveled, the faerie population was divided over how to bear it. Half of the faeries chose to attempt a different spell in order to avoid the great spell's effects. And the other young apprentice, best friend of the imprisoned faerieman about to die, discovered that if any faeries transformed into centaurs, they would escape the curse. Thus, half the population of faeries chose to transform moments before the great spell took hold.

The elder sister witnessed the young apprentice's execution from afar, along with the newly gifted white dragon, daughter of the first dragon to speak.

When the young apprentice was killed for his crime, the white dragon and the eldest sister wept bitterly. While crying the white dragon saw visions of the future in her tears. With majik and power in her words she made a great prophecy:

Curse you faeries t'ward every way,
For precious blood you spill this day.
Instead of beauty, true and fair,
Become the monsters your hearts bare.
Until the morn The One shall come,
And you accept your salvation.
For when his heart be made un-whole,
One will die by the life they stole.
Human and dragon accountable,

Unite in ways unimaginable.

Upon hearing the fate of her kin, the elder sister saw Visi's prophecy as justice enough, because she knew there would always be a fate worse than death.

1

DISTORTION

Human. Cold. Soft. Fragile. Small.

The pure black dragon, Hiro, looked down at his claw and heaved a sigh. Still a claw. He looked up at the dripping stones dripping down onto the stone floor of his cavern lair in one of the many floating mountains of the Rock Clouds.

Those should be much farther away, he thought before his mind drifted to the human men he had trained alongside in the Noble army. Squad 3-4, or 'claw' as the common term the men used, were the closest thing he had to friends among the humans, having spent so much time as a human training with them. Hiro had to figure out how to best use his ability to change from dragon to human and back again in hopes of saving both species – or living forever as only one of them.

The men in my claw would laugh at the ridiculous sight of a dragon practicing changing into a human – they wouldn't even be frightened. As he thought it, the ceiling seemed to shrink away from him. He looked down at his hand, covered in soft brown skin. Yes, a hand!

Human, he thought to remind himself how it felt. *Cold air on my skin. Soft flesh wrapping my arms and legs. Fragile bones inside those limbs. Looking up at everything and everyone. Well, almost everyone. Thinking about other humans or dragons helps too.*

He stood for a moment feeling the stone under his soft feet. Those feet had hardened in his weeks as a human, but they still couldn't compare to the comfort of the scaly pads of his dragon claws.

He scrunched his eyes. *Dragon,* he thought. *Hard. Burning. Large. Fierce.*

He looked down at his hand again. Growling inside, he bared his fangs and struck the rock under him with a claw.

A claw.

This is meaningless, he rumbled to himself, *Anna won't take me in either form.*

The moment he thought of her, he felt the cool air brush his skin. Looking down at his hand, he sighed again.

I have to figure this out, he thought, staring at his hand. *There must be a reason for it.*

"Hiro?" Tog's voice called from outside the cave. Tog, his best friend. The keeper of all of Hiro's secrets…except this one.

Hiro bolted on two legs to duck behind a small outcrop in his cavern home, only to fall onto all fours, skitter across the ground and ram the two long horns on his head against the stone wall. Dragon again.

Fear ... anger, he thought, *anger works especially well.* He remembered being angry during his training and feeling the fire burn in his belly. He felt that fire in great detail now and decided he could use that feeling in the future.

Tog, a large gray dragon known for his two toggling eyes like that of a chameleon, landed in the mouth of the cavern. "What are you doing?" he asked with a queer look on his face.

"Sleeping," Hiro grumbled, hoping being woken up would be a good enough excuse for the sour attitude.

Tog seemed to accept the answer with a shrug. "Sorry to wake you, but Prak and I need your help speaking with Rakgar."

"What do you want me to do?"

"Not entirely sure," Tog admitted, "Prak thinks you can help influence Rakgar. Some say he wants any and all knowledge of our efforts to fight the humans while keeping well clear of the action. Which reminds me," he turned one of his toggling eyes on Hiro, "any progress with the *other* problem?"

Hiro shook his head. The 'other' problem was Hiro's own personal assignment to find out who betrayed the dragons to the faeries. Flarote, a tiny, red, bulbous mushroom-like plant grew in many places, most of them warm and moist. A few caves, including Rakgar's lair, grew the little mushroom during most seasons. The ones in Rakgar's lair were used by many in the ruck to heal injuries, even those that a dragon suffered close to death. However, dragons knew to never tell the faeries or humans or centaurs about the fact that flarote could kill them if they ate too many. But one had.

The seemingly harmless plant and information had been used to make a deadly dragon poison which the humans were currently producing and using on arrows to kill dragons. Hiro had discovered this fact a short time ago while imprisoned within Kingstor Noble as the human named Owyn. Anna had helped him escape the dungeon and revealed the treacherous act at the same time. Hiro was tasked to find the culprit.

"I can't find out anything here, among dragons," Hiro said. "To find them I need to be on the surface. Follow their tracks, stalk our enemies and their friends. I need to get out of here."

"But you're still not feeling well?"

Hiro nodded. He had confessed previously to Tog that the fire in his belly, the life of a dragon, had been weak and guttering off and on for some time. What he hadn't told anyone, especially any dragon, is that the same fire sputtered out completely, and continued to do so, every time Hiro turned into Owyn, a human. It had all started shortly after he fell in love and his heart broke for the human woman, Anna. He had been forced to confess his ability to change species to Anna when she helped him escape the castle dungeon. In fact, he often pondered the fact that she had accepted his changing without much reaction, even come to the conclusion of it herself without any explanation.

He still struggled to keep the changes under control and he wasn't sure if he could trust himself on the surface. But he had no more time to practice.

"Will it keep you from meeting with us at all?" Tog asked.

Hiro rolled his shoulder, making sure to feel his powerful dragon body and fire in order to help keep his current form. "No," he said, "let's go."

He knew changing could be difficult, but staying the same was easier. He followed Tog to the edge of the cave and the two dragons leapt into the bright sky.

—

Rakgar's cave was the largest of all the lairs since the dragon ruck had many uses for it. The foremost cavern was so large it could fit more than a hundred dragons, although the ruck didn't often need that capacity. Rakgar – in faerie tongue, leader or king – used it to counsel with the dragons of the ruck he oversaw.

Inside the cavern, thousands of wet dripping stones dripped from the ceilings with mound-like mates of spilling stones jutting up from the floor. Some dripping pairs met in the middle, forming columns scattered in the chambers, many as thick as a dragon's body. Two chambers separated by rock columns led off either side of the central chamber.

In one of the side chambers, along with the ruck's supply of flarote, usually hung meat collected over the summer and autumn and dried by dragon fire. Unfortunately, with human armies surrounding the Rock Clouds as they had of late, hunting had been sporadic and difficult. The danger was that if dragons went too long without eating, the fire in their own bellies would consume them, turning them to embers as swiftly as if someone had slit their throats in the night as they slept.

Beyond the food chamber and hidden around a corner was a small chamber where Rakgar slept. Opposite the food supply, a small tunnel led away from the massive central chamber to Priya's lair but, upon Priya's insistence, neither Hiro nor any dragon he knew of had ever been down it. Most of the other tunnels off the main chamber were too small for any dragon to access. Very little light reached beyond the main chambers, with daylight coming only from the entrance and a large opening to the sky at the top of the central chamber.

Several dragons gathered with Rakgar in the main chamber of the lair, including the brown dan brothers, Milah and Mitashio. Siblings were rare among dragons, but the rivalry between the brothers and Hiro and Tog was common and well known. Although the four of them had been thrown together recently and seemed to agree more often, the brothers never stopped arguing the points opposite of Hiro's.

Behind the brothers, the sun dazzled a small pile of gold, gems and other precious items collected over their many clashes with humans. Humans erroneously believed that a dragon would spare their life if they offered it something shiny.

Since Hiro had returned from his secret life among the humans, he'd kept to his own lair, practicing changing. He hoped that maybe by feeling the expression of his body in both forms he could choose which life to live. But he knew if anyone discovered his ability, he wouldn't be able to live in either world. So he stayed in his lair, ignoring the rest of the world while he figured himself out. But he knew the war couldn't wait forever.

"The hatchlings will starve," a small red dame spoke to Rakgar. "They won't last much longer."

"They're stronger than you think," Rakgar answered. He sighed and wouldn't meet her eyes. Perhaps because his held so much malice. Perhaps because he didn't care. Hiro still couldn't believe that Rakgar didn't care. This is the same dragon that had trusted Hiro's father unwaveringly until Tusten's death. Could he really just stop caring about dragons?

Hiro and Tog stepped up as the red dame snorted flame and whipped her tail around to leave. Prak stepped up in her place.

"She's right, Rakgar." Prak's demeanor had altered recently in such a way as to make his nasal voice sound demanding rather than annoying. He was a small brown dragon, smaller than most other dragons even though he was fully grown, but he was as tough as the two rows of spikes running down his back and tail would lead one to believe. "We don't have the stores we need to wait out the humans. Now that the centaurs are on their own, they'll never get to all the human supply groups alone. The humans will be fed as they wait for dragons to descend from the Rock Clouds, and we'll starve up here on our own. The hatchlings will be first to die, then where will that leave our ruck? With no one to take up our memories? We can't just—"

"Wait," Hiro said, his brows knit together in concentration. "What do you mean the centaurs are on their own?"

"Just what I said," Prak snarled. "Rakgar has ordered that all dragons stay in the Rock Clouds. No one is allowed to leave. No hunting parties or raid parties. No one. Even the Watch perimeter is being closed in tighter."

"Not even hunting parties?" Hiro turned toward Rakgar.

Rakgar was an enormous dragon, larger than any other in their long history. Although a dull gray, like Tog, he displayed several large horns, spikes and barbels mostly around his head making him look somewhat like a lion. The bravest of dragons cowered before the intimidating Rakgar – but not Hiro. Rakgar had always been kind to Hiro. He doted on him as young Dakoon (Hiro's birth name) and let him get away with all kinds of mischief. Now, as they both aged, the older dragon seemed to diminish in Hiro's sight, in both respect and aspect. The fire in Hiro began to burn brighter.

Rakgar rolled his eyes. "I don't expect either of you to understand how to maintain an entire ruck." He looked at all the dragons present around him. "I have ordered this because I believe that the humans will get bored and leave. Especially since they can't reach their prize." He looked down on Hiro. "If the prey evades the hunter, the hunter persists. But if the prey ignores the hunter who can't reach them, the hunter leaves to find easier prey."

Hiro growled. "And what if the hunter gets help to reach the prey as the prey sits idle and slowly dies?"

Rakgar glowered down at Hiro. "Don't tell me you still believe the faeries have anything to do with this."

Hiro stamped his front left claw. "They have everything to do with it," he snapped back. Rakgar glanced down at the claw and Hiro stretched out his smallest talon for emphasis. It was the only one cut to half as long as the others. The faeries had cut it off while torturing him in the courtyard of the human castle. They physically tormented him, trying to coerce him into speaking before the humans. Hiro still believed those faeries didn't act alone.

Rakgar bent his neck and slunk down, snout to snout with Hiro. He barked, "Prove it."

Hiro's temper flared in him. He had tried to tell Rakgar and the others that the faeries were always lurking in the human kingdom of Kingstor, constantly whispering to the king, but he couldn't prove it because he couldn't pass them his human memories. Beside the fact that he wouldn't want to pass any memories of his life as a human, he also couldn't pass memories of him being friends with Princess Anna. She was the only human he trusted and who was willing to help him find out more about the humans' and the faeries' plans of attack, but he couldn't explain any of that to anyone. He had to allow the ones who trusted him to do so. He knew in his heart that the faeries would find a way to get the humans into the Rock Clouds.

"We can't," Prak spoke up, probably to keep Hiro from picking a fight with Rakgar. Successfully distracted, Rakgar swung his head to meet Prak's eyes. Hiro noted no fear in Prak when Rakgar stared him down. "We can't do anything unless we're allowed to leave the Rock Clouds. If you let us leave, we'll bring you proof that the faeries are aiding the humans."

"A few rogue faeries are nothing to fear," Rakgar said, sitting up straight again.

"No," Tog spoke this time, "but we'll find proof that all the faeries are in on it."

"Still not enough of a threat," Rakgar grumbled.

"Then," Hiro spoke carefully, "we'll prove that they have the means to send the humans into the Rock Clouds. All of them. The entire army."

The cavern grew deadly silent. All eyes hovered either on Hiro or Rakgar.

"It's not possible," Rakgar whispered.

Hiro sat up. Not knowing why he said it or how he planned to accomplish it, he said, "It is. And I'll prove it."

"Hmpf," Rakgar cracked a mocking grin, "so be it. If you can bring me proof that the faeries can and will aid the humans and get them into the Rock Clouds, I'll allow you to retaliate against the humans. With supervision and caution."

"Fine," Tog said. "Until then, we'll bring food back for the hatchlings. Then we can—"

"No."

All eyes turned to Rakgar again. Several maws hung open.

"But the hatchlings…" Tog tried again.

Rakgar sat a moment in silence, then stared back at Tog. "It would take too long and our movements would appear too much like we'd planned them ahead. It would expose too many dragons. No. The hatchlings will have to wait."

"But they—"

"NO!" Rakgar roared, slamming a heavy paw on the ground to shake the cavern walls. "You'll have to figure it out in time for them and DON'T COME BACK UNTIL YOU DO!"

Hiro pried his eyes from Rakgar and scanned the other dragons in the cavern. "Who will go with us?"

"Wait," Rakgar roared, "I didn't say—"

Prak advanced on Rakgar, much like a half-witted mouse before a lion. "You already gave us leave!" he bellowed up at the leader, something he never would have done only a few weeks ago. Then turning to the rest of the dragons, he yelled, "Who will help us?!"

Every dragon in the room roared in agreement. Prak roared, Tog joined but Hiro couldn't. He watched as the dragons followed Prak and Tog from the cavern into the shining blue sky. Even Milah and Mitashio, uncharacteristically silent, gave Rakgar one last look and walked out behind the others.

When the cave was empty except the two, Hiro walked away from Rakgar.

"Hiro," Rakgar called, interrupting the echo of Hiro's claws on the stone. "The hatchlings will only last another week without food. You might want to remember that as you go about your personal crusade."

2

DISRUPTION

The ceremonial bell chimed five times. Philip stepped up to the dais from the back. He had practiced the ceremony several times with his best friend and royal general, Torgon, and Tierni, Torgon's sister and the only woman to capture Philip's heart, helping him. Even Ruther and Murthur, brothers and his close personal servants, had taken turns helping him memorize the wording. But now at the real event he still felt as if a rock the size of a scorrand egg sat in his belly.

He motioned for the groom, Lord Dieko of Selevyn, to join him on the platform. He recited the names and titles Dieko currently claimed. The man was still dressed in furs and boots as if it were a winter day, not the sunny, breezy autumn afternoon they enjoyed. Yet he didn't sweat a drop. *He must be using majik*, thought Philip. The furs only seemed to emphasize the man's graying hair and drooping jowls; obviously near twice Anna's age, he exemplified nobility. Or, at least, he tried to in his every move. Grateful that weddings were required to take place outdoors, Philip slowed himself and took a deep breath of the warm, autumn air before focusing on what he needed to do next.

Towering over Dieko on the dais, the young king was relieved when he could step back to allow the royal high priestess to take his place. Reciting her name and customary titles, Philip stepped around closer to Anna. Careful not to touch her blue wedding gown, he extended his hand. He was grateful for his height, and hence, the reach of his arm as he took her hand. It was forbidden for all but the high priestess to touch the wedding gown. Philip had been told it would "tarnish the majik and poison the marriage". Even the king would be punished for the infraction, according to religious law. The gown's skirt was so large, he wondered if a shorter man could have even reached Anna to take her hand.

He forgot the cumbersome dress when he realized that her hand was clammy and cool despite the warm sun. He attempted a firm but gentle touch as he led her to the platform in front of Dieko and the priestess. Before he released her, he took the blue ribbon tied around her wrist and passed the end of it to Dieko's wrist, tying them together.

"That these two shall be wed in the presence of the people," Philip continued, standing in front of them with his back to the audience, "to witness their union is blessed by the High Gods." He took Anna's and Dieko's hands and joined them in front of the priestess. Behind the couple, the priestess began to murmur quietly to herself, rubbing majik ingredients, produced from a hidden pouch, into her hands. Travaith the royal majishun stood nearby, chanting quietly to assist the priestess in her majik.

Philip took another long blue ribbon from one of the men Dieko had requested be his Seven Men. The man grinned as he handed it over, but not at the couple. He and the other six watched Philip gather the ribbon, as if waiting for him to make a mistake. Philip felt their eyes on him but brushed away the suspicious feeling in order to focus on the ceremony.

"In the sky of Tartaku over you," Philip said as he wrapped the second ribbon around Dieko's wrist along with the first. He didn't watch as the sky above the couple shimmered with majik. "With the joy of Tarka to lift you," he said while wrapping the ribbon around Dieko's hand. The couple and the priestess lifted ever so slightly from the ground, Anna's golden hair swirling around her to create a halo. As the couple lifted into the air, Philip couldn't help but glance at the older man only to see his nose in the air, avoiding the eyes of the princess.

"Tarsa's wind shall whisper counsel," Philip said, returning his focus to the ribbon as he wrapped it around Dieko's fingers where they joined with Anna's. The wind stirred around the group, brushing Anna's dress and Dieko's furs. Philip wanted to murmur his own prayer of thanks that he had insisted on light clothing for his ceremonial robes.

The air became more solid, settling over them in a swirling fog. "The clouds of Kruh will soften your hearts," Philip said as he swung the ribbon over the fingers of the couple again, "and your future shall sparkle like the stars of Khurta." He passed the ribbon over Anna's fingers as specks of light danced over Dieko's soft hand covered in rings and Anna's rougher hand, now quivering. "The moon goddesses of Shurta shall bless you with fertile wealth." He brought the ribbon over Anna's hand while three beams of silver light shone onto their hands.

Before he could finish the ceremony, Philip risked a glance at Anna. She stared blankly at her husband; the fierce fire in her brilliant green eyes that Philip had grown accustomed to seeing was gone. Extinguished. Philip imagined he could see pain and even sorrow in her eyes even as her features remained impassive. The pit in his stomach jolted and he couldn't take his eyes from her face.

"And with Shurka's sunlight to purify," he muttered as a bright, golden light enveloped the couple, "these two shall be one."

As he said these last words, Anna closed her eyes and a tear slid down her cheek.

———

"Try not to stare at her too much, huh?"

Torgon's voice jolted Philip. He had been staring at Tierni again. She stood with her friends from the laundry, giggling at the juggler. While Philip had appointed Torgon his royal general on a whim, knowing he could trust the man, Torgon's sister and the rest of his family remained at a lower station. It wasn't exactly illegal for the two young people to have a relationship, but some in the kingdom might not agree that his attraction to her befit his noble role. A difficult position to be in when you led the Noble Kingdom. Philip wished Tierni could be sitting next to him at the wedding feast. He imagined holding her hand and smelling the sweet scent on her dark brown hair. Most of all, he wanted to stare into her intoxicating blue eyes. But Dieko had put his foot down, citing law. Servants weren't allowed to sit with nobles at a celebration. Philip ground his teeth and reluctantly tore his eyes away from her.

"How could I let this happen?" the young king leaned in toward his best friend. "How could I let Dieko dictate whom I sit next to at a wedding?"

"It *is* his wedding," Torgon replied. He nodded and smiled as dancing girls flashed past, but the royal general's eyes flickered toward the newlyweds. "He does have the final say, no matter what the king wants."

Philip allowed his eyes to drift to the couple as well. Dieko sat with his back to Anna, smiling and talking with his Seven Men. With only a wan grin, Anna watched the dancers silently. Philip's stomach churned again and his gaze slid onto the untouched plate of food in front of him.

"Philip," Torgon grinned at the courtiers seated around them. With little movement to his lips he said, "Try to look like you're having fun. Smile. Be happy."

Trying not to grimace instead, Philip picked up his wine cup, the only thing he'd touched all night. "I can't," he said behind it, "I feel like I'm going to be sick."

Torgon turned, inspecting Philip's face briefly, but looked back at his food. He stabbed a thick slice of beef and twirled it in front of him. "Sick or not, you have to remain present for your sister's wedding party or it will appear you don't approve."

"I performed the wedding myself," Philip countered, "Isn't that approval enough?"

Torgon shrugged. When he put the fork back on his plate with the meat uneaten Philip realized Torgon had no appetite as well. "What have I done?" Philip whispered.

"What's done is done," Torgon said. "You have every reason to be happy. You have kept your word to the faeries and not told Anna anything about the poison or the plans. But you told them that you would no longer keep it from her once she was married." He turned to look at Philip with a genuine smile on his face. "You can tell her everything now. Perhaps she is on the other side of that imagined locked door. Perhaps she has insight to help you."

Philip sighed, feeling some sense of relief, but stifled it. "That's true, but that also means I have to tell Dieko."

"And how do you feel about that?"

"To be honest," Philip glanced at Dieko again as the man brushed food off the table away from himself and onto Anna's lap, "not good."

"Me neither."

Philip's eyes met Torgon's, then together they glared at Dieko.

———

The call came in the small hours of the night after the wedding party finally dwindled.

"DRAGON! DRAGON! DRAGON!"

Philip leapt from his bed on the second call and threw on some nearby clothes. After he tied a heavy cloak around his shoulders, he pulled his sword from its sheath and marched out into the corridors.

"Where?" he shouted to the nearest guard.

"In the upper town," came an answer from down the hall.

Philip ran behind the guards as they led him to the tower overlooking the town. Instead of scrambling to the top of the tower where the guards shot at the beast, he stopped atop the open battlements. A small, smooth, green dragon belched flame onto rooftops of the houses below, then landed on them and tore at the stonework.

"Shoot her!" Philip bellowed to the guards on the tower. But he knew they didn't have a decent target from their vantage.

He looked down below to see who might be available to help. There in the street stood Dieko, in his nightclothes and a cloak. He held a sword before him, but stepped back toward the guards gathering around him. As Philip watched, the man shoved the guards roughly in front of himself and backed away toward the castle.

Philip's eyes swung to the building the dragon was currently attacking. "No," he whispered. "NO!" he yelled as he ran for the stairs that would take him out to the street.

He screamed for someone to find him a bow and quiver as he unlatched every door until he ran into the street.

"Anna!" he bellowed as he ran for the home into which she and Dieko had retreated for their wedding night. "Anna!"

As he watched in horror, the dragon tore at the rooftops of Dieko's home and those nearby. Someone tapped Philip on the shoulder and exchanged his sword for a bow. Finally feeling useful, he ran forward, firing repeated shots at the green monster. Unfortunately, they weren't poison-tipped arrows, but she was low enough that they pricked her side and wings. Feeling the sting, she hovered in the air above the homes, then wheeled around and dove away from her foes.

Once the dragon was out of sight, Philip burst into the newlyweds' house. With the guards' help, he tore through the rooms searching for his sister. The first floor was littered with pieces of the structure, charred and scattered. The tops of the walls still crackled with fires the guards rushed to douse. No one could reach the second floor in the grand house because the staircase was gone, open to the night sky above, with the walls and roof torn to shreds. The only portion of the home still intact was the kitchen and servants' quarters in the lower section.

"She's not here, Sire," a man finally said as a large group of guards dug through the remains of the house.

"Perhaps she got out," another man offered.

"Pray to the gods that she did," Philip muttered.

"If she did," the first guard said, "she would have run. Possibly to another home."

Philip nodded. "You're right," he said. "Spread out. Knock on doors, search the streets."

He ordered a few men to stay behind and continue the search and clean up as well. As he returned to the street, Torgon ran up to him. "Did you find her?"

Philip shook his head.

"Maybe Dieko knows where she is or which way she might have gone to escape."

"Where is Dieko?" Philip asked. When Torgon shrugged, they both scanned the growing crowd of guards, nobles and people around them.

"I…I think he might be in the castle, Sire," one guard answered sheepishly.

As the group headed back to the castle, Philip looked at Torgon. "Where did it come from?"

The royal general shook his head. Philip assumed he must have been on duty because he was wearing his daily uniform after having changed from his ceremonial uniform following the wedding party. "I have no idea," he answered. "She appeared out of nowhere. The first sign of her was when the guard saw her attack Dieko's home. I was directing from the walls when I saw you run into the street."

Before Philip and the group reached the castle entrance, Dieko ran toward them.

"Sire," he said, breathless, "I was coming to look for you. I—"

"Where's Anna?" Philip asked, ignoring the comment.

"I don't know," Dieko answered. "I was more concerned for my king."

"Your king? Not your new wife?" Torgon growled. "Where was she when you last saw her?"

"She," Dieko hesitated, his beady eyes bouncing between the younger men, "she was upstairs when the dragon appeared."

Silence.

"Did you not go after her?"

Torgon shouted to the guards to get more men to search the area, then the two men turned back to Dieko. Silence.

"Philip?" It was Anna's voice. Weak, but Anna's.

They heard her, but didn't see her immediately. They followed the sound to see her appear from the shadow of a small alley between houses. Her night clothes and robe torn and singed, she stumbled toward her brother and fell into his arms.

"She's hurt," Torgon whispered, indicating her arm and side.

"They're just scratches," Anna mumbled. She righted herself, gingerly covering the wounds.

"I'm pleased you're safe, my dear," Dieko muttered, not at all sounding pleased. "Come," he said, placing his arm around her shoulders and turning her toward the house.

"Dieko," Philip said, grabbing the man's arm to stop him, "she needs a healer."

"I'm fine," Anna said.

"I'm her husband," Dieko said, "I'll see to her. We won't let this interrupt our wedding night."

Philip's grip on the man's sleeve tightened. "It already has," he said, but he tried to calm his voice. "Your home is in shambles. Your wife is in shock. Come and stay in the castle until all is put to right."

Dieko bobbed his head in agreement and led Anna back toward the castle.

Torgon placed a hand on Philip's arm to wait. Once the couple and most of the guards were outside of hearing, he leaned in toward Philip's ear. "One of the guards just told me," he glanced toward Dieko who was no longer supporting Anna's weight, "he was waiting out the attack in the castle!"

Philip ground his teeth. "What does it mean?"

"That he's a coward, for one," Torgon whispered, "but whatever else, I don't know. Did he somehow bring on the attack? I'm not sure."

"One thing is certain," Philip said as he began following, "he's a coward that warrants watching."

3

CONSPIRING

"We need to go to the other rucks," Milah said.

"He's right," Prak echoed. "We need help, but we also can't spare the dragons." Prak had sent the other dragons who had accompanied them to rejoin the centaur groups attacking the humans and searching for proof that the humans could get into the Rock Clouds. Then Hiro joined Prak, Tog, Milah and Mitashio to meet the centaurs.

Joss, the leader of the centaurs, only denoted himself as leader with a single leather band around his black hair. His brother, Rylan, one of the few centaur majishuns, wore leather straps twisting up his bulging arms and his brown horse's body was adorned with pouches full of majikal ingredients. His only weapon, the brilliant Silver Sword of Allegiance, which his sister had stolen from the humans, was sheathed on his back. Ashel, their sister and leader of the warrior centaurs, wore numerous knives and swords strapped to her brown body, as well as a leather binding across her bronze chest. But her real weapon she wore slung over her shoulder, and the quiver and arm bracer with it indicated her powerful use of the bow. Pure black and intimidating, with a massive scar running the length of his face, Vikal, Ashel's right-hand comrade and friend amongst the warriors, waited on the banks of Centaur River.

"I don't need your approval," Milah sneered at the younger dragon. One of two brown brothers, neither he nor Mitashio had ever esteemed Hiro or Tog or, by association, Prak.

Prak rolled his eyes. "And I don't need to agree with you, but I do. However, we can't spare many."

"It hasn't been easy without your help," Ashel grumbled, catching Prak's attention with her large eyes. "I don't know if we can spare any at all."

"We've made do and we will continue to do so," Joss said, "because we'll need every claw later. It's more important that we have help when the real fighting starts and not just these skirmishes."

Ashel nodded, swinging her black hair. "Milah and Mitashio should go," she said, "one to each ruck nearby. Then each move on to the next ruck. Deliver your request for help to all of them and come back as quickly as possible."

"Desert Ruck!" Mitashio shouted, laying claim to first visit the most comfortable location.

Milah twisted his face at his brother. "Fine, I'll go to the Ice Ruck."

"Don't bother," Hiro said. "The last time I saw them, they weren't willing to help. I'm going that way, so I'll try again to convince them."

"Alright," Milah grumbled, "I'll go to the Island Ruck. But if they drown me trying to make me catch fish, I blame you!" he yelled at Hiro as he and his brother slapped tails and leapt into the sky.

"Where will you go?" Ashel asked, turning to Hiro.

"Where else?" Tog grumbled, sitting off to the side of the gathered group.

Ashel bared her teeth in a very dragon-like manner. Hiro knew Ashel hated the idea and risk of a dragon meeting with a human. But she couldn't argue about it with Vikal present because he didn't know the situation. Hiro still didn't know if she had told Joss and Rylan, but neither of them asked questions.

Hiro sighed. "She's the only one with any information at this point."

"Why?" Ashel growled.

Hiro shook his head to cover the rumble of his shoulders. Thinking of Anna made his body want to change into human form again. But Ashel's loathing helped him maintain his current state.

"She's married by now," Hiro lowered his voice, "that was the deal. If she married, she'd learn—" he glanced at Vikal "—everything."

Vikal sat in stone-still silence. He might have been an ebony statue for all the response he gave. Either he knew more than he should or he had been tutored not to ask questions. Joss and Rylan, however, listened with intent, not hiding their curiosity.

"As much as I hate to say it," Prak grumbled, "she might be the only one who either has answers or can get them. We can't exactly interrogate random humans."

"In the meantime, what do we do here?" Ashel asked, indicating herself and Tog and Prak. "Lie back and wait for you to return?"

"The hatchlings only have a week," Tog said.

"Then we'll search here," Prak offered. "We'll use all our senses to search the trees for traces of faeries or their majik. We won't stop until we either find proof of them or hear from you, Hiro."

Hiro stared at him and waited. He knew Prak had more to say.

"Ok, ok," the little dragon finally said. "Of course, we're also going to sneak food to the hatchlings. It won't be easy and it may take some time and I don't know who will be here when you get back, but you know we're going to try SOMETHING. I just felt you needed to focus on what you need to do. I didn't want to say it so you could tell Rakgar that you had no idea about it. But don't worry about Rakgar or the hatchlings. Leave them to us."

"Keep a messenger on the riverbank or stay nearby," Hiro said as he moved to an opening in the trees.

Ashel trotted after him. "Wait, how will you…?" She let her voice trail off.

Hiro assumed Ashel wanted to know how he would get to see Anna. "Don't worry," he said as he opened his wings, "I have a plan."

—

Ok, not really a plan. Maybe just an idea, Hiro thought to himself. *But it will be enough. It has to be enough.*

Soon enough, the small village came into view. It was as if the troubles of the rest of the world hadn't touched it. Jarek's farm spread all the way to the mountains, his fields waving lush green at the black dragon as he flew over. The people of the village, called the Hamees, were different from other humans in more ways than one. Not only did they believe in only one god, but they were also friends with a dragon.

Months ago, Hiro, in dragon form, had helped Anna save these people after they had risked everything to save him. As he flew over the houses, the humans in any other village would scream and run for cover, but the Hamees looked into the sky with smiles. Some even waved at the dragon.

Although he trusted Jarek, Hiro knew he couldn't just land and take human form. He decided instead to let the village see the dragon first, then he would change and ask for help as a human. Owyn, his human persona, could claim to be friends with Anna if they had seen her "pet" dragon first. Hopefully.

After circling the village a couple times, Hiro flew in behind Jarek's barn. The first time he was there he'd given himself away by leaving claw marks. This time he wanted to leave human prints as well so it would appear as if he was traveling with someone as Anna's pet. He rolled his eyes at the debasing thought, then rolled his shoulder and began altering his form.

He had practiced changing along the way and improved the process by focusing on making his fire burn or extinguish. It wasn't perfect, as his emotions still tried to overtake his control, but he was getting better. Once he had tried to change in mid-air and learned the painful way that he needed to account for distance.

Just as he landed behind the barn and before Jarek could show up, Hiro changed into Owyn, focusing on the fire in his belly cooling and dying. He limped back and forth with bare feet in the soft dirt. Then he changed back into a dragon by imagining the fire reigniting in his belly. After trodding the ground a little with his claws, he changed back into a human. With a grin, he realized he was getting better at changing faster and easier by focusing on his fire. Then, not watching where he was stepping, he tripped on a rock. His leg twisted under him and he fell, face first, into the dirt.

"Aargh!" he yelled as he crumpled on the ground. *Stupid human feet!*

"Who's there?" Jarek's voice came from the other side of the barn.

As Owyn lay rubbing his sore leg, Jarek came from around the corner. "Please," Owyn stammered with forced humility, "I need your help."

"I can see that!" Jarek laid aside the large pitchfork he held in one hand. The other hand lay against his side covered in a glove. "Wait here."

By the time he returned, the pain in Owyn's leg had subsided. Jarek draped a large blanket around Owyn and helped him to his feet.

—

The conversation was not going well.

"You know Anna?" Boorda, Jarek's wife, repeated for no one in particular. She sat across from Owyn at a little wooden table in their home. Her soft brown hair was pulled into a neat bun at the back of her neck.

"Yes," Owyn answered again anyway.

"And you need to see her?" Jarek asked again. He stood behind his wife, occasionally pacing and fidgety.

"Yes."

"And you want us to help you get into the castle to see her?" Boorda said.

Owyn sighed. He had explained everything he thought he could without attracting undue curiosity. He knew Princess Anna. He'd arrived here on her dragon, and he needed to speak with her. About what, he couldn't say; it was a private matter.

The couple had been kind and patient. Boorda made him some food to eat and Jarek gave him clothes to wear, although they were obviously too small and fit him poorly. But something clearly bothered both of them about Owyn's story, and Owyn couldn't figure out what.

"Why can't you just go to the castle on your own and ask to see her?" Boorda stared into his eyes without blinking. She hadn't turned her kind, round face from him once during the conversation, as if trying to read him.

But, no, he couldn't tell them why. "It's difficult."

Jarek nodded. He leaned against the wall behind his wife, his one gloved hand tucked under his arm. His brown hair had grown since Owyn had last seen him as Hiro. He tucked the edges behind his ear. "I guess it would be," he finally said, "seeing as you're a wanted man in the entire Noble Kingdom."

Owyn glanced up at Jarek and lowered his eyes again. "I didn't want to share my troubles with you, but—" he looked into Boorda's inquisitive face "—I mean no harm. It was all a misunderstanding."

"Threatening Princess Anna?" Jarek asked, while Boorda seemed to stare deeper into Owyn's eyes. "How is that misunderstood?"

Owyn hung his head. *How am I going to get these humans to help me? They risked much more helping me as a dragon. Why won't they help me as a human?*

"I'm sorry I can't say more," he said, "but I had to get out of there. And I need to reach her again, now. She should know I have her dragon, and I – I just have to talk to her… I…" He let his voice trail away. What else could he say? How could they be convinced to help him?

Boorda reached her hand across the table to touch Owyn's. When he looked up, her eyes, the color of Anna's green eyes and Jarek's brown eyes mixed together, stabbed like a knife while sparkling with intuition. "You care for her, don't you?" she asked.

Owyn could only nod. He remembered her knowing gaze and gentle touch when he had surprised her as a dragon. He could tell she wasn't afraid of him then and she wasn't afraid of him now.

Jarek finally stood up straight. "Owyn," he said, "allow me to discuss this with my wife."

They left Owyn sitting at the table with the empty plate in front of him. He listened to them leave the small kitchen and go into another room. The home reminded

Owyn of Adair's – the first man Owyn met as a human – except Jarek's place was much larger. The walls were made of wood and mud and very little adorned the rooms except furniture. Tables and chairs, but no beds made up in the corner. Owyn assumed the beds were in the upper level of the house. Fortunately, Jarek and Boorda had no idea of his extraordinary hearing, so they only stepped into the adjacent room.

"He's clearly insane," Jarek mumbled. "How do we get rid of him?"

"By helping him."

"You can't be serious," he whispered back. "He was naked and covered in dirt."

"So was Anna when you found her."

"Yes," he answered, "but we should just send him away and be done with him. I don't want him to hurt her."

"He doesn't mean to," Boorda whispered back.

"What do you mean?"

"He loves her," Boorda said.

"There's no dragon in him?"

"Oh no," she countered, "he's almost *all* dragon. Practically a dragon in human form. But he's not deceitful and he's not here to harm her. I'm certain."

"He's still a criminal, no matter what the circumstances are."

"And you've never helped anyone else who was afraid of the guards," she said, "have you?"

"I learned my lesson then," he said. "We're risking everything just taking him in."

When Owyn heard this, he remembered Jarek's scream as he, in dragon form, blew white hot flame across his hand to destroy the earth wraith. That scream haunted Hiro's and Owyn's nightmares. With that, Owyn realized that he couldn't put them in any more danger.

"You know," he said from the next room, loudly scraping his chair across the floor and standing, "I shouldn't have bothered you. You've been very kind, but I can't keep you from your lives any longer." When Jarek and Boorda stepped back in, Owyn met Jarek's eye. "I'll figure it out without asking any more of you," he told them.

Jarek nodded, "We'd like to help you."

"You have," he indicated the empty plate, "and I'm grateful."

As he turned to leave, Jarek spoke up again. "Remember, you're a wanted man in Kingstor. Your face is posted. With or without a dragon, the guards will arrest you the moment they see you."

"I'll be careful," he said and pulled the door open.

"Oh, spit in Tarsa's eye!" Boorda exclaimed. Once she had the men's attention, she turned to Jarek. "You'll be going there later today, won't you? On Dugger's wagon? To deliver goods to the market? Right?"

Jarek seemed a little confused, but finally nodded. "Oh, y-yes," he stammered, "yes, we'll be going into Kingstor. Would you…uh…like a…ride?" Boorda placed a hand on her husband's arm. "Oh, that's right," Jarek said, "they check all the wagons going in or out of Kingstor."

"Except," Boorda said slowly, "maybe the saddle box."

Owyn held back a smile. "No, thank you," he said, "no, I think I'll walk."

Boorda and Owyn shared a knowing grin.

4

SEPARATION

"I don't like it," Kradik growled at Philip. "You swore you wouldn't tell her anything of our plans."

"And I won't," Philip answered as he put a couple last-minute items into his saddlebag. "I'm going to show her."

"That was not part—"

Philip tugged on his horse's girth a little hard before he decided not to take out his frustrations on the animal. He spun to glare down at the black, vacant cowl of the faerie. The faeries covered themselves with the darkened garment to hide their transparent skin. But Philip didn't need to see their judging eyes and sneers without feeling them.

"Look," he muttered low enough for the others around them not to hear, "I made her a promise a long time ago. She has met my requirements to show her trustworthiness. I gave her my word and you have no right to say otherwise. Nor choice in the matter."

Kradik grunted but stalked away from the king.

Philip took a deep breath. *That felt good,* he thought.

"I don't like it," Torgon said, joining Philip alongside, holding his own horse's reigns.

"What now?" Philip muttered, but allowed Torgon to speak his mind.

"I don't like your departing with Dieko and me leaving for the Rock Clouds tomorrow," Torgon said while watching the older man mount his own horse. "You saw how he…" Torgon lowered his voice further, "how he dealt with a dragon attack. He left his new wife behind!"

Philip sighed. He watched the couple – who didn't act much like newlyweds – while he spoke with Torgon. Word had reached Philip that the two hadn't slept in the same room since the wedding night, and others had noticed they didn't even look at each other if they were in the same room. Anna spoke with Tierni while Amethyst, her maid, filled her saddlebags. Dieko barked orders at the guards from atop his mare.

Amidst the chaos of departure preparations in the courtyard, Philip noted that Amethyst turned abruptly and went back into the castle. Everyone seemed to be upset about the party leaving and who was coming and going. Everyone had something to say or complain about. Amethyst and Anna were normally inseparable, except when Anna disappeared into the mountains. Even then, Amethyst often went with her or at least knew her whereabouts. This time, she simply nodded and left without saying goodbye. Philip brushed the thought aside to address his royal general's concern.

"Torgon," Philip said, "you're the leader of the Noble army. You must go to the Rock Clouds and join the army there. I promised Anna she would learn all of our plans if she married. As for Dieko," they both glanced at the man, "he'll need to learn everything anyway. For better or worse, if anything happens to me, he'll have to run the Noble Kingdom. He needs to know what's going on."

"Murzod and Dieko? You'll be surrounded by bullies and cowards!" His eyes fell on Dieko.

"Don't worry," Philip said, "I'm leaving you with Kradik."

Torgon grunted. "Keep an eye on the old fool," he said as he stepped away.

"I will if you will."

"I don't like it," another voice said behind him.

"No one seems to!" Philip exclaimed, but spun at the words to face Tierni, her lips pressed firmly together and her arms crossed over her chest. He didn't realize just how intimidating those Black Saber uniforms were until he came under the scrutiny of the wearer, no matter how small she was.

"Don't like what?" he finally spluttered.

"I don't like you leaving with my lady, the woman you assigned us to protect, without the Black Saber accompanying her in order to fulfill our duty."

Philip looked around to see everyone watching the conversation from the corners of their eyes. Except Dieko, who blatantly stared at them. Philip reached out and touched Tierni's elbow, indicating she follow him to move away from the audience.

When she finally moved aside Philip leaned in close. Perhaps noticing it wasn't totally necessary, but he could smell the scent of flowers on her while they spoke. "I'm sorry," he said. "I know you don't approve, but we're bringing Hilde as a maid and protector and Anna can use a sword for herself as well."

"I'm her second," Tierni insisted, "I should be alongside her and you know it."

Philip glared at the ground. He could feel anger and frustration welling inside him. When he felt it almost ready to overflow, he finally looked into her blue eyes. "I know it," he said, barely able to keep his voice steady, "but I also know this will be a dangerous journey. Not just the journey, but the destination is dangerous as well. I haven't had any control over anything for a very long time, not the faeries, not the war, not a single decision has been completely mine. So the one decision I am making now is to keep you from danger."

Expecting another outburst, Philip had to blink hard when Tierni's countenance softened. She looked down at the ground momentarily before meeting his gaze again. "I suppose Hilde's presence will suffice for now."

Philip, slightly baffled, turned toward his horse again.

"Majesty," Tierni said, and Philip turned back. "You can't keep me from danger forever." She stood on her tiptoes and leaned in as if she wanted to whisper in his ear. When he bent toward her, she pecked him on the cheek. "I'll see you in the Rock Clouds," she said before striding back into the castle.

5

TANGLED

Are we there yet? Owyn asked himself for the thousandth time. But no matter how uncomfortable he was, he didn't dare move. The bottom of the wooden box on the wagon smashed against his face. He could feel tiny slivers of wood working into his cheekbones with every bump. He couldn't move away because the top of the container sawed into his shoulder on the other side. His knees pressed into his chest. He felt like a hatchling crammed into an egg, but he couldn't explode from this one whenever he desired.

The saddle box was the only enclosure on the entire wagon, hidden underneath where the men sat, with a hatch on the side of it, next to Owyn's head. While Jarek visited with Dugger inside his home over drinks, Owyn had removed most of the contents of the compartment, with the exception of a thick blanket, then stuffed himself inside. He kept the blanket, hoping it would cushion or warm him, but instead sweat dripped relentlessly from his nose and the blanket smelled of animal waste, turning his stomach. In the end, he had shaped the blanket against the hatched door and around him as much as possible to hide his form.

After the one-thousandth-and-forty-second bounce that jammed his cheek further into the walls of the wooden box, the wagon slowed. Owyn heard the wheels rattle over the bridge outside the city gates, then they stopped altogether, and he heard the two drivers talking to the guards. They were informed of the need to search the wagon and Owyn's spine prickled worse than the slivers digging into his face.

One guard poked around in the back of the wagon, but the other walked around the outside.

"What's in here?" Owyn heard as the door to the saddle box swung open. Owyn's heart jolted. Ice spread through his lungs as he stopped breathing. The blanket puffed out of the door, but miraculously clung to the edges of the opening without falling out entirely.

"Extra saddle," the man accompanying Jarek answered. "In case the wagon breaks."

"Huh," the guard grunted and shoved the blanket back in before closing the door on it.

With the door shut again, Owyn closed his eyes and took a shallow shaky breath. Heat washed over him, but he no longer felt hot. He could feel his blood pounding against his ears. The fear of being discovered threatened to change him into a dragon again. He felt his tail pull away from his leg ever so slightly before he took a deeper breath.

Anna, he thought, *I'm going to see Anna.* The thought seemed to get his form under control. He focused on the cool sensation in his stomach.

Finally, the guards cleared the men to leave. Owyn breathed easier as the wagon rolled on into the city. When they eased to a stop again, Owyn noticed the quiet and lack of clamor around them. The men jumped down from the wagon and Owyn heard the area quickly go still when their footsteps and voices faded away. Braving a look, Owyn shoved the hatch and pushed the blanket out of the opening.

Not seeing anyone around or hearing any reaction to his motion, Owyn gradually wriggled himself free of his hiding place. He checked his surroundings before making sure to replace the blanket and close the small hatch on the saddle box. The wagon was pulled alongside one of the buildings in the center of the town and he assumed the men had disappeared into it. Streets slanted off at angles, but he couldn't see a way that led to the castle.

He rubbed and stretched his legs slightly as he hobbled down the street away from the wagon. No matter what happened next, he didn't want to get caught in Jarek's company. He couldn't place any suspicion on the man. He owed Jarek too much already.

Owyn remembered the layout of Kingstor Noble from flying overhead. All the major roads seemed to slant away from the castle and wandering on foot through those same streets now made it much more difficult to find his way. Houses and buildings towered over his head. He stumbled up a street that he assumed would eventually wend its way to the castle gate. However, he reached an end where the only option was to turn to either side. He could smell horses on the other side of the wall in front of him, but there seemed to be no way over the blockade, as it reached almost a full dragon-length taller than he was. His choice of direction only led him into another street that curved away from the castle.

While getting more and more frustrated with the confusion of the streets, Owyn's stomach began to distract him as well. Several buildings he passed displayed shelves full of meats and breads and things Owyn had no reference for, but they smelled delicious all the same.

When he stepped into one of the buildings to ask for some of the food arranged to see from the street, he came face-to-face with a picture of a man on a wall near the door. Since Addil had taught Owyn to read, he was able to quickly interpret the description. A wanted criminal, at least three dragon claws tall, dark skin, black hair, "to be arrested on sight for threatening bodily harm to Her Royal Highness Princess Anna." He slipped back out the door before the man inside could notice his resemblance. He decided his rumbling stomach wasn't nearly as important as not being arrested. Then he wondered how much the picture of the man really looked like him.

He bumbled along through the jumble of streets, hoping he would find some way toward the castle, but the layout of the town seemed determined to send him away. He would follow one way only to come to a dead end, and turning back he would find another way where he hadn't seen it before.

He eventually figured out the jagged roads that didn't appear to follow through to another road would eventually lead to the castle. It took the keen vision of a dragon to find them. Owyn was on his way but suddenly found himself blocked by a large gate with guards standing in front of it. Hanging on the wall behind the gate was another picture of himself, the fugitive. Luckily his quick movement away prevented the guards from seeing his face, but Owyn's progress was thwarted and he was forced to head back into the maze of Kingstor Noble streets.

Still lost, Owyn accidentally slipped into an alley between buildings and found himself navel-to-nose with a short, round little woman in an apron.

"Who are you, then?" she snapped at him.

"I—um—I just—"

"What'd you think you're doin' wandering int'a private residence?"

"I'm—uh—lost."

"Too well, you are," she looked straight up at him. The top of her head barely met his chest, but she brandished a large wooden spoon as if she could lop off his head with it. "You're not the one bin nippin' my loaves, are ya?"

"Loaves?"

"Don't think your size'll save you if you 'ave." She jabbed the spoon against his chest so hard he backed up. "Keep your grimy 'ands off and stay out!" Owyn backed into the street and set off at a run to avoid the dangerous little spoon-wielder.

Before much longer the sun began to descend in the sky. As it dipped, Owyn's stomach gurgled outright. The smells from the many buildings enticed him. With or without his picture on the wall, he would have to find something to eat soon and, hopefully, someone who would help him.

He came to a building with a large sign above the door showing a moose with the wings of a falcon. The sign read, "Public House: Food, Drink, Rooms to Let", and he stepped inside.

A short hallway led to a large room that opened up before him. Several tables were arranged in front of a cold, unlit fireplace. The room was warm and multiple lighted candles hung overhead and were attached to the walls. A few people sat at the tables murmuring together, and two sat on tall chairs alongside a long, raised table with a solid front that stood along the side of the room. A skinny man stood behind the tall table, close to the door.

"Need something?" he grunted, while focusing his attention on something behind the table top.

"Your sign said 'food'," Owyn said, hanging back in the hallway. "I was hoping I could get some."

"Long as you have money," the man said, without looking up.

Owyn shook his head. "I don't have any money."

"Well," the man finally put down whatever was in his hands and looked up at the newcomer, "I can't rightly give—"

When he stopped, Owyn's stomach clenched. The man's eyes widened, then darted to something on the wall beside him.

"You!" he said.

Owyn stepped forward to look around the corner of the opening and saw the familiar notice with his face hanging on the wall.

"You insulted the princess," the man's voice rose with each word. Two men and a woman looked toward the disruption.

"You don't understand," Owyn began as he slowly backed toward the door.

"You threatened her life!" the man yelled. He raised a shaky finger to point at Owyn and three men stood, the two at the tall table and one from near the fireplace.

"I didn't—I would never—"

Before Owyn could concoct a defense, the three men rushed him. He fled toward the door but got pulled back into the common room. A woman yelled. Men grabbed at him. Fortunately, Owyn's size and swift dragon reflexes helped him push off the hands.

"Get the guards!" the man behind the tall table yelled as Owyn launched himself over a shorter table to the back of the room. He pulled one of the men coming at him, used the momentum to spin him around, and shoved him into the other men pursuing him. At the back of the room he saw another door and threw himself at it.

Through another door after that and Owyn burst into a small courtyard with stables. He jumped over the fence into an empty stall. He heard the shouting of the men in pursuit. His heart pounded in his chest as he ran through the stalls toward an opening to the outside at the far end.

"Stop him!" a man behind him yelled.

A young boy with wide eyes stood in Owyn's way, but Owyn pushed past him, knocking him into a stack of hay.

Once in the street again, Owyn ran from the flying moose sign only to bring himself to an abrupt stop, seeing one of the women at the end of the street with two men in blue tunics. Owyn knew those tunics. The woman pointed at Owyn and the Kingstor guards headed for him.

"Stop!" they yelled as Owyn ran the other way.

He squeezed into a small alley for cover to gain some distance, but the guards followed at the scream of a woman he ran into on the other side. Shoving past her he burst through another door into the next street, but he nearly tripped over a dog who growled and barked, and the guards followed.

Still able to run at top speed, he praised the training he had received in the army until he realized that the guards behind him had the same advantage. Plus, the guards had armaments – long staffs with sharp pikes on the ends. He urged his feet to move faster.

Owyn fled as fast as he could down the street, hoping to out-distance his chasers. He thought he had gained on them until he heard them shout.

"Stop him!" the guards yelled.

Owyn looked ahead and saw four more guards duck around the corner. He swerved to the left to avoid them and jumped over a wall with the use of a barrel sitting to the side. Another alley zig-zagged behind the buildings. Owyn knew that the alley ended at the side of the castle wall and would turn in both directions, so he stretched his legs to get there before his pursuers.

When he reached the castle wall, Owyn could smell horses and animals on the other side. The wall rose higher than the adjacent rooftops, but the stacks of crates piled in the alley alongside the adjacent building gave him an idea.

He turned to the right just as the guards yelled at him again to stop. Using every ounce of his given strength without actually changing into a dragon, Owyn jumped off the crates, kicked off the castle wall, pushed from a window ledge and kicked off the castle wall again to finally pull himself onto the building rooftop. He didn't dare look down but he heard the guards come around the corner in the alley just as he rolled onto the shingles and out of their sight.

"He can't've gone far," he heard them say below. As the guards below scrambled through the alleys, Owyn crept across the rooftop to hide behind a chimney, avoiding the castle guards looking out from the towers.

The guards below pounded on doors and asked the occupants if they had seen the fugitive. Owyn lay still, not daring to peek from his hiding place until he heard something that would force him to move.

"Inform the castle guards," one of the men in the alley said to another. "Perhaps they can search from the wall. You, search the rooftops!"

Owyn craned his neck around the chimney. While the streets were cast in shadow now, the sun still shone enough to reflect off the helmets of the guards on the castle towers. He watched as they paced back and forth, only occasionally throwing glances at the sky and earth and town.

He watched them until he heard movement in the building below him. The guards were coming up to the rooftops and the castle guards would be searching for him soon as well. He had to move. Making certain the tower guards were looking away before he budged, Owyn stood and ran across the roof toward the castle wall. As he scrambled, he remembered how his tail had begun to pull away from his leg when he felt the same kind of fear in the wagon box. He wished he could use his strong back dragon legs now, just strong enough to propel him off the roof. He didn't look down, but he felt power surge through his legs stronger than he knew his human legs could push him as he jumped. With the strength he could muster, he threw himself from the roof across the alley and up to the edge of the castle wall. He caught the very edge of the wall with his fingers, but that would be enough.

Pulling himself up to the edge, Owyn waited. He peered over the side of the battlements. The curved merlons hid him perfectly while he watched the tower. Once the tower guards turned away again, Owyn threw himself past the merlons to the walkway atop the wall.

Landing on the walkway beyond didn't afford him the relief he sought. He felt exposed. At any moment the tower's guards would turn and see him. He searched his surroundings, first glancing at his legs to make sure he wasn't in part-dragon form. On the other side of the wall was a long row of covered stables. Landing from a jump would make noise and he would have to depend on the neighing inside to cover for him. But to get any further into the castle he knew he would have to run across the roof of the stables, revealing his presence in the waning sunlight.

He lowered himself carefully onto the stable roof, but slipped on the awkward angle of the shingles. In order to stay silent, he allowed his body to roll with the momentum. Unfortunately, he rolled onto his side and slid into a narrow crevice between the stable wall and the castle wall. He jostled down the small opening until his shoulder bumped against dirt at the bottom. With his body wedged and his bottom arm pinned under him, he listened to the tower guards run up and down the wall in the search. He heard orders being shouted. He even heard men running through the stables on the other side of one wall that held him.

Quietly, Owyn twisted his shoulders but they were held fast and wouldn't move. His top hand could stretch but he couldn't reach anything beyond scraping the walls with his fingers. He could wriggle his hips but they were also stuck fast. Even his chest could barely expand to breathe comfortably. When he tried to inhale deeply, his chest pressed into the boards in front of him. Guards peeked over the battlements toward the stable. Owyn froze – not that he could move anywhere, nor could they see him wedged below – until their gaze moved on. While a remarkable hiding place, he couldn't help but compare it to the cell and chains he had previously endured in the dungeon. And if he couldn't get himself out of this predicament, he would probably be returned to the cell soon enough.

Once the guards on the walls moved on, Owyn began to methodically work against his walled confines. He knew the guards in the stables were closing in on his position so he pressed harder into the stone behind him, pushing his feet to budge himself. Looking ahead toward the far end of the stalls, he used his only free arm to reach up and pull himself along. His chest and back unexpectedly scraped against the stone and wood and he couldn't stop a gasp from escaping. Out of Owyn's sight on the other side of the stable wall, a searching guard stopped and turned toward the sound.

Owyn held his breath at the sudden quiet. He closed his eyes, silently praying to Khurta to save him. When the guard finally moved on in his search, Owyn almost prayed thanks to Khurta, until he remembered the deadly trap he now lay in.

6

INTREPID

As the horses clambered to a halt, Philip dismounted quickly. He checked his horse to see wide lids and darting eyes. The ride had been fast because the faeries had given Travaith, his majishun, a concoction for the horses and for the men who walked to speed them along. His horse had run at a steady gallop the entire way to the halfway-point encampment, as had the men on foot. Philip felt the horse's sides heaving and the beast's heartbeat pounded a faster-than-healthy rhythm under his palm. He silently decided he would never ask to try the potion himself.

Dieko stepped next to him, having handed off his own horse to a guard. "Where's the commander of this hovel?" he said, wrinkling his nose.

"I'm sure he'll be along shortly," Philip answered, although he was certain Dieko wasn't talking to him.

Philip saw a guard take his horse's reins and pull him away faster than normal to lead the animal to a rough pen. All the other men in their group had used the majishun's speed potion, as had Torgon's group and the majority of the Noble army. As far as Philip knew, the armies from the other kingdoms were using it as well.

He turned to watch the others in their party and stepped over to Anna. She and Hilde stood together, stroking their horses. Anna calmly whispered to soothe hers. A guard stood nearby, bouncing slightly on his toes as he waited for the princess to relinquish the animal. She looked into the beast's eyes with concern before she allowed it to be led away.

"Doesn't seem natural, does it?" Philip said as Anna watched it go.

"No," she said shaking her head, then her eyes flitted to the guards around her. "I can only wonder how it affects the men."

Following her eyes, Philip noticed many guards twitching while they unloaded gear. Most rubbed down the horses with surprising vigor. Some wandered into the woods and back again for seemingly no reason except to keep moving. Before he could comment, a short man in a blue tunic with two swords embroidered on his shoulder, signifying him as a captain, walked quickly toward the party.

"Your Majesty," the man said with a small bow. The man's brown hair melted into a receding hairline lower than Philip's gaze, but Philip tried to remember to keep their eyes connected. "Welcome to our humble waystation. Please, come inside."

The group was ushered into the closest and largest of the rough encampment buildings. Inside, the captain indicated a large table with chairs for the king and his officers. Having been in the saddle all day, Philip declined the proffered chair, but stood beside it. Dieko took a seat with Anna beside him. Anna's companion, Hilde, stood behind Anna's chair. She looked impassive, neither uncomfortable nor interested in the proceedings.

"I'm Captain Leo Eisley," the short man said with another bow. "I welcome all of your royal highnesses to our small outpost. If there is anything—"

"Refreshment," Dieko said before the man could finish.

Captain Eisley nodded to a guard by the door, who stepped into the next room.

"We're so happy to host your highnesses," Eisley continued with a smile.

"A map!" Dieko barked as if he had been thinking of something to yell at the smaller man and only waiting for the opportune moment.

"Of course," Eisley said graciously with another bow. He shuffled to a cabinet against the wall and withdrew a large diagram of the Noble Kingdom. After laying it out on the table, Eisley motioned for the guard to set the tray of goblets and decanter he'd fetched next to it. Although the decanter was positioned directly in front of him, Dieko lifted a goblet and jiggled it slightly, expecting service, while his eyes wandered to the map.

"Where, exactly, are we?" he asked no one in particular.

Philip accepted a full goblet from Eisley and stood over Dieko to point at the map. "Here," he said, wishing he could "accidentally" spill the contents of his drink on the man's head. When had Dieko become so arrogant as to appear intentionally unpleasant? "We're on the eastern edge of the Torthoth Range, halfway to the Great Northern Mountain." Before he might fulfill his own wish, he stepped away from the older man to remove the temptation. "We should arrive tomorrow night if we use the faeries' speed potion on the horses again."

"Must we?" Anna said, accepting her own beverage. "It doesn't seem good for them."

"They'll be fine, Anna," Dieko said.

Anna's jaw clenched when he addressed her and she looked at Philip for a response.

"Unfortunately," he said, "I think we must. We need to hurry our progress so we can join Torgon at the Rock Clouds."

"Why are we wasting time and resources going to the Great Northern Mountain?" Dieko grumbled. "Why don't we go directly to the Rock Clouds? It would be preferable to sleeping somewhere that smells like a stable that hasn't been cleaned for months."

Philip took a deep breath and tried not to appear exasperated by the older man. "I need to inspect production before we leave for the Rock Clouds, and I want to explain our plans to you. And my sister, too, of course." He nodded to Anna and received her small nod in return.

"What is it you're going to explain?" Dieko asked. "What are these mysterious and brilliant war plans you have that you're keeping to yourself?"

There hadn't been an appropriate time along the road to divulge the information about where they were going. As well, Philip hadn't been comfortable, yet, with filling Dieko in on the details of his plans. He had held off until the last possible moment. Pressed by Dieko as he was, that moment appeared to be now.

"We have a secret weapon against the dragons," Philip said.

"Numbers aren't enough?" Dieko snipped.

"Against one dragon, never mind an entire ruck?" Anna said. "Do you remember our wedding night?"

As Dieko turned and opened his mouth to speak, Philip cut him off quickly before he could anger Anna further. "Exactly," he said. "All the Kingstor guards against a single dragon and it still escaped. But when we get to the Rock Clouds, we'll have a more powerful weapon."

Dieko turned back to Philip. "Like what?"

Philip looked at Eisley, who now stood silently nearby. "Do you have a sample, Eisley?"

From behind the cabinet, Eisley produced a quiver of arrows. Pulling one out, Philip showed Anna and Dieko the blackened tip.

"I don't understand," Dieko muttered. "Dragon killer bolts would be more effective. They do more damage to a dragon than an arrow."

"Not with this," Philip said, pointing to the black tip. "This black substance is dragon poison." Dieko's face slackened. Anna's seemed to harden.

"The faeries," Philip continued as Dieko plucked the arrow from Philip's hands, "researched it in the castle at Kingstor. They found an effective recipe and have been producing the poison in the Great Northern Mountain with men from the Noble army to assist. Bolts have a higher chance of bouncing off a dragon's hide if not properly aimed. The smaller arrows are better at slipping between dragon scales. These arrows are being produced in the mountain and sent to our armies and our allies' armies in preparation for the attack on the Rock Clouds. We're going to check on production and escort a supply delivery to our own armies."

"What if we get attacked?" Anna said, with a trace of fear in her voice.

Dieko nodded. "I've heard the centaurs are attacking supplies and caravans."

"We'll have the arrows with us in case of dragons," Philip answered. "And I plan on bringing men from the mountain to join us at the Rock Clouds. We should be a sufficiently large number for the centaurs to leave us alone."

Dieko shook the arrow. "Are these safe? Around humans, I mean? Won't they harm centaurs too?"

Remembering Torgon's lack of fear when he drew the blackened arrow tip across his palm at the faeries taunt, Philip pointed at Dieko's hand. "Try it and see," he said with a grin.

Philip stared at Dieko, testing the man's mettle, until Dieko reached his other hand toward Anna, palm up.

"Anna?" he said.

"What?" Anna gasped.

"If it's safe for me," Dieko said, turning to his young wife, "it's safe for you, yes?"

"No!" Hilde pushed herself between the newlyweds. "I'll not allow it!"

"How dare you!" Dieko hissed. He stood to confront Hilde, but the woman's size made him halt.

"You want to test it?" Hilde said. She yanked the arrow out of Dieko's hand and drew the point of the blade across her own palm.

Everyone flinched from the perceived pain, but couldn't take their eyes off her hand. The cut, just as Torgon's had so long ago, slid back together seamlessly. Hilde threw the arrow on the table and, wiping her bloodied hand on her black shirt, stepped away from Dieko to move back behind Anna. She never once took her eyes from Dieko.

After an awkward silence, Philip cleared his throat. "We have no means of knowing how it would react with a centaur, but an arrow is still an arrow. Tomorrow, I'll show you how it's made."

After another moment, Dieko glared at Eisley. "Where are our quarters?"

Eisley wrung his hands. "I'm sorry," he said, "but we only have one room with a bed besides the barracks for the men. We're still rebuilding. I assumed the king would use those quarters."

"No," Philip said. "I'm having my tent put up."

"Then," Dieko said, lifting his chin, "Anna and I will take the quarters."

Philip shook his head. "And what," he said, "let Hilde sleep in the barracks?" Before Dieko could balk, he spoke to Eisley. "Let the ladies use the bedroom. Dieko and I can sleep in our tents. I'm sure Dieko agrees that any other arrangement would be rather inappropriate."

Philip could see Dieko's jaw grinding his teeth together. Finally, the man drained his goblet and stormed from the building.

7

SHROUDED

Feet. Hips. Shoulders. Hand.

The guards had quieted their search some time ago. They wouldn't have been able to access the tiny hidden space where Owyn lay trapped anyway. The sun was fully down and Owyn crept along by the feel of his one hand groping the wall and his body scraping against it.

Feet. Hips. Shoulders. Hand.

Owyn fell into the rhythm after another short break. Bare feet flat against the stone wall behind him, he used the pressure to push himself ever so slightly along the wall. He wriggled his hips to shift himself and push his shoulders a little farther. Then using his free hand to grip whatever he could against the rough wooden wall of the stable stall in front of him.

Feet. Hips. Shoulders. Hand.

One week. The hatchlings only had one week. He might not even be out of these stables by then.

Feet. Hips. Shoulders. Hand.

Focusing on the rhythm helped distract from the pain. Every claw's length of movement of his shoulders felt like sword blades drawn across his back. The shirt and breeches Jarek had given him tore away easily as he scraped along. The stench of the horses and their excrement threatened to turn his stomach and the pain in his back doubled the pain in his stomach.

Feet. Hips. Shoulders. Hand.

Feet. Hips. Shoulders. Hand.

Several times he debated whether to turn himself into a dragon and burst from the confines. Each time he remembered there was no way to know if the guards at Kingstor Noble had poison-tipped arrows that would kill him. So he inched along.

He was actually closer to the other end of the stables, if only he could move backward. In fact, he'd tried to move himself to the nearer escape, but had found it easier to use his feet to propel him forward. So he scratched and squirmed toward the far end of the stable wall.

Feet. Hips. Shoulders. Hand.

Feet. Hips. Shoulders. Hand.

After what felt like an eternity, he stretched his arm to reach a vertical post between two stalls. Hooking his fingers on the edge, he pulled hard to gain more distance, but almost cried out as he felt small portions of skin peeling from his back. In the back of his mind, he wondered if his wings would survive.

He took another short break. Feeling pain as a human was slightly different from feeling pain as a dragon. The stabs of icy pain were similar, but burning often followed. As a dragon the burning would be a good sign; but it would only bring more pain to a human. The throbbing would usually briefly subside into numbness, but what he felt now didn't subside. It burned until the pain concentrated itself into stabbing prickles.

Resting and trying to hold in his screams, he tried to see the area around him. It seemed the guards had given up on finding him. From his place between the two walls, the sky appeared fully dark. Even the horses had stopped much of their chomping and clomping noises. Somewhere, though, a light burned, giving Owyn just enough vision for what he needed to see.

Once he started inching along again, he noticed a crack in the stable wall just over his head. He could see the horse's hooves through the slats of the wall. Part of the wooden slats had been shaved away, weakened by the horse's chewing or scratching perhaps.

Owyn rested quietly for a moment. He remembered a piece of information he had been taught as a soldier in the Noble army. Horses, especially those untrained to be a war horse, spooked easily. And never walk behind a horse in case it becomes scared and kicks you. He realized this horse must not be a war horse or it would already be at the Rock Clouds.

The horse stood with its head down and one hoof resting directly in front of the weakened part of the wall. Bringing his free hand up higher along the wall, Owyn swung it down quickly to bang on the wall. Although the noise wasn't enough to alert anyone else to his presence, it was enough for the horse. The scared horse's head jerked up and his back leg struck the wall behind him, opening a large crack.

Owyn lay silent again, wondering if anyone would come to inspect the noise. No one came. The crack in the wooden slats wasn't large enough to free him, but it was significantly close. Owyn waited until the animal quieted. Again, he banged on the beams and again the frightened horse kicked the wall behind him. This time the wall cracked in another spot and a small piece fell away.

Before Owyn could inch closer, he heard footsteps coming. Some of the other horses had woken and were snorting and neighing. The horse before him stamped and protested at being disturbed.

"Shady," whispered a voice, "quiet there. What's wrong with you?"

A stable hand fumbled to open the stall door on the other side of the wall from where Owyn hid. He could hear the person walking around the stall, probably inspecting the horse. Would they examine the wall? See the crack?

"What did you do?" Apparently, they would. "Did you hear a mouse or something?" the person whispered to the horse. "Well," they sighed, "we'll fix it in the morning. No extra oats for you if you're going to make more work for me." The person closed the stall and stalked away, grumbling.

After he was sure the stable hand was gone, Owyn pulled himself up to the cracks in the wall.

"Don't mind me, Shady," he whispered to the horse. The last thing he needed was to scare the animal again and get kicked in the face. "I'll just work on this hole a little more myself."

He wiggled the boards back and forth and after some effort the cracks grew bigger. After more work the boards cracked and pushed out of the way. Eventually, Owyn wriggled himself through the hole and into the horse's stable.

He lay in the hay at the horse's feet for a while, feeling the sting in his back, chest and arm. Sitting up, he rubbed life back into the flattened arm and his legs. Standing up, he rubbed the horse before turning to leave. "Thanks for your help, friend. Hope I've never eaten one of your friends."

The horse snorted as Owyn unlatched the door and tip-toed out of the stall.

———

Carefully slipping from shadow to shadow, Owyn regularly glanced up at the guards on the towers. Only sparsely placed torches lit the pathways because three bright moons gave more light than a fugitive might desire. Caught off guard as he crept along, Owyn saw one guard marching straight down the pathway from the castle to the stables toward him, but he ducked into the shadow of a barrel just in time not to be seen. A small glowing cube hung from a chain around the guard's neck, the cube a common majikal item that humans used to see better in the dark. As the guard passed Owyn, the shadows and light shifted around him, threatening to expose him. Owyn knew he would have to keep to the deeper shadows.

He had no idea where Anna's chambers might be or any idea how he would get there. He assumed he would find the tower where she placed the red banner as a sign to him that she needed to speak with him, but with as many guards as he had seen prowling around, he doubted he could get there tonight. Especially without being seen.

Another guard with a cube of light crossed the path in front of him between two outdoor walkways. More guards peered over the edge of the battlements. More watched from the towers. Owyn began to move from one of the shadows but caught sight of a guard peeking out from a window. Was it always this busy at the castle? He didn't remember nights with this much activity while he was chained here as a dragon. Perhaps more guards were on watch because word had passed around of Owyn's appearance in town.

Owyn shifted to another shadow only one dragon claw away. Moments after he flattened against the wall, another guard crossed in front of him. He had to stifle a cry of pain as he leaned against the wall on his torn back.

By the time I get to Anna the armies will have attacked the Rock Clouds, he thought as he rolled his eyes to the night sky. Seeing the black sky speckled with stars gave him an idea. But it wasn't without risks.

When enough time had passed that Owyn thought the guards had cleared the area, he moved away from the wall to the middle of the pathway.

Anger. Dragon.

Silently, he jumped into the air and spread his wings. Aches and pinpricks of pain speckled Hiro's wings. They felt as if someone had tried to use them as a talon sharpener. His borrowed clothing fell to the path beneath him. Beating his wings against the air, he gained height until he rose above the lower rooftops of the castle.

Using one of the shingled roofs, Hiro kicked off to gain more altitude. Surprisingly, he didn't hear the call until he flew toward one of the towers.

"DRAGON!"

The call echoed from all the towers in turn, then the walls, then the ground. Hiro flew close to the towers as the guards slung their bows. On the second tower, one of the guards took a swing at him with a sword. He didn't taunt them too much for fear of poisoned arrows.

Hiro shot into the night sky. He hoped the men would lose sight of him in the dark. He gained as much altitude as he dared before plunging to the ground. Aiming for the front of the castle to keep his pursuers in chase, he dropped a wing at the last second and spun in mid-air. Streaking toward the far tower, he flew up the side facing the castle courtyard and slipped silently over the top. The men on the tower ducked as he skimmed over their heads. When they recovered their senses and ran to the other side of the tower, the black dragon had disappeared.

Dragon, dragon, dragon, dragon… Human!

However, a naked man clung silently to a window ledge partway down the tower. Luckily it was still the warm side of autumn. The window remained open in the nighttime to allow a gentle breeze. Owyn waited until he heard the tower guards report that they had lost sight of the black dragon. He finally pulled himself level with the window ledge and unexpectedly met the eyes of a young maid with soft brown hair and a blue apron. But rather than scream with alarm, the young woman waved one hand at Owyn and shook her head. "Not yet," she whispered.

Still shocked by the encounter, Owyn lowered himself back under the window ledge just in time to hear the guards from the tower rumble down the stairs past the window. While he waited for them to clear, he wondered, *Who is this woman?* She had almost seemed to expect him. She certainly wasn't shocked or frightened at his presence, as he had been at hers. Once the guards passed, he mustered his courage to peek over the window ledge again. When he pulled himself up, the maid gestured for him to climb inside.

Clambering through the window into the stairwell, he could see the young maid holding a long black cloth in one hand and a glowing cube in the other. Once Owyn's feet found the floor, the maid stepped in front of him.

"You are the black dragon, are you not?" she asked, looking directly into his eyes without wavering.

Owyn scrunched his face, unsure how to answer her.

The maid took a step closer to him. Her face, devoid of fear, appeared hard and determined. He remembered her now. She had flirted with one of the guards to distract him so that Anna could free him from the chains keeping him in the courtyard. She must know many secrets. Perhaps all of Anna's.

"You *are* the black dragon, are you not?" she repeated.

"How do you…? Who…?" he stuttered.

The diminutive maid pursed her lips, transferred the cloth to the other hand and grabbed Owyn by one arm. She turned him enough to see the black outlines of his wings and tail on his back and leg.

"Of course, you are," she said as she released his arm.

"How do you…"

She held up her cube to stare into his eyes. "Your eyes," she said, "they're as black as a dark cave on a starless night."

Owyn pulled his head away from her inspection. "I need to see Anna. Can you take me to her?"

The maid lowered the cube slightly. "My mistress's eyes are green."

As Owyn tried to discern whether he could trust a young woman who couldn't or wouldn't explain herself, the maid began wrapping the cloth in her hand around his waist, showing no hesitation despite his nakedness. Perhaps Adair, who had taught him much about being human, wasn't exactly right about the body parts that shouldn't be shown to other humans. Or perhaps the important point wasn't that they shouldn't be shown, but when.

"Wrap this here," she said, using deft hands to secure the cloth. The cloth clung to itself at the top around his waist, allowing his legs to move freely. "Follow me. Quickly."

She led him into the castle by the light of her small cube. She walked so fast that Owyn thought he might lose her if he blinked. Twice she stopped him, counted to herself, then whipped around corners before he could ask questions. Finally she led him through a door into what seemed to be a bed chamber.

"I'm Amethyst," she said, leading him to another door. "My lady told me to wait for you."

"How did she know—"

"In here," she motioned. She led him into a large room filled with gowns. Owyn recognized many of the gowns he had seen Anna wear before. In the back of the room, behind all the others, stood a large blue gown held up by a frame to keep its shape. Owyn immediately recognized it as the gown she had worn in his visions. The ones in which a blue ribbon was wrapped around her wrist. It was her wedding gown.

Amethyst set down her cube to pull a couple of long metal hooks from the wall. Without a glance at him, she ordered Owyn to follow her to the back of the room.

"What are those for?" he asked, trying to indicate the hooks.

Using the hooks, she lifted the skirt of the blue wedding gown at the bottom hem. "I'm not allowed to touch it. Get under," she ordered.

Owyn pointed with a question on his face. "Am I allowed?"

She stood holding the skirt of the dress up and glared at him. "Don't let them find you."

Owyn took that as a 'no'.

"Hurry," she said, "the guards will be here any moment."

With one more glance at the door, Owyn dove under the garment and she dropped the skirts around him.

He squeezed his knees in tight, but even so, he could feel his legs, feet and shoulders brushing against the soft fabric. No sooner had he ducked underneath and the maid dropped the hem with the hooks, they both heard a knock at the door.

Owyn heard Amethyst replace the hooks on the wall, pick up her glowing cube and leave the room. She closed the door behind her, but he listened as she walked to the other door in the outer chamber.

"Sorry to bother at this late hour," the man's voice said as he entered, "but we're inspecting the entire castle."

"What do you think you're doing?" Amethyst insisted. "My lady isn't even here. And thank Shurka she isn't."

"If she isn't here," the man said as Owyn heard more feet enter the room and wander around the bed chamber, "why are you attending to her quarters?"

"Not that it's any of your business," she answered, "but there's always work to be done. I find it easier to get tasks done while my mistress is away."

"At night?"

"Sometimes."

After a moment, the man ordered, "In there." The man's voice sounded familiar, but Owyn didn't have time to think about it before he heard the door to the room where he was hidden open.

"Shurta's tangles!" Amethyst exclaimed. "What do you hope to find in there?"

After a startled pause, a couple men entered the room. "A dragon flew overhead only moments ago."

"Ah," Amethyst said, "and I have, of course, hidden the beast in my lady's petticoats."

Silence among them. Then a few snickers.

Owyn could hear their heartbeats inside the chamber. He thought the men must have brought more light with them because he could see a faint shadow falling across the cloth in front of his face. His own heart beat a rhythm so loud he thought the men might hear it.

Finally, Amethyst broke the silence. She must not have liked the look on the men's faces.

"No," she whispered. "How can you even consider such a thing?"

Footsteps walked toward Owyn's hiding place.

"It's forbidden for all but the high priestess," Amethyst insisted.

The shadow on the fabric grew small.

"Not even the king can grant you quarter if the high priestess finds out!" she shouted.

Owyn saw the form of a hand come clearer into focus as it reached for the skirt.

"General!" Another man's voice called to him from near Amethyst. The hand halted. "Please, sir. The men and I would rather not lose a good commander. There's no dragon under there."

The hand drifted away.

Owyn exhaled silently. He listened in relief as the general backed away and the guards left the area. Before leaving the chamber where he hid, Owyn heard the general mutter under his breath, "Why is it always this dragon?"

8

TROUBLE

"How do you know who I am?" Owyn mumbled through mouthfuls of slices of cold meat, cheese, bread and even some juicy round red vegetables. He preferred the meat over the others, but his human stomach rumbled so loud that he ate everything the young maid placed in front of him. He surprised himself by rather enjoying the red plants.

"You're the reason I'm here instead of with my lady," Amethyst grumbled, "as I should be," she added quietly. She sat on the bed behind him, gingerly dabbing at his cuts with a cloth. Her eyes never fully connected with his even when he turned to look at her.

That didn't quite answer his question, but he let it slide. She hadn't answered any of his questions directly. She had only permitted Owyn to come out from under the gown after she counted to one hundred. She told him – more like ordered him – to sit on the bed so she could tend to his wounds, but she also pulled out the large plate of food. She hadn't spoken much, only enough to dodge giving answers that would satisfy Owyn.

"Anna must have a crystal ball," he said between gasps of pain and mouthfuls of meat. "How long have you two been planning all of this?"

"She's not here," Amethyst said, after once again waiting for Owyn to hold still.

Owyn waved at the empty room. "I can see that." He thought that maybe by simplifying his questions he might get a straight answer. "Where is she?"

"She has the answers you seek," she said putting the cloth down and grabbing a small vial of liquid.

"Did she tell you anything? Does she know what Philip is planning?" he asked. Anna obviously knew more than she would have told anyone else. But why would she leave her maid behind without a message for him?

Glancing over his shoulder, he saw Amethyst shake her head.

"If she hasn't told you anything, then I must find her," he answered. "Immediately."

"You'll sleep here tonight," she said as if she hadn't heard him. "The remainder of the army and complement, including me, will leave in the morning."

"And me?"

The young woman stopped; after another beat, she splashed the liquid on a different cloth. "If I told you to go to the Rock Clouds and await her there, would you?"

Owyn gasped again as the liquid she applied seared into the skin on his back. The extra pain didn't help his thoughts, but he focused on his questions as best he could.

Why would Anna be in the Rock Clouds? Could he just sit and wait for her? Should he? How much does she know? Where are the poison arrows? Did the humans have a way to get into the Rock Clouds? How could they stop the spread of the poison? But most importantly, does Anna know who the traitor is among the dragons? Has she found out yet? Does Philip even know who it is? The hatchlings didn't have long to live. If Anna had the answers, he had to get them. Now. Could he stay away until then? Could he wait with nothing else to do but hope to see Anna soon?

And how in the world does such a small vial of liquid spread a blinding icy fire across his entire back?!

"Owww!" he whispered loudly.

He realized Amethyst had gathered the rags and stood, but she stopped next to him. He turned to her and she glared back in frustration, almost to the point of anger. She ground her teeth and turned her head.

"I have a uniform for you," she said. "You'll need to blend in with the men until everyone leaves."

"Where am I going?"

Amethyst shook her head slightly, still not willing to give away what she knew. "You will find her at the Rock Clouds, but for now, she has gone to the Great Northern Mountain," she finally said. "She's gone with the king. He swore to explain everything to her when she married."

"Anna is with the king?" he asked.

"Yes," she nodded, "and her husband, Lord Dieko of Selevyn."

Owyn stiffened.

"They have no idea," she grinned, staring at something across the room, "they'll get much more than they wished for."

"What?" he asked. When she didn't answer immediately, Owyn left the plate and stood in front of her. "What will they get?

Amethyst smiled up at him. "A dragon, of course."

Owyn nodded. Of course they would. He would follow that blasted woman to the gates of the World of Souls.

———

Amethyst woke him before the sun came up, a pattern he remembered from his training in the army. She had ordered him to lie down and rest for the night, then slipped into an adjacent chamber. But he didn't sleep well, and not because of his back. No, whatever she had applied to his wounds had helped them heal faster than they would have done on their own. Amethyst had kept the doors locked and the windows closed and covered. Through his fitful night, Owyn had worried about Anna and the hatchlings and the dragons and the centaurs, but each time he woke and slept and woke and slept, he stayed human, thank Shurka.

Amethyst threw a uniform at him but told him to keep the cloth she had wrapped around him the previous night. "Wear it when you change and it will change with you. It was made for your black scales."

"Who made it?" he wondered aloud, not really expecting an answer.

She shook her head at him. "I can only assume you are the reason all of this has been so difficult."

She went back to ignoring him as she packed several large trunks. But she didn't seem to be concerned about what went into them as she threw in some empty tonic bottles and what looked like an old hairbrush. After sunrise she fetched two plates of food; the larger one she passed to Owyn.

While they were eating, she suddenly jumped off the bed, threw the plates into a trunk, and slammed a helmet on Owyn's head.

"Tell me I can't take all these trunks down," she said. Her eyes flitted to the door. "Now!"

Before he could question her, the door opened.

"You can't take all of those," Owyn said quickly, trying to sound demanding.

"He's right," the guard said as he came through the door. Owyn pretended to scan the trunks surrounding them to keep from facing the guard. He knew his old claw's rival, claw 7-2, had been stationed at the castle. It was a good guess that one of them might recognize him if they saw him.

"She is a lady!" Amethyst shouted at both of them. "She's a princess and if the worst should happen, she'll be the queen! She needs to be at her best at all times!"

"Doesn't she already have everything she needs with her?" the guard said.

"One trunk," she pleaded. "Just one more trunk."

"No, not one more," he said. "Only one!"

Amethyst huffed, punching her fists on her hips. The motion caught Owyn's attention, reminding him very much of Anna.

"Fine!" she threw up her hands. Checking the trunks, she pointed to one. "Take that one down."

Without another word, Owyn hefted the trunk in his arms.

"And take that with you!" Amethyst yelled, throwing Owyn's long black cloth, bundled into a roll, on top of the trunk.

Owyn pushed past the guard, carrying the trunk down to the courtyard, leaving the bickering servants behind him.

Walking the halls and wandering amidst the army of men preparing to leave, Owyn folded and unfolded the black cloth to make himself look busy every time someone came by. Owyn went unnoticed in the scurry to get the last of the castle's complement on the journey. Finally, several minutes later, with everyone except the bare minimum castle staff being left behind, the large group was ready to depart. Unbeknownst to the men of the army, Owyn, the Noble Kingdom's fugitive, marched out the castle gates behind them.

9

OMISSION

Philip dismounted his horse in the large cavern opening. They had ridden far, but the men and horses still seemed jittery to continue. Instead of trying to soothe the beast, Philip was distracted by the enormity of the view under the mountain.

The cavern opening could easily allow two dragons to fly inside. Deep into the vast space, paths wound past cauldrons of different sizes, racks filled with rows of arrows, ladders, tables filled with bowls and scales, all covered in ash. Rivulets of molten lava flowed under the cauldrons. Men climbed ladders and stirred pots of bubbling black fluid. Black-tipped arrows overflowed large crates near the entrance.

To one side of the enormous space, stairs twisted up to several doors. The barracks and rooms for officers.

Philip headed that direction when a familiar face came into view.

"Welcome, Sire," Murzod's slimy voice intoned. His beard was much longer than last Philip saw him and he looked more unkempt than ever. His receding hairline emphasized the heavy beard. "We're so pleased you could take the time to inspect our humble facility." Behind him a faerie drifted away toward the cauldrons.

"I'm sorry I didn't come sooner," Philip said. And he meant it.

He noticed the haggard glances from the guards around him. How long had they been here? Their clothes were torn and thinning. Their faces, dirty and dripping. Dozens of men had bandages wrapped around their hands, wrists and feet.

The heat intensified as they walked farther into the cavern. The rivers of lava flowed from the back of the cavern into the ground along the sides. When the streams were too wide or too many ran together, a small bridge hovered over them, allowing access to the other side.

"If you'll follow me, My Lord," Murzod said, ignoring Philip's wandering eyes. "I'll show you to your quarters. I know how arduous the journey can be."

"That sounds perfect, Murzod," Dieko said, stepping forward. "Do you have any rooms with windows? It's stifling in here."

"Of course," Murzod said. "The two large rooms next to the side of the mountain are for that purpose. Our special guests receive fresh air to cool them from the heat generated by our production."

Dieko insisted they move on to their rooms but Philip stopped. Bothered by the ignorance of Murzod and Dieko, Philip walked away from them.

"I wish to see the facility first," he finally said. He wasn't going to wait. He didn't like the idea of the dragon poison. He didn't like the idea of the war to begin with. The one thing he cared most about and the one thing he could do something about, he would. The men. He inspected the men working and their surroundings.

Murzod caught up to the king and began pointing out the different functions of the many apparatuses around them. Philip already knew the basics of making the poison, but he didn't realize the intricacies. However, he couldn't listen as Murzod explained the process. He saw haphazard ladders that someone could easily fall from. He saw tables propped on large boulders. Steam drifted from the boulders and the floor. Sweat dripped from the men and sizzled on the floor around them. Several times, Murzod warned Philip away from unsafe areas where men were clearly laboring.

As they came to the back of the cavern, Philip saw the point where the lava flowed in a huge river from the back wall. The light from the lava blinded his eyes in the dark surroundings. As he began to turn, Anna, who he had almost forgotten was there, called out.

"What are those men doing there?" she said, pointing.

Philip turned to where she indicated and after his eyes adjusted to the darkness, he saw a small group of men huddled next to the wall beside the thickest of the lava flows.

"Nothing of note," Murzod grumbled. "If you'll follow me, Your Highnesses?"

Philip didn't move, gazing intently at the men. "That can't be safe."

Anna walked closer. "Are they chained?"

"Only one of them," Murzod answered, as if that was acceptable.

Philip ground his teeth and turned to the captain. "Explain yourself, Murzod."

When Philip looked into his eyes, Murzod straightened his back. He didn't quite meet Philip's height and Philip stood up even taller.

"It is a means to discipline my men," he said. "We need to have order. Especially in such a dangerous environment."

That made sense to Philip. He had been raised with Bragon teaching him the challenges of how to discipline. He knew that punishing someone was often more difficult for the punisher, and was reasonable only if it achieved justice.

"Only one violated a rule," Murzod answered. "He hit a superior officer."

Ignoring warnings to keep her distance from the searing lava, Anna walked briskly toward the men. Philip and Murzod followed her, knowing the danger. Dieko stayed back, well away from the fiery heat.

"You there," Anna pointed to one of the men, the largest man among them. "What's your name?"

The man stood respectfully with his head lowered. "Name's Thaddeus, My Lady. I had the honor to be sworn into the army by Your Highness."

"And what happened here?" she asked. "Why are you men being punished like this?"

"My Lady," Murzod blurted. "You don't—"

"SILENCE!" she yelled at him. Turning back to Thaddeus, she said in a firm, but kinder tone. "Please explain. Everything."

Thaddeus glanced at Murzod, who shook his head ever so slightly, but that only seemed to embolden the larger man. He stood up straight and spoke clearly.

"Addil," he said, pointing to a small man with broken spectacles on his nose, "he's not the strongest in the group. He was struggling one day. When Murzod came over to beat him, Maelin, that's your man chained to the wall, stood between them. When Murzod tried to hit Maelin, Maelin took the first swing. He was only standing up for the men in his claw, my lady."

"Maelin hit Murzod?" Philip said. While understanding the need to discipline the men and the rule that a subordinate must never hit a superior, Philip knew something else must be going on.

Thaddeus nodded.

"Why are all your claw's men together over here?" Philip asked. "Why aren't the rest of you working?"

Thaddeus shifted uncomfortably. "We take our punishment as one in claw 3-4. Seeing as any of us would have done the same for another."

Anna paced closer to the lava and back. "You're also trying to shield him from the heat."

Philip noticed most of the men sat between Maelin and the heat of the lava. A few rested on the more temperate side of their leader.

Thaddeus stared at the ground a moment, then said, "We take it in turns, Highness."

"And how long will they be like this?" Philip asked.

Murzod tilted his head. "It depends. Only one man is under punishment, the others are disobeying orders by staying here and not working. If their behavior doesn't improve, they'll all take a turn in the chains."

"For how long?" Philip asked again.

"Several days."

Anna huffed, crossing her arms over her chest. "The heat could kill them."

Murzod shrugged. "It happens," he said with stony features.

Philip struggled to keep his teeth from grinding. "Well," he said, when he found his voice. "you'll have to find some other means of punishment, because production won't be able to stay in this location much longer."

"Unless you plan on trapping them here," Anna added. "The ice on the surrounding sea is melting. The facility will have to be abandoned for the season or else you'll have no way out and will be forced to stay here much longer than planned."

Murzod glanced at Anna, then looked over at Philip. "Kradik said we need to produce enough arrows to fill the quiver of every man in the five kingdoms' armies. That total is much more than we have now. We plan to continue the work here and deliver supplies by eagle."

"Eagle?"

"Who cares about supplies when these men are likely to die under these conditions?" Anna almost shouted. She marched to Murzod and held out her hand. "The key," she spat.

Murzod looked to Philip. The young king could see both sides of the debate but he knew he wouldn't be so hard on his men. How long had this treatment been going on? He knew it was much too dangerous and Anna was right. These men had certainly suffered enough for being loyal to each other. He finally shrugged noncommittally, not wanting to exacerbate the situation, and nodded to Murzod. "She has the power to grant pardons," he said.

Murzod handed the key to Anna, who spun around fast enough to whip him in the face with her hair.

As she freed the man from his chains, Philip and Murzod joined Dieko on the cooler side of the lava. "I'll need good men at the Rock Clouds for the battle ahead of us," Philip devised. "I believe you should accompany us when we go, Murzod. We also need a strong contingent to escort us to the front lines. We'll have to pull most of your men away from their duties here." From the corner of his eye, Philip noticed some of the working guardsmen nearby perk up at these words.

Murzod seemed thoughtful before asking, "How will we maintain the production we need to continue supplying the weapons?"

"I'm sure we have plenty for the time being," Philip said. "You've been operating at the highest possible efficiency and our quivers will be plenty full for this battle. Make no mistake, production will return to 100 percent when the lake is frozen over again, but I think we can put someone else in charge of this place. I'd rather have good men and strong leaders with me during the battle ahead. Wouldn't you agree… General?"

Murzod's eyes widened a moment, but he smiled quickly at the change in title. "Of course, Sire," he said with a bow.

Philip gazed at the men while Anna attended to Maelin's discomfort after standing up without his shackles. "Where is your lieutenant?" he asked. "We should let him know that he'll be in charge when you leave."

"Uh," Murzod hesitated, "he…um…he passed…a while ago."

This time Philip didn't bother to hide his shock and Anna's eyes flashed again. "Passed?"

"Yes, Sire," Murzod said. "He died from exposure."

Murzod tried to hide his glance to Dieko, but Philip caught it. Dieko quickly straightened to confront the young king and defend Murzod. "He said it happens," the older nobleman said. "I received a few reports from Captain—I'm sorry, I mean General Murzod—at the request of Royal General Torgon. He's been doing his best here but some of the men aren't as hardy as they need to be for this assignment."

Something clicked into place in Philip's mind. A little louder, he said, "Someone will need to be in charge of moving these men to the Rock Clouds. We don't have the luxury of them resting while we do the fighting." Before Murzod could counter him, Philip called to the man being half-dragged toward the barracks. "Maelin, is it?" he said.

The men of claw 3-4 stopped as one and turned to their king. The men didn't salute as they probably should have otherwise, as they didn't seem to even be able to lift their feet to walk. The two men carrying Maelin shifted so he could look at the king. "Yes, Sire," he croaked through parched lips.

Philip stood to his full height, hoping the other men around them could hear everything he said. He needed witnesses and allies. "You'll be in charge of getting all of these men and their belongings to the Rock Clouds. I expect—"

"Sire," Murzod began to argue quietly.

Philip glared him down until he dropped his gaze. Returning his attention to the men, he continued. "I expect you and all of these men to depart here in two days. You will leave hours behind us and maintain the pace *without* faerie potions to speed you. Am I clear…Lieutenant?"

Silence followed, only punctuated by the bubbling lava around them. After a moment, Maelin lifted a shaking hand from the shoulder of the man carrying him, closed it into a half-fist, and placed it against his chest. The other men in the claw gathered their height and saluted as well. Philip noticed a grin tickle the lips of the smallest man in the group, his eyes darting to Murzod, but away again before it could be noticed.

As the men stumbled away to the barracks, Philip and his group moved toward the cooler rooms set aside for guests. As soon as they were behind closed doors, Murzod scoffed, "You're putting him in charge? And promoting him? How is that a punishment?"

Dieko rolled his eyes, but Philip couldn't be certain if it was at the whole situation, or in agreement with Murzod's assessment of it.

"I think they suffered enough, Murzod," Anna hissed.

"You shouldn't get involved, Anna," Dieko said without looking at her. "You have no idea how to keep order in a man's army."

Hilde leaned forward, but Anna placed a hand on her arm. The two women glared but said nothing.

Philip couldn't help but see Dieko's remark as an insult to his leadership as well. After all, he hadn't been ruling long and had never led men into battle. But he didn't let the comments deter him. "You're both right," he said, attempting to placate both sides. "If Maelin can't get to the Rock Clouds fast enough, he'll be demoted. But he'll need the authority to organize the men here. Besides, how better to teach a man the importance of discipline than to make him oversee the unruly? Maybe it's selfish of me, but I want both you, Murzod, and you, Dieko, by my side in the Rock Clouds, and I prefer not to leave either of you behind to complete such a distasteful task.

"Now, if this business is settled," he continued, seating himself at a table in the guests' quarters, "I'd like Murzod to describe to us exactly how the poison is made."

The group settled into an uneasy silence as Murzod cleared his throat. Philip allowed the older, more frustrating man to condescend to explaining the functions of the facility as he dwelt on how to get his hands to stop shaking from standing up to him.

10

ABDUCTION

CRASH!

"AAAAUUUGGGGHHHH!"

Philip sat straight up in his bed as the wailing screech tore every living being from their sleep. A guard shot through his door.

"Are you alright, Majesty?" the guard asked.

"I'm fine," Philip answered. "What's going on?"

"Not sure yet, Sire."

The guard left the room and Philip jumped to his feet. Pulling on a robe, he rushed from his room and saw several guards gathering at Anna's door in the common area between the two guestrooms.

"What's wrong?" he asked as the guards and Murzod arrived, but no one answered.

"Anna!" Hilde barked, pounding on the door to Anna's and Dieko's room. A crash and a muffled cry issued from within. More crashing erupted as Hilde shook the door's handle and leaned against the door. She spun on the watching guards. "Help me!" she yelled. As if only waiting for the order, the group of guards and men leaned against the door with her and each other. Philip followed, pressing his shoulder into the crowd.

"Ready!" Hilde yelled over the noise. Philip felt the bodies sway back and forth. "One, two, three!"

As one, the mass moved together and the door gave way. They had to continue pushing with force for it to fully open. Someone passed forward a lighted cube to illuminate the room and Hilde wailed. Philip pushed to enter as the crowd poured into the room.

They saw that such force was required to open the door because the entire bed had been thrown against it. Bedding and clothing were strewn across the floor, much of it charred or burning, mostly dripping in red. Trunks and furniture had been smashed or displaced and destroyed. Down from the mattress and pillows slowly fluttered to the floor with spatters of blood soaking into the remains. Glass shards splayed across most of the floor as pieces of the window dangled loose from its frame. Large chunks of the frame lay outside, burning along with the vegetation around the opening. Many items inside smoldered and water was called for, but the majority of the burning remained outside. Philip's legs shook as he took in the sight.

"Over here!" a guard called from the far wall. He pulled away the canopy drapes that were still attached to the ceiling but torn to shreds. Dieko lay there, slumped against the wall. Large swaths of red stretched across his upper and lower body, as if he had been thrown against a sword rack. Only a messy stump existed where one leg was missing and one arm was as black as charcoal. His eyes stared into the World of Souls.

"Anna," Philip whispered, feeling the blood draining from his body. His hands shook as he reached for the wall to steady him.

"She's not here," Hilde said. She knelt in front of the mutilated window, her rumpled uniform and hands covered in blood and soot. She sagged as she pointed to a piece of Anna's night dress stuck on a glass shard. Blood dripped onto the floor from handprints on the sill. On the ledge and carved against the walls, furniture and torn clothes, the rest of the marks couldn't be mistaken for anything else. Dragon claws.

A guard rushed to the window, pushing past the broken glass and daggers of wood. Three bright moons lit the night sky. After peering out, he pointed. "There! I see movement!"

Another guard joined him, holding a majik lens against his eye, a tool of the night watchmen. "I see it, Sire," he said with little enthusiasm. "But I...I can't be certain..."

"The night watch," Murzod grunted. Before Philip could ask, the man pushed past everyone.

Murzod led the way out of the room. Almost everyone followed, but Philip was closest on the older man's heels. They darted past the stairs and ignored the guards coming from the barracks to inspect the commotion. Murzod practically ran outside.

Just outside the entrance to the mountain cavern, several guards stood with arrows nocked, some posed as if they'd already fired.

"What happened, man?" Murzod barked. "Why didn't you give the alarm?"

One of the men turned to face his commanding officer. "She must have come around the far side of the mountain," he said. "There was nothing we could do. By the time we saw her, things were already..." The man trailed off waving a hand in the direction of the destruction.

Philip's knees felt weak. His stomach curled and his breathing came in short, ragged gasps. Someone nearby grabbed his arm to steady him. "She?" he asked, staring at the ground. "It wasn't the black dragon?"

"No, Majesty, to be sure ..." a small man with spectacles stepped forward. When Philip met his eyes, he recognized the little man from the loyal claw that had defended Maelin inside. On his face, the spectacles shimmered with multi-colored light. They were enchanted. "It was a female. A small, green dragon, Majesty. And..."

"What?"

After a moment, the man added, "She had a bundle in her claw."

The weakness in Philip's knees disappeared. Anger replaced his fear and raised him to his full height. Blood returned to his head and burned through his veins. His teeth ground together at the thought of the dragons who haunted him and his family and his people. His vision swam with thoughts of killing every dragon until he could find his sister again. Turning to Murzod, he growled through clenched teeth, "Get these men moving. Forget waiting two days. We leave at first light."

11

COMRADES

Little vials of potion got passed around amongst the men of the army. The women of the Black Saber refused the potion as they would all be riding, then the large group left the city behind. Owyn only pretended to take a sip, not knowing what it was or what it would do to a part-dragon. But the remains he licked from his lips sent a tingle down his throat. It tasted awful and his hands shook. He noticed the men at the front of the lines marched faster than their normal pace. It took him a moment to realize that he shouldn't follow them. His heart raced, urging him to move ahead, but he stayed at the back of the formation.

As the contingent marched, he shifted to the side of the group. His eyes darted from the effects of the potion and he could perceive that no other eyes were on him. He ducked into the trees to the side of the path so fast that he knew no one had seen him. The men kept moving ahead without him, their eyes forward. He could hear their hearts pounding as fast as their boots. With difficulty, he fought the urge to spring into the air. He waited until he knew no one would come back and look for him.

When all was quiet around him, he undressed. Assuming he would need human clothing later, he wrapped the uniform in the black cloth Amethyst had thrust on him and secured it to his back leg. Returning to the path, he jumped into the air.

Dragon, he thought, and he spread his wings. It was finally getting easier. He flew away as a dragon.

The lick of potion pumped through him, urging him to lift higher and move faster. He felt his wings shake when he tried to slow or glide. His wings pressed harder against the cold air, so cold that he shouldn't have been able to feel it. But he did feel it. Then his snout numbed and his wings seemed to move on their own. His tail whipped in the frozen air as his legs clawed to move him faster. Before long, Hiro watched the distant mountain range of the Ice Ruck approaching. His wings finally began to slow.

He knew he had flown much farther, much faster than humans could move. The residue of potion had urged him on. He didn't know when he would get to the Great Northern Mountain, but he assumed he had plenty of time to stop without losing track of Anna. Surely, she couldn't leave the mountain so quickly. He would catch up to Anna soon enough. His eyes drifted toward the Ice Ruck. He had told Milah that he would try again to get their help, so he dipped his wing and shifted course.

I'll have plenty of time, he told himself as he flew into the mountains of the Ice Ruck. It was a completely different scene than when he had visited before. On his first visit, the mountains were covered with snow and ice. No matter how much the ice dragons assured him it wouldn't remain that way, he hadn't believed them. Now, he couldn't deny it.

He remembered the sight of a frozen waterfall. That same waterfall now roared down the mountain. Around him water poured in rivulets, pooling, then splashing down further. Green grass and tall trees covered the mountains. The grass was a darker green than even in the Rock Clouds, but the summer landscape looked the same as it did there, only here it was rooted to the earth. The sun beat down on dragons lounging in the warmth outside of their caves. Groups of hatchlings chased some deer. Six dames flew out to hunt. Rabbits, deer, lydik, even a scorrand could be seen wandering the many forests and green carpeted areas. The land was alive and thriving.

"Welcome back, floater!" Maggoran, the pale bluish-gray young dragon that had greeted him last time fell into his wake.

"Shining days, Maggoran," Hiro answered, ignoring the slang term for 'stupid visitor'. "I need to speak with Rakdar."

"Again?" Maggoran's eyes wandered to the bundle attached to Hiro's leg, but Hiro pulled his leg in tighter to his body and Maggoran lost interest in it. "Don't you ever just come to visit?"

"I wish I could. This place is just as magnificent as you described it could be the last time I was here," Hiro said, and he truly meant it. This might be the perfect place to get away from a war or a rejected love or anything else that might darken his days.

"Then what do you need to see Rakdar about?" Maggoran asked, turning and taking the lead to the dame's lair.

"War," he said. "I've come to beg for help."

"Not you too," Maggoran whined.

"Me too?" Hiro started. "Who else has been here?"

"Your friend, Priya," he said.

"Priya? When was she here?"

"Yeah," Maggoran's eyes glazed over slightly, "the gorgeous green one. She was here a few months ago. Claimed a war was coming and she would need our help eventually. I would certainly follow her into war!"

Hiro's own heart pinched with a hint of jealousy at the sentiment – or was it just protectiveness – before he remembered Anna. For the briefest moment he wondered how it was possible for him to feel any jealousy about Priya. But he shook his head and dismissed the thought.

"Well," he said, "the time for that war has come and this might be your chance to fight alongside her."

They had reached the narrow chasm where Rakdar's lair was situated at the bottom. Hiro didn't stop to wait for Maggoran or anyone else – he flew straight to the lair. Landing at the entrance, he crawled into the glowing cavern. Maggoran and the watchers outside followed him in.

"Hiro Tekla!" Rakdar said with surprise, looking up from the lydik she had been sharing with a few others. Her lair was much the same as that of Rakgar's in the Rock

Cloud except for the glowing green spilling stones that gave this one light. She pointed her angled eyes at Hiro. "What are you doing here?"

Rakdar hadn't given Hiro a friendly welcome and he knew why. She didn't approve of the fact that he was so flippant about speaking while on the surface or among the humans. She didn't know about Anna, but she had blatantly refused to help him hunt down anyone from their joint attack on the humans. Without a reason to kill them, she saw no need for a hunt. She needed a reason to kill, which made her a logical leader. But she also needed a convincing reason to take any drastic actions at all. Which could make her unreliable.

"Shining days, Rakdar," Hiro gave her a polite greeting, realizing that, at the moment, he respected her more than his own Rakgar. "I've come to beg your assistance."

"Beg?" she asked, her purple, feathery scales rippling as she sat down. "I don't believe you the type to beg. I don't believe your Rakgar should let you out of the Rock Clouds either, but that's not my decision to make."

"Humans are surrounding the Rock Clouds," he said. The statement was met with silence in the cavern. "So, yes," he said, "I'm willing to beg."

Rakdar stared at Hiro. "Explain," she finally said.

Hiro explained about the humans gathering and Rakgar banning the Rock Cloud ruck from the surface. He explained that the faeries were helping the humans and his quest to figure out their plan to get into the Rock Clouds.

"The poisoned arrows that you helped destroy were only a part of the supply," Hiro finished. "Without your help now, the rest of the supply will get through to the human army."

"Again, Hiro," Rakdar said. "I will not forbid anyone in my ruck from joining you or assisting you. But, as I told Priya, sending our full force to join you against the humans would show intelligence and planning."

Hiro hung his head. "If you don't help us, we'll all be killed and the secret of Avonoa won't matter anymore."

———

The sun was only one or two dragon lengths into the sky when the Great Northern Mountain came into view. Hiro's heart burned as he beat his wings harder against the cold.

While the Ice Ruck Rakdar hadn't promised anything, Maggoran and others had offered a place for Hiro to stay the night while they discussed what they might do for him. In the morning, Hiro had awoken early after having another fitful night. He had abandoned any more attempts at sleep in the dark hours of the morning and at sunrise he'd sent off the few dragons who agreed to help him to meet with Ashel and the centaurs.

Before a warning of his arrival could be made to the humans at work inside the mountain, Hiro dipped toward the ground. The frozen sea, which acted like a moat around the mountain, offered him no cover to change, so he swung closer to the tree line. As he descended, he realized he wasn't as close to the mountain cavern opening as he'd thought he was, and he still had farther to go. He landed and continued on claws, covering the stretch of slushy snow quickly, being careful to stay outside of view from the opening.

Once he was close enough to see human movement inside, he used the coverage of the sparse vegetation, wagons, boxes and human paraphernalia outside the entrance to change into a man himself. He dressed with the clothes he'd carried tied to his leg, and added the layer of the black cloth under his tunic. He was extremely grateful to Amethyst for including boots in the bundle.

Owyn slipped inside the cavern and crept behind some crates before shuffling past tables laden with arrows. Knowing he wasn't completely hidden, he picked up one of the black-tipped arrows and pretended to inspect the tip. He knew what was on the tip. He knew the damage it could do. He remembered the piles of ash and ember and felt the burn of the poison seeping into his blood.

"What are you doing?" a harsh voice shook him from his thoughts.

Looking up, he met the eyes of a guard across the table. "Uh," Owyn hesitated a moment, then grabbed a fistful of arrows. "I was told to move these arrows into the crates. For transport."

The guard looked him up and down. "Clean uniform? You must have come in with the king's group. You obviously don't know how things work around here." The guard yanked the arrows from Owyn's grip and slapped them onto the table. "These don't go into the crates. Faerie couriers deliver them in satchels."

Owyn, not wanting to miss an opportunity, looked at the table laden with hundreds of arrows. "Satchels? Must be lots of faeries and giant satchels."

"Only one," the guard said. "One faerie. One satchel. At least, one at a time. The satchels are enchanted to hold thousands of arrows. Expanded majikally or something like that. Centaurs are attacking large parties, but the faeries knew they would. One faerie traveling alone doesn't seem like a threat." The guard looked around, then continued. "Why didn't you leave with the king at first light?"

Owyn shrugged, hoping he could lie his way through this interrogation. "I stayed behind to help."

The guard grunted, "Slept in, huh?" he shook his head. "The effects of the potion can be draining like that. You're lucky I found you instead of one of the men who brought you. Go outside and help haul the feed."

Stumbling back outside he met several men loading large barrels into wagons. He recognized some of the items the dragons had come across while raiding the human parties. Now, at least, he knew where the arrows came from and how they were being distributed.

"…not the black one?" one man finished his sentence as Owyn approached.

Two men in dirty tattered uniforms rolled a barrel toward a wagon. One man had bright orange hair and freckles all over his body. The other had dirty yellow hair with hairy patches on his chin. When Owyn approached, they eyed him warily.

"I was sent to help," he said.

"We could use a fighter to lift these," the orange-haired man said. Owyn struggled a little with the weight but heaved one of the barrels into the wagon.

"I'm Brack," the orange-haired man said. "That's Dergin."

"Owyn," he said, introducing himself. He paused, worried that someone might recognize the name, then he remembered that Adair had claimed it to be a fairly common name when he gave it to him.

"I'll stack," Dergin said, climbing into the wagon.

With a last glance at Owyn, Brack sauntered back to the barrels to roll another one toward him. "Anyway," he said as he grasped one and rolled it, "it wasn't the black dragon."

"What wasn't the black dragon?" Owyn asked in shock before he could stop himself. He knew the guards often discussed happenings in the kingdom, but he didn't know why they would be discussing him here.

"The attack," Brack said with a sneer. He looked Owyn up and down again, almost in disgust.

"Attack?" Owyn feigned ignorance. His mind immediately remembered the many past coordinated attacks with centaurs and dragons. Perhaps the men were discussing one of those. "Which one?"

"Which one?" Brack choked.

"Where have you been?" Dergin questioned.

Owyn, desperate not to give himself away, mumbled, "I came in with the king's group. I haven't been here long."

Brack shook his head, "Then you were here last night, weren't you? Or did you slip away and come back before dawn?"

When Owyn could only stare back in stunned silence, Dergin saved him. "It's probably the potion. I bet you're one of the cracks that slept through all the commotion. Haven't you heard everyone talking about it all morning?"

Owyn just shook his head. So much for blending in. As he passed the barrel up, the man in the wagon relayed everything with great passion.

"The night watch didn't even see her coming," Dergin said. "I heard it was a small green dragon. She swooped in, killed Dieko, destroyed their sleeping chamber, then flew out the window with the princess!"

Owyn stopped, paralyzed with the realization. *Why would Priya kidnap Anna? What was she doing here? Could it have been someone else? No, only Priya would think to take Anna. But why? —Ouch!!*

"Hey!" Brack smacked Owyn on the back of the head. "Keep moving, the lieutenant's coming this way."

Owyn lifted the next barrel to the wagon as another man joined them. He started turning toward the newcomer but stopped when he recognized the man's face. Instead of acknowledging the superior officer like he had been taught to do, he turned back and pretended to struggle with the barrel to prevent Maelin from recognizing him.

"If you don't get these wagons harnessed immediately," Maelin barked, "we'll leave you and the horses to the centaurs. We're leaving now, with or without you."

"Yes, Lieutenant," the other men said while saluting with a fist to their chest.

Luckily Owyn couldn't salute without dropping the barrel, so he remained bent over and watched from the corner of his eye as Maelin stalked away.

Brack rushed Dergin off to return with the horses and harness them to the wagon while he and Owyn shoved the rest of the barrels on board. When time ran out, Brack left several barrels behind. They barely brought up the rear of the trail of men leaving the Great Northern Mountain for the Rock Clouds. As they hurried to catch up to the others, Dergin pointed out the large dragon claw prints in the melting snow.

"Keep an eye out," he told Owyn. "You're taller, so you can see more."

"They're probably from the one last night," Brack said, "but be aware, just in case."

"Do you think the other men saw them?" Owyn asked.

"Who could miss them?" Brack said. "We're probably just too far back for any of the others to warn us."

"We'd better get moving if we're going to catch up," Dergin said.

Owyn could barely see the men ahead in the main group. "Are they using the faerie potion? Aren't we all going to?"

Dergin shook his head. "Nope, not allowed, are we? Part of Lieutenant Maelin's punishment. We gotta move just as fast as if we had used it, though."

"Punishment," Brack snorted. "If you ask me, king doesn't care how fast we get there. It's a blessing getting us out of there."

The two men did urge the horses on to join the main group because the wagons would need the protection of the guards around them. But Owyn lagged behind.

What was Priya doing here? he thought as he trudged through the melting ice. *Amethyst said I would 'find' Anna in the Rock Clouds. Did she know Priya would take her there? Why wouldn't she just tell me?* He snorted to himself, thinking of his frustrating conversations with Amethyst, the maid who couldn't – or wouldn't – speak straight.

He decided something had to have happened that led to all this, and he had to find out what it was. He would have to, once again, break away from the group of men and guards to disappear into the forest and mountains. He would find Anna using his own devices, but would he ever stop chasing her?

Owyn had fallen behind, but he stayed close enough to the men still trudging to the Rock Clouds. His claw marks finally fell behind the group and after traveling much of the day the soggy, frozen mush turned to soggy, muddy grass. Suddenly Owyn stopped. He looked up and – momentarily forgetting his worry about Priya and Anna – searched their surroundings. They had been walking at a good pace for a long while and just entered a narrow canyon pass that would take them through the Torthoth mountain range. He knew this pass. He had used it. Surveyed it from above. Watched and waited. From above.

Owyn's breathe caught in his throat. The few men walking on the outside of the caravan searched the mountains around them. Owyn noticed Koris, one of the first men to befriend Owyn when he changed into a human and one of the men in his former claw, watching the trees. On the other side of the caravan, he could see Thaddeus. His huge fighter bulk could be seen for miles. He searched the trees on the other side. They would be among the first to die.

Rooted in place, Owyn's better-than-human eyes also searched the trees around them. The centaurs were good at concealing their presence. Even as a dragon, he couldn't locate them when they wanted to stay hidden in the forest. Then he realized, the centaurs wouldn't be the first to attack. The centaurs would come from one side only after...

"Dragon!" the call came.

As all the human heads went up, Owyn realized he didn't have any time. He would have to chance being seen.

He changed just as the centaurs erupted from the trees with knocked arrows on bows. He leapt from the back of the caravan to the front with only a few swipes of his wings. He landed on his side, facing Koris, as the arrows bounced off the scales along his back.

Standing, Hiro unleashed a burst of flame toward the centaurs. He looked into the sky to see Prakyndar. The small brown dragon wheeled away toward the side of the canyon opposite from where the centaurs had come. He was retreating.

Bow in hand, Ashel skidded to a stop in front of Hiro. Hiro stood his ground between her and the humans until she finally lowered her bow. The centaurs flanking her did the same, albeit slower. Hiro could see her teeth grinding. Her large eyes flashed between Hiro and Koris. Hiro snorted at her and her eyes locked on his.

Finally, after a moment of silent argument between the two, Ashel straightened her back. Her eyes met Koris's. "You have fortunate allies," she bit at him. Then she turned and galloped back into the trees from where she'd come.

As the centaurs left, Hiro turned to look at Koris. Then, seeing their human weapons half-drawn, Hiro inched backwards, away from them. He saw Maelin step forward, watching him carefully. Slowly, Maelin extended one hand to signal the men to stay their weapons.

Finally, Hiro launched himself into the sky. Behind him he heard someone say, "Aren't we supposed to kill dragons?"

The last voice he heard was distinctly Maelin's, saying, "That dragon just saved our lives."

12

CUT OFF

"What happened?!" Ashel yelled. She had obviously given up caring if the humans heard her. Or else she knew their hearing wasn't as good as the dragons'. "Has your heart hardened for the humans?"

She doesn't know how close she is to the truth, Hiro thought.

"There's no need to kill them," he said.

"No need?" she said. "This is war. That's how you finish it."

Hiro had flown farther down the canyon after the confrontation, hoping the humans wouldn't associate him with the centaurs. He'd also wanted the group of humans, which included his old claw 3-4, to feel safe enough to continue on the path they were going.

Back on ground, however, Hiro had doubled back to meet Ashel and Prak in the trees overlooking the canyon. The men had advanced much farther by the time he met the leader of the warrior centaurs, but he still thought her yelling might carry to the Rock Clouds and beyond.

"What's going on?" Prak said as he landed next to them. His route back to them must have been even longer. "Hiro, where have you been? What did you find out? Why did you stop us? You appeared out of nowhere. I didn't see you until you were there. What happened?"

"Apparently, Hiro has grown a conscience," Ashel growled at Hiro. "He says we don't need to kill the humans."

"You don't," Hiro said.

"Why not?" Prak asked.

"Those humans didn't have the arrows," Hiro finally answered.

"So?" Ashel said. "They're still reinforcements."

"And it's fun," Vikal mumbled from behind Ashel.

"We're not going to win this war unless we act," Prak said. "That's what you said. That's why we're doing this at all. What else are we supposed to do?"

Hiro shook his head. He had to give them something, some reason to spare the humans. "The individual travelers," he said, "usually faeries. They're the ones carrying the arrows. They have enchanted satchels to transport supplies. They knew you would let lone travelers through."

After a moment of silence, Ashel broke her bow with a resounding CRACK! "Shurta's tangles and Khurta's claws!" she cursed as she threw the bow and added more curses into the sky.

"We've been spitting in Tarsa's eye," Vikal grumbled as the other centaurs cursed and shook their heads as well.

Prak shook his head and closed his eyes. He opened his mouth to speak but nothing came out. He closed it again and opened it a couple more times.

"Prak," Hiro began, but he didn't exactly know what to say.

"Let me think. Let me think," Prak said. He stared into the sky and mumbled to himself, getting louder and louder. "We've been chipping away at them. Bits and pieces, yes, but…fewer men is fewer men. We were going to have to withdraw back to the Rock Clouds soon enough anyway. We knew it was a risk…"

"What was a risk?" Hiro asked.

Prak sighed. "We risked staying out here longer. Being closer to the humans' waystation. We knew the humans might beat us to the Rock Clouds, but we thought it might be worth it to find the arrows. We were hoping to find the chain of transport."

"Break camp!" Ashel yelled, spinning on the other centaurs. "Send a message by eagle and wolf for all groups to retreat back to the Rock Clouds." Several centaurs, including Vikal, galloped into the trees. She turned to face Hiro and Prak. "Let's hope they're slower than we thought and we can still get through."

―――

"We can't get through!" Vikal yelled as he galloped toward Hiro.

After only a day and a half, the groups of dragons and centaurs had gathered on the east side of Centaur River. Tog and Prak and many other dragons had joined them, including the Ice Ruck helpers. Vikal, Tog and a few others had scouted ahead before the sun fully set, only to come back with dreadful news. They had arrived just after sunset at the banks of the river. Now the groups rested in the darkness of the Black Forest to decide how to proceed.

"Human camps stretch for miles in either direction," Vikal reported.

"We're cut off from Joss and Rylan," Ashel said. "So they have no idea we're here and they can't get any help through to us."

"We can fly you over," Prak said.

"We've discussed that," Ashel said, as they had debated back and forth for the entire previous day and a half. "It would take too many trips and too long. You would look like you're either highly trained pack animals" – Tog growled low – "or you're organized to know exactly what you're doing and expose the dragons' higher reasoning."

"I know, I know," Prak mumbled. "The humans might strike early, change tactics, or any number of countermeasures, each more fatal than the last."

"Besides…" Ashel looked into Prak's eye, "flying over would be too dangerous for all of you, now that we know they have the arrows."

"That's not all," Tog said. He admitted to taking a few low passes over the trees to distract the humans from the scouting centaurs. "I saw large wooden structures beneath the trees."

"I saw them too," Vikal said.

"What are they?" Ashel asked.

"I don't know," Tog answered. "They look like huge, flat platforms. Looks like they could hold several dozen humans or…"

"…or a handful of dragons." Vikal finished.

Hiro shook his head. Prak searched everyone's eyes, but no one had an answer.

Ashel shook her head. "Now what do we do?"

"We fight on two fronts," Vikal said, puffing his chest. "It could be a tactical advantage."

"Only if Joss knew where we were and what we're planning," Ashel said.

"You can go back to your land," Prak said. "The other centaurs might need protecting. Follow the river and protect your people. The faeries might go there next because they know you've been helping us."

"Oh, yes," Ashel rolled her head along with her eyes for emphasis, "the leader of the warrior centaurs scampers off home instead of defending her allies." She snorted. "I wouldn't be leader of warriors much longer."

"But you'd be alive," Prak muttered.

Ashel growled low, "I'd rather die defending you." She seemed to catch herself and her eyes skipped to Hiro's. "All of you."

"That," a deep voice grumbled, "is what I needed to hear."

Hiro recognized the voice, but couldn't say anything before the small, gray-skinned king of goblins appeared out of nowhere in the middle of their circle. He wore an adorned circlet atop his dark red hair but his brown clothes stood out for their plainness. As soon as he materialized, a knife pinged off a majikal shield around him. Ashel's hand dropped in consternation.

"King Svorgh," Hiro said, stepping toward the leader. "What are you doing here? How did you find us?"

Shvika appeared next to her father. "Anna," she said, spitting the name like a curse. She continued to glare through the frame of her blood-red hair at the centaurs surrounding her, hand on her sword.

"Is she ok?" Hiro asked before he could stop himself.

Shvika shared a look with her father before answering only, "She's in the Rock Clouds."

Svorgh stepped toward Ashel and Prak, his hands turned toward the centaur. Ashel's hand inched toward another knife strapped around her belly.

"We've come to help," he said.

Ashel's hand stopped. She shared a glance with Prak and they simultaneously leaned down to inspect the king, not hiding their intrigue at the little man's gray skin, red hair and circlet bedecked in gems.

"Who are you?" she asked him.

"More like, *what* are you?" Prak said.

"How are you going to help us?" Ashel asked without waiting for a response.

"How can we trust you?" Prak said in turn.

Hiro realized that Ashel and Prak must have spent an awful lot of time together, speaking in turn the way Milah and Mitashio did.

Svorgh held up his hands to slow the questions. "We are goblins," he said.

"Phantoms," an invisible presence near Vikal was heard to say.

"Ghosts," another presence said from behind Tog.

Snickering swelled around them. Ashel didn't stay her hand. Before the giggling subsided, she held a long dagger in each fist. Vikal and the other centaurs did the same.

Svorgh waved a hand. "Enough," he said, loud and firm. When all eyes returned to him, he looked to Hiro. "We are allies," he announced.

Ashel swung her dagger to point at Svorgh. He was just tall enough and her blade long enough to point it at his throat. Shvika tensed, but was as steady as a stone carving. "Hiro," Ashel said, "do you know this creature?"

"Yes."

"Do you trust him?"

"Well," Hiro hemmed, "he did choose to not kill me."

Ashel raised an eyebrow at Svorgh, who shrugged. "It wasn't his time," he said.

Ashel's eyes darted as she slowly put away her blades. "Let me see you," she said. "All of you."

A blue gem glowed briefly on the side of Svorgh's circlet. Shvika's also glowed. She moved her hand from her hilt as several goblins materialized around them.

Svorgh indicated himself, then Shvika. "I am Svorgh, King of the Goblins. This is my daughter, Shvika, she is the leader of our warriors."

Hiro recognized Keeahrspi, his bulging arms covered in glowing tattoos, and Mlika and Morkni, with their fluorescent yellow hair, as they appeared before them.

Keeahrspi came to stand beside Shvika while most of the goblins gathered behind Svorgh.

Ashel looked to Prak, who stepped forward. "Other than the ability to be invisible," he asked, "what help do you offer?"

"We'll fight," Shvika said.

"You're not suggesting," Vikal sneered, indicating the short swords on their hips, "that those little pins can do any real damage?"

"I suggest nothing," Shvika said, "but I can show you." She took one step toward Vikal and a purple gem glowed on her circlet. With her next step, there was a flash of purple and she became a large white centaur with the same blood-red hair. As she pulled out her small silver sword it extended from its sheath and grew into a long, two-handed blade of pure black — handle, hilt and blade. She held it to Vikal's throat before he could move.

"Is that what I think it is?!" Ashel shouted. Hiro thought she should be more concerned about Shvika holding a blade to Vikal's throat rather than being captivated by the blade itself.

Prak began to bounce in one spot. "Is that the Just sword? Where did you get it? How did you get it? Is it real?" He remembered himself and calmed down even as his eyes bounced between Svorgh, Shvika and the sword, waiting for an answer.

"Shvika claimed the sword last night," Svorgh said, "from the human king's own tent. She's using an illusion to hide it."

Shvika's eyes imitated the mischief in her voice. "Call me a dragon, but I just can't resist something shiny."

Her words quoting the same previously from Ashel's own mouth.

Ashel gasped and threw a hand to her mouth. Turning to Prak, she exclaimed, "I like her. Can we keep her?"

A grin spread across Vikal's face that agreed with the sparkle of admiration in his eye.

As Shvika returned to her original form and position by her father, Prak turned to Svorgh again. "You obviously have impressive abilities," Prak said. "What are you proposing?"

"You have tunnels," Hiro said, remembering them. "Passageways. Can you, somehow, get us to the Inner Mountain? To where the others are gathering?"

"We don't have anything close enough or that can transport all of you. But we do have these," Svorgh reached into a small pouch at his side, producing a handful of silver circlets, each with a brilliant blue gem embedded in them.

"I always wanted to ask you about these circlets," Hiro said. "What are they?"

Svorgh tapped the circlet on his head with the simple ones in his hand. "These are dragon gems," he said. "Different gems with different powers. They are gems created from thousands of years of dragon ash. Each gem has a unique power derived from the dragon whose ash created it. The blue sapphiragons are connected to each other to allow concentrated thoughts to move between them.

"There will be a distraction," he said, offering the circlets to Ashel. "My troops will move ahead invisibly and guide you through the human camps. The sapphiragon will allow us to communicate to navigate the dangers efficiently. We can regroup and plan on the other side. With your brothers."

Ashel accepted the tiny silver bands. She kept one and handed the others to Vikal. She threw a questioning look at Svorgh, who simply tapped his own head. Although the circlet was no bigger around than Ashel's arm, she lifted it with both hands over her head. As she lowered it, it grew to fit her head perfectly. With grudging acceptance, she looked down on the little king and said, "I want one like yours."

The diminutive king grinned up at her. "Maybe someday, my dear."

"You said there will be a distraction," Prak said as the centaurs fitted their circlets. "Will you provide one? Or can you tell the future? When will we know?"

Svorgh turned to Hiro. "I know many things," he said, staring deep into Hiro's eyes. "Nothing distracts like a criminal."

A distraction, Hiro thought.

"No," Tog said, shaking his head, "a dragon flying over the humans' heads will only alert them that more might be coming or passing."

"Agreed," Prak said, "we can't have the humans looking up."

A criminal, Hiro thought as he stared back at Svorgh. "Don't worry," he said, "they won't be looking up."

13

EXPECTATIONS

"Lieutenant Maelin, squad 3-4 reporting, sir."

Philip looked the lieutenant over. He seemed to have healed well and quickly from his ordeal in the Great Northern Mountain. He may have brought the report specifically for Torgon, but Philip wanted to listen in. He couldn't help but respect this man and his squad after what they'd suffered.

"Is all in order, Lieutenant?" Torgon asked.

"All men and supplies from the Great Northern Mountain and laboratory are accounted for, General," Maelin said, standing at attention.

"Then why is a lieutenant reporting to me instead of your captain?"

Without hesitation, Maelin answered, "I technically don't have a captain yet, sir. Murzod was my superior—"

"And you obviously don't have any respect for him," Philip put in, noting the absence of Murzod's title in the lieutenant's reference.

"No, Sire," Maelin said. "I would request a different superior."

Torgon nodded. "I'll see to it. Is that all, Lieutenant?"

"No, sir," Maelin hadn't hesitated to complain about Murzod, but for the first time he seemed nervous. "There was an incident."

"Explain."

"While we were traveling through the Torthoth mountain range, at the Pass of Scurlyn, we were attacked by centaurs."

Philip sat up. "Centaurs?"

Torgon glanced at Philip, but asked Maelin, "Your men survived?"

"Yes, sir," Maelin said. "All survived, as did our cargo."

"How is that possible?" Philip couldn't help himself. "Centaurs don't leave humans alive."

"I'm not entirely certain what happened either, Your Majesty," Maelin stood tall and noble, and managed to look Philip and Torgon in the eye. "In one second, centaurs were dashing from the trees to attack; in the next, a dragon stood in the way. The centaur female only said we have 'fortunate allies' and they all left."

"What is that supposed to—"

"What color?" Torgon blurted.

Philip, barely noticing Torgon's interruption, glanced over at his royal general and a knowing look passed between them.

"What color was the dragon?" Philip repeated.

"It was a black dragon, Sire."

Torgon dropped his head to bang his forehead on the desk next to him. "Why is it always that dragon?" he mumbled.

"Wait," Philip held up a hand, "a green dragon kidnaps Anna and kills Dieko. Now the black dragon is protecting humans from centaurs? What in Shurta's tangles is going on?"

Torgon sat up, a visible red mark in the middle of his forehead. "Why is it always that dragon?" he grumbled a little more forcefully.

Maelin didn't twitch.

"Why would he protect you?" Philip said. "Why would a dragon," he placed a hand on Torgon's arm to stop him from repeating the same question, then continued, "*any* dragon spare, no…*protect* humans?"

"I don't know, Sire," Maelin said. "Honestly, Your Majesty. We all discussed it in our travels here. Four different claws made up our group. The only difference between any of the claws was…"

Torgon sat up straight. "Yes?"

"Well," Maelin hemmed slightly. "Please understand," he hesitated, "I'll submit myself for any discipline necessary, but I don't feel my men, or myself for that matter, have done anything wrong."

"But?" Torgon barked.

Maelin stood up taller. "When my claw took our oath to the Noble Kingdom and the Noble family, there was a man among us that was…well…different."

"Different?" Philip asked. "How?"

Maelin sighed. "Name's Owyn, he was the man who insulted Princess Anna."

Philip and Torgon stared at Maelin. Finally, Torgon said, "That's it?"

"Is he the man Dieko wanted killed?" Philip asked.

"Yes," Torgon nodded. "Then this man, whoever he was, threatened Anna and used her to escape the dungeon."

"What did he call her?" Philip asked. He had never bothered to get the whole story before Dieko had taken charge of the problem.

"He said she was disgusting, Sire," Maelin said. He didn't seem at all bothered by answering truthfully. "But she said we could say whatever we wanted. She said he had the right to speak his thoughts."

"And he did leave her behind unharmed when he escaped," Torgon added.

Philip nodded thoughtfully. "Do you think she's disgusting?"

"Of course not, Your Majesty," Maelin said.

"I can't decide," Philip said, as only a brother would.

"That's not the point," Torgon said, pursing his lips at Philip. "The question is, why did the black dragon choose to put himself between your men and the centaurs?"

"I don't know, sir," Maelin said. "We thought a beast like that might be provoked by the markings Owyn, the escaped man, had on his body. Brilliant markings of dragon wings that spanned his entire back, as if a dragon had folded them up and placed them there. And markings of a tail that ran the length of his leg down to his ankle. The tattoos were black as a moonless night."

Torgon nodded. "And the man, Owyn. What do you make of him?"

Maelin shook his head, unable or unwilling to answer.

"Speak, man," Torgon said, not unkindly. "This is your chance to be heard."

"I…" Maelin hesitated, then cleared his throat. "He was different, but I trusted the man with my life. I believe I still would."

Philip and Torgon shared another glance. With promises of no disciplinary actions against Maelin or his men, Torgon excused him.

After Maelin left, Philip sat pensively biting the inside of his lip.

"What is it?" Torgon said, facing him.

"Do you trust him?"

"Who, Maelin?"

Philip nodded.

Torgon sighed and slumped back to his chair. After a moment he said, "I'd like to hear what you think first. You're a better judge of character than most men I know."

Philip paused before answering. Maelin carried himself nobly. He was confident, honorable, brave and loyal to his friend. He stood up for the men he'd trained and fought alongside. He acted with respect toward his king, but wasn't afraid to look him in the eye. Maelin hadn't looked over Philip's head the way Dieko had, but he didn't lower his eyes, either.

"Yes," Philip whispered, "yes, I do trust him."

"So do I," Torgon said.

"Good," Philip said. "I'd like Maelin and his men with us when this disaster starts."

With a nod of agreement, Torgon slipped from the tent.

14

POISONOUS FAITH

How could he know, Owyn thought to himself, *and how much does he know?*

Owyn distinctly remembered Svorgh telling Anna he knew more about her than she would like him to. How much could he know and of what?

He picked his way through the trees on the northwest side of Centaur River, moving ever closer to the human armies. He had flown away from the group as a dragon and landed in the trees as a human. The black cloth Amethyst gave him did, indeed, change with him. He hadn't thought about the human clothing ripping to shreds when he changed to save Koris and the others. He didn't once think about the need for clothing while he was a dragon.

But thank Shurka, Anna had thought of it. Anna knew that Owyn would come for her. She left Amethyst behind to help him. Anna was the one with the foresight to give him the cloth. Had she procured it after she found out that he could change into a human? How did such a cloth even exist? If she knew so much about Owyn, about Hiro, did she also know how to contact Priya to fly her away from the Great Northern Mountain? Or did a different green dragon come to Anna's rescue?

No, he concluded, *any other dragon would have killed her if she had tried to contact them.*

Was it Anna's idea to get Priya to take her to the goblins? Had she pled with them to help the dragons? Did she know what the large platforms were to be used for? But most importantly, where was she?

"You will find her at the Rock Clouds," that's what Amethyst had told him. Even Shvika said Anna was in the Rock Clouds. He had to continue on course to send everyone to the Rock Clouds, then join them there. Priya was probably there with Anna at this moment. If only he could get everyone else to the Rock Clouds as well.

Through the trees, Owyn saw the lights from a fire. He saw a few men ahead staring into the trees. Lookouts. Behind them, other fires were dying down. Only a few men appeared alert in the deepening darkness. Most men were probably in their tents asleep by now. The human camps were dark and mostly quiet.

Owyn stepped carefully on rough bushes and fallen branches. When he had noisily broken quite a few of them, he was finally discovered.

"Who goes there?" one of the men shouted into the dark trees.

"No one," Owyn answered. He had wrapped the black cloth around his waist to cover what Adair claimed to be the more 'private' parts of his body. Owyn's own darker skin helped obscure him from the men's view.

"Who are you?" the man shouted again. "Show yourself!"

The men pointed their long staff weapons at Owyn as he emerged from the trees. He held up his hands as if placating the men. "I'm just passing through," he said.

"Through to where?" the man asked. "What's your name and what's your business?"

An idea struck Owyn. "I've come to see the king," he said.

"The king?" The men looked at each other and looked Owyn up and down. "And why would the king want to see you?" The man asked him again, "Who are you?"

Owyn stepped forward enough for the light to catch his face. He glared down at the men until he saw the recognition in their eyes. "Oh," he grinned at them, "he doesn't want to see me."

Without waiting for an attack, Owyn grabbed the bottom end of one of the guards' staffs. Tucking it under his arm, he used the fact that the guard still clung to the weapon to swing him into his companion, knocking both guards over. He leapt over the small fire behind them as they untangled themselves to pursue him. He uprooted tent poles, threw boxes and barrels at the men behind him and made as much noise as possible.

The two guards yelled behind him and tried to keep up. But their legs being shorter than Owyn's didn't give them much chance. Their only chance would be to alert someone ahead of Owyn.

"Traitor!"

"Catch him!"

"Stop him!"

"He's after the king!"

"Traitor!"

The calls drifted behind Owyn as he scrambled through the camp. He picked up a sword and staff and began slicing tents as he ran. Occasionally checking behind himself, he saw heads and bodies jumping from tent openings toward the ruckus. They weren't looking up.

Over the trees in the distance, Owyn could see stars winking. Meaning the dark shapes of dragons must be slipping overhead unseen.

Owyn continued to make as much noise and trouble as possible as he ran through the field of tents and humans. He knew roughly where the king's tent might be, having viewed the camp from a distance in the sky. He tried to move in a straight line toward it to fool his chasers about his intention and direction. Finally, when he found a stretch where no one was in view, he dropped the weapons he'd gathered up. Then forgetting everything else, he sprinted in the opposite direction.

He almost made it to the trees before he saw men running along his previous path toward the king's tent. When they weren't looking in the direction he'd gone, he slipped into the trees on the fringes of the camp. But as he jogged away with a smile, another tent came into view.

Set off but still in view of the others, this tent was different. It was taller, round rather than square and was lit inside. The decorative scrolling around the bottom made Owyn stop. Faeries.

"What is it?" a voice came from inside.

Owyn heard movement on the far side. Someone was coming out. He ducked closer to the tent but avoided touching it. He knew he couldn't stay here. He was exposed. The light from inside the tent spread his profile in shadow beyond for anyone from the human camp to see if they looked in that direction.

Listening, he heard one of them walk around the side closest to where he had sent his pursuers, so he slipped around the opposite side.

"I don't know," a voice said. It sounded distinctly female. "I can't see anything."

Crouching, Owyn watched his feet and tried to avoid twigs and rocks. As he snuck past the tent, hoping to get away, he heard something that made his heart stop.

"It's probably centaurs," the other voice said from inside. The one was a male's, dripping with bitterness, and familiar. It could only be Kradik inside. "We don't have any information on their whereabouts or what they're doing."

Information? Owyn thought. *What other kind of information do the faeries have?*

Painstakingly slowly, Owyn lowered himself to the ground beside the faeries' tent while the female went back inside. The bottom created a wedge as it pulled away from the ground slightly over a depression, providing a small hiding spot. Had Owyn been a smaller man, he might have been able to squeeze into it fully. He imagined Addil or

Taka would fit better, but he wedged as much of himself in as possible.

"As the representative of the council," the faerie woman said, "I need to tell you that not many are pleased with the position you've put us in."

"I've told you everything I know, every step of the way," Kradik said. He didn't sound happy about it. "What else can I do?"

"Is there no way to gain more control over the dragons? By majikal means, maybe?"

Control the dragons? How would they even try that?

"No," Kradik answered. "He's done everything he can for us without being discovered."

"So you've been telling the council all along," she said. "But surely you've been researching spells with your time. The situation isn't ideal, and the council wants to know if you have a plan or if we must prepare for defeat? Certainly, you've been experimenting on him to find more and better ways to control a dragon."

Who? Owyn begged silently in his mind. *Who is the traitor? A name!*

"Time to research? Control a dragon?" he retorted. "Are you mad? What time have I had? Flying back and forth between you, the council, the humans, the mountain. What resources? Other than those the humans have to offer. What good would it do anyway? As the situation stands, he said Visi knows everything and watches everything. And the black dragon, Hiro, is the one causing the most trouble." When Kradik said it a smile tickled Owyn's lips. "Hiro is everywhere he shouldn't be, riling the dragons. Making them fight. He desperately wants Hiro dead. Almost as much as he wants Priya dead. If we have the chance, we must kill them first. You want to control the dragons? Take out their leader. Maybe that will take the fight out of them, but I have no more courses of action."

The smile disappeared. *Priya isn't the traitor, but for some reason the traitor wants her dead. But* who *is the traitor? Does Anna know? Did she find out and alert Priya somehow?*

"Well," the faerie woman sighed, "I can't say your efforts are enough for the council, but no decisions have been made as to your fate. If the massacre goes off without a problem, you might even gain a seat on the council. But if the dragons fight back and they're not all killed, you might be…punished."

Kradik growled. "How is this my fault? It was Skorkot who started it all! She and Rakgar!..."

The rest of the tirade drowned in Owyn's ears by the pounding of his own blood. His stomach churned. It couldn't be.

Rakgar. Traitor? No. Never.

He didn't want to fight the humans, but he had good reasons. Tell the faeries about the flarote? He'd always protected the secrets of the dragons. Why would he want Hiro dead? He was like another father to Hiro. He had spoiled him when he was young, allowing him so much leniency that other dragons protested.

Want Priya dead? Why? She's his daughter! He couldn't be the—

"Rakgar sought out Skorkot," the woman bit back, "he gave her the key ingredient for the poison. It was

Rakgar's plan to kill the dragons with flarote; Skorkot was nothing but a messenger for his vengeful ideas.

"You discovered how to use those ideas. You created the poison. You positioned the humans to kill the dragons. You pull the king's strings even now. How are you not to blame if the dragons aren't killed? Or worse, if the curse doesn't end." She lowered her voice and Kradik's fight seeped out of him. "Many faeries have died trying to end this curse. If killing the dragons doesn't work, you'll just be next in a long line of failures. The council will move on."

"Then we must see that it doesn't fail."

As the two began arguing about who was in charge, Owyn burst from his hiding place. He didn't care if they heard him escape. They couldn't stop him. His heart burned as hot as the deepest embers of a fire as he exploded into the sky. In the back of his mind, he knew he should be concerned if the centaurs and other dragons made it through to the Inner Mountain, but he didn't care. He had to face the *real* traitor.

15

TESTIFY

"He's disappeared," Torgon announced, entering Philip's tent. "Again."

"Too bad," Philip grumbled. "I was kind of hoping for a physical altercation with someone who might actually fight back."

"You wouldn't want to fight this one," Torgon said as he found his chair next to the king. "He's huge."

"That's good, I wouldn't suffer as long."

Torgon sighed. "You're suffering now?"

Philip put the papers down on the little table in front of him. Reports of how many men were assigned to each platform, how many arrows were assigned to each man, how long it would take to get into the Rock Clouds, and the last page was an estimate of casualties – dragon and human. Far too many casualties in Philip's mind – on either side. He noticed there was no estimate of faerie casualties.

"We shouldn't be here," Philip grumbled rubbing his face. "We should be looking for Anna."

"You said yourself that she's here, in the Rock Clouds."

"She's survived a dragon kidnapping before." Philip had been searching his own feelings. Anna disappeared all the time, often of her own accord. But this was the first time he saw evidence of destruction where she'd last been. The chaotic remains of their sleeping quarter and the lifeless body of Dieko had scared him. He felt his own mortality. He realized that his people might face the same threat. "Hundreds could die because I want to retaliate against one dragon for taking one person, and we don't even know if she's dead or alive. How will any of this improve the situation?"

"Don't forget," Torgon almost whispered, "a dragon took my father too."

Before Philip could respond, the captain stationed at his door stepped in.

"Sire," the man saluted. "There are men outside requesting to see you."

"Who is it?" Torgon asked, standing.

"The man said his name is Jarek. He's one of the Hamees."

Torgon turned to Philip, mirroring the same quizzical look on Philip's face. Philip shrugged. "What do they want?"

"He said he has information of the black dragon," the captain said.

Torgon threw his hands in the air in exasperation.

"Let him in," Philip said.

"Perhaps," Torgon whispered as the captain slipped out, "they hold the answers to that riddle of yours."

My ever-present riddle, Philip thought. He and Torgon had argued the point many, many times. This situation was like Philip standing at a locked door. Kradik wanted him to raze the "building" to the ground, but Philip had the burning desire to discover what was on the other side.

Philip straightened himself. Torgon adjusted his tunic and stood at his king's side as three men entered. They wore simply stitched clothing. Their hair and boots bore no marks of stature or nobility. They removed their hats upon entering and held them in their hands. The man in front wore a glove on only his left hand.

"Your Majesty," the first man said. He fell to his knees and wouldn't look Philip in the eye. The two men behind him did the same without a word.

"Your name is Jarek?"

"Yes, Your Majesty."

"Please stand, Jarek, and look your king in the eye."

Slowly the man stood and the other two did likewise. Jarek's eyes wandered about the room, to the table, to Torgon and finally to Philip. Although the other men kept their eyes cast downward, when Jarek met Philip's eye he seemed to gain his confidence.

"I've come to talk to you about the black dragon," he said.

"Yes," Philip answered. "What information do you have about it?"

"We've seen it," Jarek said. "We've had more than one dealing with it."

"I seem to recall," Torgon said, "that a group of Hamees reported sighting the beast before we captured it almost a year ago."

"Yes," Jarek nodded at Torgon. "That was our village. But we've seen it more since."

"Sightings?"

Jarek shook his head. "More than just sightings." He looked to Philip again. "I've taken an oath of honesty and I wish to tell you all, but there are aspects of my story that would do harm to others. That would conflict with my other oaths."

Philip nodded. He knew a little bit about the Hamees' oaths but apparently not enough to get around them. "You obviously came here for a reason," he said. "Tell me what you can."

Jarek took a breath. "The black dragon isn't your enemy. He saved our village from the wraith last fall. He saved my life. He's a tame dragon."

"Tame?" Torgon asked in shock.

"Tamed by whom?" Philip asked.

Jarek pursed his lips.

"This would cause the harm?" Philip asked.

After Jarek nodded, Torgon said, "You think we would do them harm?"

Before Jarek could answer, Kradik entered. "And you would be right," he said. "Any man who…tames…a dragon is our enemy."

The blood drained from Jarek's face. The other men got fidgety.

"No one is going to harm you, Jarek," Torgon said.

Jarek swallowed. "I hoped to dissuade you. I don't think the dragons are—"

"—are what? The enemy?" Kradik spat. "You have no idea what they are capable of."

Jarek looked into the dark cowl of the faerie. Without a word, he dropped his hat on the ground, reached up and pulled the glove from his other hand. Under the glove, the skin on his hand was shriveled and black. He held it up to the faerie.

"I have felt dragon fire," he said. "It saved my life and the lives of those I love most."

"Peculiar alliance," Kradik said, partially echoing the centaur's suggestion of an alliance with the dragons, as reported by Maelin. "Dragons rampaging wild is dangerous enough, but if someone can use...that power...harness it...somehow... All the more reason to be rid of the beasts and anyone who might be sympathetic toward them."

A thought struck Philip. "Captain," he called, standing. When the man entered, the king indicated Jarek. "Take these men and give them food and shelter for the night. They may rest here until their journey home. Jarek, I thank you for the information. You have shown fealty to the Noble Kingdom."

When the Hamees men had been shown out, Philip turned to Kradik. "Is that what this war is about? The feud between faeries and centaurs?"

Kradik snorted. "Don't be absurd."

"The centaurs are protecting dragons," Torgon said.

"Joss and those drivel will have their time," Kradik hissed. "For now, this war is about you doing what I tell you. And I'm telling you to kill dragons and anyone else who gets in your way!"

The air seemed to be sucked from the tent as the faerie stormed out.

16

WHY

He'd told the faeries about the effects of flarote on the dragons. He'd helped them make the poison. He even now was plotting to keep all the dragons in the Rock Clouds to await a massacre. How could he betray all dragons? He was a blood and ash traitor! *That's why the Allegiant Sword had such a strong effect on him,* Hiro realized as he remembered the encounter with the centaurs and the majikal sword. He was plotting to have all dragons killed!

Suddenly a memory assaulted his mind.

Hiro and Tog entered the cave together. "He gets worse every day," Tog, Hiro's best friend, grumbled next to him. Tog scrubbed smoke out of his protruding eyes as an orange dame scurried out of the cave opening they had come through and took off into the air. "He sent Trakillyn and Sanatab to cut down fifty oak trees," Tog whispered once she had gone. "He gave no reason for it. He sent

Makki to stack them, again with no explanation, he just ordered him to do it. Then he forced Burrabill and Hakkil to carry the same trees into the Black Forest and leave them there. No explanation, and ordering them around like a human king. Like he has the authority." Their claws beat a rhythm against the stone as they walked through the cave toward Rakgar's lair. Tog lowered his voice even further in the silence, ensuring that only Hiro could hear him. "He told Makki not to tell anyone, and insisted on his wyrd. The only reason I know any of this is because I stumbled upon Makki while he was at it."

That had happened months and months ago. At the beginning of spring. Cutting down trees. Stacking trees. Delivering trees. Probably more than anyone was aware of. The platforms. Rakgar had been planning these platforms for several seasons.

The fire in Hiro's belly burned brighter and hotter as he flew. He would challenge Rakgar. He would force his leader to confess, if it was true. He flew higher and faster than he ever had before. He didn't feel his wings or legs. He didn't see the night sky. He didn't feel cold or warm. He only saw the Inner Mountain. He saw the Rock Clouds. His home. He would protect it.

He flew high enough that even the Watch didn't stop him. He flew straight past them, directly to Rakgar's lair. Rakgar had stationed two of the Watch at the entrance. Hiro roared and blasted them with flame as they tried to intercept him.

"HIRO, STOP!" Visi jumped in front of him, spreading her wings. Startled, he stumbled to a halt. When he righted himself, he only glared past the old seer at Rakgar. The leader, although confused, narrowed his eyes.

Anger. Hatred. Hiro realized that he had been seeing an increasing amount of these emotions in the leader's eye. He *did* want Hiro dead.

"Go home, Hiro," Visi growled at him.

"He's—"

"I know!" she yelled, cutting off Hiro's words.

Hiro allowed his eyes to find Visi. The fragile dame pleaded with her eyes. "You know?" he asked. "Of course, you do. How can you—"

"He'll kill you," she whispered. "Without the help of your friends," Visi continued, "he'll kill you and then his plan will succeed." Then, leaning in close, she put her nose to his. A warm breath of memory overlaid his vision.

His father lay on the ground in a forest, a hole torn through him and pieces of his body falling away into ash. Hiro, called Dakoon then, stood over his dying father.

"I must," Tusten forced through clenched teeth. He drew a long breath through his nostrils then allowed his eyes to rest on Dak. "Ido," he whispered.

"Dromdan," Dak replied. He remembered their pleading sorrow as they used the revered titles for father and son in faerie language.

"Ido," his father forced out. "Of all the things I taught you, I failed you in the most important matter."

"No, Dromdan."

"You must understand," Tusten groaned. "The most important question in the world is…why?"

"'Why,' Father?"

"Yes," he nodded. "You must ask 'why' – always. There is a reason for every action. A purpose to every word. Understand why I taught you the things I did and you will understand me."

The memory faded and Hiro allowed his eyes to slip from Visi to Rakgar and back. She must be reminding him of this, the most painful of his memories, for a reason.

His fire burned hotter, if that was possible, as another thought came. "Is he the reason my father is dead?" he growled low to the old dame.

"You'll never know," she whispered back, "unless you do as your father told you."

Why? He fought through the fog of anger. *I must figure out why he would do this. And alert the others.*

Hiro glared at Rakgar a moment longer, then turned and ran out.

———

Hiro landed in his cave with a roar so loud the walls shook and a few dripping stones fell to the ground. One of the spilling stones in front of him absorbed the fire from his angry roar and burned red hot to light the cavern, much like the green stones did in the Ice Ruck lair.

"Well, it's nice to see you too."

When Hiro could clear his vision from the anger and see again in the darkness, he saw Priya stand up from the bed of grasses he left in the corner.

"Where have you been?" he growled at her.

"Believe it or not, Hiro," she said, a sneer in her voice at his name, "I've been doing something about this war too."

"Like what?"

She sat on her haunches haughtily in front of him. "Seeking allies."

"Like Anna?" he barked. "And the Ice Ruck?" he added at the last moment.

"Perhaps."

"Where is she?" he snapped at her.

Priya stared at him.

When she didn't answer, he snapped again. "Her maid said I would find her here. What did you do with her?"

"She's safe," she answered. "And so am I, by the way. And what were you doing talking to her maid?"

"By Kurta," he roared again, "what have you done with her?"

Priya crouched in an attack posture. She hissed. "She's safe on her own. She doesn't need you and neither do I!" She roared and swiped a claw across Hiro's nose.

Hiro blinked. His snout stung. Her claws were small but sharp. "What's wrong with you?"

"What's wrong with me?" she yelled back. "What's wrong with you? You tear in here full of anger, only caring about your precious little human."

"I don't have time for your feelings," he growled. There wasn't time for anything; he needed to make sure Anna was safe and he needed to tell the others about Rakgar. If Anna was anywhere in the Rock Clouds, he needed to get her away quickly. "I don't have time to apologize, again, for not loving you. We've got to find Prak and the centaurs and end this war. I need to know where Anna is."

"Since she's all you care about, she's in my lair," she hissed. "And as to your love," she shook her head. The muscles in her jaw clenched. She bunched her legs and spread her wings. Hiro could see the fire building in her eyes. "Don't speak to me of your love." Her voiced climbed with every word. She lifted into the air with a final scream echoing, "You're in love with a human!"

As he watched her tail whip out of sight around the edge of the cave, he noticed Tog sitting silently outside the cave entrance. Tog's normally gray scales were lit with a bloody red glare from the burning, spilling stone. He must have heard everything. He blinked at Hiro. "It's not true," Tog said, but Hiro could hear the doubt in his flat tone.

Hiro couldn't answer. There was no more time for lies. He knew his best friend would have to find out about his broken heart sooner or later. He had hoped to explain how it happened and why. He wanted to heal relations between the humans and dragons before it came to light. He was out of time.

Tog swung his head slowly, seemingly attempting to expel what he was holding inside. The revelation and anger visibly rose in his belly in the form of burning fire. Eventually, realization forced him to meet Hiro's eyes. He bared his fangs at his best friend and turned away.

"Tog, wait," Hiro called to him before he could leave. The memory of the vision of this moment stung at his heart.

"No!" Tog snapped around to face Hiro and roared, "YOU'RE A BLOOD AND ASH TRAITOR!"

Hiro watched, helpless as his best friend disappeared into the dark sky. He hung his head. His best friend had abandoned him, as Visi had predicted. At the time when he needed him most.

Rakgar wanted him dead. Hiro's anger turned to fear. His knees felt weak. He couldn't protect himself against the massively powerful dan. His breath came ragged from his throat when he thought about fighting Rakgar. Visi had saved his life by stopping him.

He couldn't protect all the dragons from the waiting hoard of humans at their doorstep. He had seen what the poison could do. It hadn't killed him, but only because he'd been able to change into a human. The other dragons couldn't change. They would all be killed by poisoned arrows. At any moment, he would be surrounded by dragon ash. He couldn't protect the woman he loved from the angry dragon now probably on the way to kill her.

"Hiro?"

Hiro's head jerked up. He sucked in a breath.

Prak.

"What are you doing here?" he asked the little brown dragon.

"We heard you roar," came the answer.

We. Prak must have been with Tog and they'd both heard him roar at Priya. They'd probably come to Hiro's lair together and heard everything. At least he knew they'd made it through to the centaurs.

"You should go," Hiro told him. "You shouldn't be seen with me." He knew the information that his heart had broken for a human woman would spread among the dragons faster than fire on a dry plain with a high wind. He would be exiled, if not killed. Rakgar would have justification to kill him now. His original reasons, whatever they were, wouldn't matter anymore.

Prak stepped further into the lair. "I'll be seen with whomever I choose, thank you. Nothing stopped me before. Why would it stop me now?"

Hiro flopped onto the ground. This is the last time he would probably be in his lair ever again. "Didn't you hear what they said?" he grumbled. "I'm a blood and ash traitor."

"I heard," Prak said. "Everything."

Hiro studied him as the little dragon who had annoyed him so much over the years laid down next to him.

After a moment of silence, Prak looked up at Hiro. "I know why everyone calls me 'Prak', you know."

Hiro just blinked. His name was Prakyndar. His dame named him that because he was so smart. Prakyndar meant 'point or pinnacle of knowledge'. But everyone called him 'Prak', meaning 'point', 'pointed' or 'thorn'. As in…annoying.

Hiro shook his head, "I don't know—"

"Yes, you do." Prak grinned. "Everyone calls me Prak because I'm annoying. Obnoxious voice. Ask too many questions. Follow you around."

Ashamed, Hiro dropped his head.

"I forgive you," Prak mumbled.

Hiro lifted his eyes. He saw a new dragon in front of him. The small, nasally little brown dragon had the eyes and claws of Prak, but he was confident and strong while also meek and merciful.

"The thing with friends," Prak continued, "is that you have to choose who you're willing to forgive, how often, and for what. I've forgiven you every time you called me Prak, Hiro. You've always treated me as more of a friend than others have. So, I won't call you Traitor. You haven't done anything to me to deserve it. Besides," he said standing up, "we still have a war to fight. We need you."

Prak was right. Hiro stood next to the little dragon. "Thank you," he whispered. "Visi told me that I was the blade on a dangerous weapon and I must be mindful who wields me." He met the small dragon's eyes. "I choose you, Kodoran."

Prak smiled, "Don't call me 'commander' yet. Maybe when we win this war and find the real traitor."

Hiro almost choked as he remembered. His own pain had rid it from his mind. "But I have," he said, "I know who the real traitor is. I know who wants the dragons dead."

17

IN CONTROL

"This is what you want me to see?" Philip asked, not hiding the annoyance in his tone. "The platforms?"

He stood at the edge of the Noble Kingdom's camp, just outside the firelight. Considering the number of men in their contingent, it was no small journey to get here. Kradik had requested Philip's presence and naturally he'd brought Torgon with him as well. The three stood admiring the large wooden platforms tucked under tree cover. Each could comfortably support fifty men. With five platforms, they would send two hundred and fifty men into the Rock Clouds at a time. As thrilled as Kradik seemed, the sight only served to depress the young king. The night was late and Philip wished for his bed to delay dealing with the war until the morning.

"They're all ready," Kradik said proudly as he waved his hand.

"All of them?" Philip asked. He knew when the platforms were finished and enchanted they would be fully prepared for the attack. He was running out of time and holdup tactics.

"We have five more sets like these," Kradik said, admiring his workmanship. "One for each kingdom. The faerie council arrived yesterday. We now have the majikal power to finish this war."

Twelve hundred and fifty men could reach into the Rock Clouds at a moment's notice. Philip's stomach churned. The first wave would carry approximately two humans for every dragon, each with at least twenty poisoned arrows in their quiver. They might not even need a second wave. Then they'll move onto the next ruck.

"We attack at first light," Kradik said.

Even with his face completely blacked out in the cowl of his cloak, Philip could hear the smile in Kradik's voice.

"I beg your pardon?" Torgon said, at Philip's side. "Your Majesty!"

Before Torgon or Philip could demand an explanation from Kradik, the three turned toward a set of newcomers.

A man in a black tunic with a silver sword embroidered across the front of it announced the small party. "His Royal Majesty, King Grisivere Ido Griffin of the Just Kingdom requests to speak with King Philip Ido Paudie of the Noble Kingdom."

The servant stepped out of the way as the short, round king stepped forward. The top of his bright red hair barely reached Philip's chest, but somehow Philip always felt the urge to prostrate himself in front of this man. But this time, he felt no such urge. He glanced at the black sword hanging from the other king's hip.

Grisivere noticed the glance. "Yes," he nodded, placing his hand on the hilt. "It is a fake. The real Sword of Justice was stolen."

"Stolen?" Torgon asked. "I thought the Just Sword couldn't be stolen."

"Unfortunately, there are ways," Grisivere answered him.

"By whom?" Philip asked. "When?"

"We haven't discovered the thief," Grisivere answered, "but rest assured, when we find them, they will be punished to the full extent of the law."

"Is this what you came to discuss?" Philip asked. In the back of his mind he considered other options.

"Not fully," Grisivere said. "While I have my doubts as to any of my kingdom being the culprits, I believe the theft was not a coincidental event. We are also plagued by some form of…attacks…"

As the man's voice trailed off, Philip's brow furrowed. Grisivere had never been the type of man to be uncertain. The nature of the Just sword provided him with answers to questions most people would find unanswerable.

"Attacks?" Philip asked. "From the centaurs? They have certainly been plaguing us as well."

"No," Grisivere crossed his arms. "We're not certain what's going on, to be honest. Men have disappeared in the night, only to turn up in the morning bound and gagged. Under their own beds. That very thing has happened several times over the past few nights. Food has gone missing, and many of our weapons – including the poisoned arrows – are either gone or destroyed. In fact," he grumbled and shifted on his feet, "my own tent disappeared while I slept. That happened last night, and the sword disappeared with it. I knew the only Just thing to do would be to confess to you that I have lost control of my soldiers, my camp and my resources."

"Your soldiers?" Torgon asked. "Surely they haven't turned on you because of these attacks?"

Grisivere glanced at the few men who had accompanied him to Philip's camp. "Not all," he said, "but some. Most of the men are terrified. They claim they've heard voices and threats, with no one around to be seen saying them. They've seen horrible things too, visions, ghosts and phantoms. All of the ghosts and voices have one thing in common…they threaten the men, saying they'll kill them if they attack the dragons."

"Majik?" Philip asked.

"Of course, it's majik," Grisivere said. "No one knows who's doing it or why. But my men know they can believe the threats."

"Why?"

"Because my majishun tried to fight back when the ghosts attacked him. He ended up hanging from a tree by his ankle with no ropes and a sign attached to him that said…" the stalwart king hesitated and muttered, almost embarrassed, "'I can't majik'."

Philip grabbed his nose and pinched his face to keep from laughing. Glancing at Torgon it seemed the general had better luck controlling himself. Then he turned to Kradik. "The attack will have to wait until we get the Just camp under control," he said.

"I'm afraid not."

"I beg your pardon," Torgon said, his voice dangerously low.

Kradik stepped closer. "This war will end tomorrow, whether Grisivere can control his men or not," he hissed.

Philip's teeth ground together. "I'm the king here."

Kradik cackled. "Do you still think you're in charge?" When Philip didn't answer, the faerie went on. "You want something to be afraid of?" He reached up and yanked back the cowl of his cloak. Everyone gasped except Philip, whose voice stuck in his throat. As Kradik spoke, Philip watched the muscles on his cheeks pull away to bare his teeth. "You're only here to do as I say. If you don't, I'll see to the destruction of your entire kingdom." He glanced over Philip's shoulder to Grisivere. "Hopefully for you, your men will see that the faeries are the real threat, not your phantoms." Turning back to Philip he hissed, "Have your men ready to attack at dawn."

The faerie didn't wait for a response. He lifted into the air by his wings and flew away, leaving Philip helpless to do anything but stare after him.

18

TENUOUS TRUST

"We have to warn the others," Prak said, or Kodoran as Hiro would call him, as he and Hiro dashed from the cave. He lifted into the air to hover in front of Hiro. The hour was late, but the moons offered some vision. "I don't know if Milah and Mitashio have gone to speak with him yet. I don't know where Priya has gone."

"She's probably gone to her lair," Hiro answered. "I'll try to get anyone else away from him and back to the centaur camp."

"Are you sure you can resist the temptation to fight him?" Kodoran asked.

Hiro set his teeth. "I will try…for now."

Kodoran nodded. "I'll go back to the camp and wait for you and the others there."

"If I don't return…"

"I'll know what happened," Kodoran finished the thought.

With a final nod to the little brown dragon, Hiro flew in the direction of Rakgar's cavern. He didn't know what he would do if the enormous gray leader was there to meet him. He didn't know how he could convince the others to leave Rakgar's counsel and go back to the centaurs with him, but he had to try. Rakgar wanted Priya dead too and he would kill Anna without a second glance. He had to assure their safety.

As he had divulged what he knew to Kodoran feira Prakyndar, the fire of anger swept through him, burning brighter with every word. Now, while that fire pushed him faster toward the cavern, Hiro had to remind himself not to engage the treacherous leader. Kordoran had warned Hiro not to fight Rakgar. "He'll kill you," he had said. "We have to make a plan first."

So Hiro landed on the lip of Rakgar's lair quietly, hoping not to see the massive dragon. He knew he wouldn't be able to resist a fight if they came fang-to-fang. Tip-taloning into the huge cavern, Hiro didn't see anyone. Passing the side caverns, he noticed a large pile of flarote in one. The cave in which stockpiles of dried meat was usually stored for barren months was completely empty. Hiro realized Rakgar must have avoided sending hunting parties out so the ruck would remain consistently low on food and threaten the hatchlings. It made his fire boil again.

As he passed the large empty rooms to the sides of the main cavern, Hiro spotted the tunnel that led to Priya's lair. He had never been in her lair, she had made sure of that since a young age. She was very strict and never allowed anyone inside. He knew she used a couple of ways in and out of the Inner Mountain, but he also knew that Anna was probably down in Priya's lair now.

He checked to make sure no one was visible from the opening, then darted inside. Priya might be fuming mad, but he had to get both her and Anna out of there. He wandered down the tunnels as a dragon but got turned around easily. With several branches in many directions, he had to choose carefully and keep track of the ones he'd been down. Many were too small to enter as a dragon, so he could only follow the larger ones. Those didn't lead much of anywhere, and some looped around. He knew he'd passed a few smaller openings closer to the entrance. Priya might have told Anna to go into one of those so no dragon could get to her. With a smile, Owyn headed back up to the lair's entrance.

Getting closer, he could hear voices in the main cavern. He stayed in human form, knowing he could hide much better and even slip into one of the cracks in the wall to avoid any dragons.

"…Hiro claims to know them," Milah growled as he entered the large lair.

Owyn couldn't be certain but it sounded like he and others had come from the opposite direction of Priya's lair. They must have come from Rakgar's sleeping cave. The brothers probably woke Rakgar.

"Of course, he does," Rakgar grumbled. "But, honestly, how much can you trust him?"

"Not much." That voice most certainly belonged to Tog. Owyn's heart pained at the sound of his former best friend counselling against him to Rakgar. "He has lied about many things. Some of which I'm only learning about now."

"Like what?" Rakgar asked.

"Many things," Tog said. "I'll have to verify before I claim anything."

Owyn heard the hesitation in Tog's voice. His best friend had yet to betray him entirely, but he seemed to be working up to it.

"He's been to the surface several times," Mitashio piped up.

Milah fluidly continued his brother's thought, "He could have met these…"

NO! Owyn shouted in his head. *No! Don't tell him of our one secret weapon!*

"…creatures…"

"…goblins," Mitashio finished. He said it like it was a dirty word.

"Goblins?" Rakgar asked. "Are you sure what you saw was real?"

"They were real," Mitashio said.

"They're ugly," Milah said.

"And dangerous," Mitashio said.

"And powerful," Milah said.

"Please," Rakgar grumbled. "I hate it when you two speak like that. Just one."

"Sorry," Milah said, without much sincerity. "The goblins are very real. Now that we have their help, we might actually be able to fight back. They can disguise themselves…"

And now that Rakgar knows, Hiro thought, *he will tell the faeries and they will stop the goblins.*

"They could possibly even disguise the dragons so we can look like centaurs and fight," Mitashio interjected, forgetting the apology.

"We can fight the humans," Milah said.

"We *should* fight the humans," Mitashio insisted.

"No," Rakgar said. "What if the disguise fails? What if these goblin creatures are just a ruse of the centaurs? Have you met these goblins, Tog? Did you know of them?"

"No," Tog answered, "I've never met them or heard about them. But they could be another secret Hiro has been keeping."

"They're certainly no ruse of the centaurs," Milah said. "With the goblins' help we might actually survive this attack."

"NO!" Rakgar roared. He took a breath, but it didn't seem to calm him. "In fact, in the morning I want all the dragons gathered here. Spread the word that the entire ruck, everyone, must gather here in the morning."

"Everyone?" one of the brothers asked quietly.

"Everyone," Rakgar growled. "Unless they answer to a different Rakgar."

Owyn could hear the anger and hatred in the leader's voice. He didn't understand how the brothers and Tog couldn't hear it. Then he remembered that he hadn't heard it before now either.

As the brothers left the cave, Owyn prayed silently that he would catch up to them before they went very far.

He couldn't spend any more time looking for Anna in this maze Priya called a lair.

Rakgar sniffed briefly at the entrance to Priya's space. Owyn held his breath, hoping the huge dragon couldn't hear or smell him. Before Rakgar turned away, he whispered into the lair whose opening was too small for him to enter. "You'll be dead soon."

Owyn froze. He listened as the leader-turned-traitor trundled back to his own sleeping chambers. Owyn could tell he wasn't hurrying, and he didn't bother looking back on the chance that Priya might appear and attack him. Then he wondered how many times her own father had whispered those words to her through the darkness when no one else was around?

Carefully controlling his temptations, Hiro waited until the massive dragon was gone before tip-taloning from his hiding spot.

Tomorrow, he decided silently, *tomorrow this will end.*

Then it hit him like a blast of ice water. Tomorrow. He's gathering the dragons. Tomorrow. The humans must be attacking.

———

"Kodoran!" Hiro shouted as he neared the center of the centaur encampment. "Kodoran, they're coming!"

Dragons and centaurs came running as Hiro landed in front of Kodoran, who was meeting with the centaurs Joss, Rylan and Ashel and the goblins Svorgh and Shvika. Milah and Mitashio were already there nearby and followed the sound, grumbling as he landed.

"Please," Milah moaned, "tell me we're not calling him *that*."

"Are you sure?" Kodoran asked, ignoring the comment. "How do you know? What makes you think so? What did you hear?"

Ok, Hiro sighed to himself, *maybe he hasn't completely grown up.*

"Rakgar is gathering the dragons," Hiro said. "First thing in the morning."

"We've already told them, Hiro," Mitashio said.

"Prak," Ashel said, but then hesitated with a glance at the dragon, "I mean, Kodoran, just told us as well."

Hiro shook his head, unable to speak what he knew into existence, but Kodoran answered. "You don't understand … it will be easier for the humans to kill all the dragons if they're gathered in one place," he said with utter realization.

"Wait," Milah stepped forward, "what are you talking about?"

"Rakgar is setting us up," Kodoran hissed, "or as I should call him, Taynor." He used the faerie word for traitor to indicate his deception.

The brothers were suddenly stunned to silence along with several dragons surrounding them. Hiro's heart chilled a little when he noticed Tog wasn't there.

"It's not possible," Milah said.

"Unfortunately, it makes sense," Rylan said to growls from the dragons. "Who else would have known about…I mean," he glanced at the other centaurs around him, "…how to make the poison?"

"He had them gather logs," Mitashio whispered to his brother. In the silence, everyone heard it.

Milah ground his teeth. "The platforms."

"Skorkot," Hiro offered, "the faerie who counselled with him, tried to kill me."

"We remember," Milah said.

"I heard the faeries discussing it," Hiro said. "It's all been Rakgar, from the start."

Milah lifted his eyes slightly to Hiro's. "Show me," he said.

Hiro shifted and rolled his shoulder. "I can't."

Milah met Hiro's eyes with defiance this time. "Why not?" he asked. "You call our Rakgar 'traitor' but don't have proof?"

"I give you my wyrd," Hiro said. "May you strike me down if I'm lying."

Milah's maw worked as if he were about to scream back at Hiro. Before he could open his mouth, Kodoran spoke up, "And you have mine," he said.

Milah, Mitashio and Hiro looked to the little dragon. "You have my wyrd," he continued, but he indicated all of the dragons surrounding him. "You all have my wyrd that Hiro is telling the truth. Rakgar is a blood and ash traitor to all dragons." He added the last to Milah's face. "I'll stake my life on Hiro's claims, with or without proof."

Milah's jaw stopped. After a moment longer, he turned to Hiro and inclined his head.

"So," Ashel barked, "what do we do about it?"

Kodoran looked at Hiro, who looked at Milah, who looked at Mitashio, who looked to the other dragons surrounding him. No one wanted to say it, but Kodoran stepped up again.

"We kill him."

Silence.

"Wait," Ashel said, "didn't you say the humans are going to attack? Shouldn't that be our first priority?"

"They're attacking at first light," Svorgh said. When Hiro shot him a questioning glance, he shrugged his shoulders. "I was prepared to report it when you arrived."

"You seem to know a lot," Hiro said to the minute leader. "Did you know of Taynor?"

Svorgh's gaze didn't waver. "We knew a dragon would betray dragons. However, we don't have the time or resources to search the past, present and future of every dragon. We knew it would happen how it should."

"What about you," Hiro asked, trying to keep the pain out of his voice when he looked at Ashel. "You watch the stars. They didn't warn you?"

Ashel lifted her chin slightly. "Stars are difficult to interpret. For example, I told you your star was being surrounded by five others that I believed represented the five human kingdoms. I now believe they represent the five intelligent species of Avonoa. I just didn't know one of them existed."

Her large eyes dropped to Svorgh and Shvika.

"Did your stars tell you what to do about the humans?" Milah grunted.

"No," Ashel glared at him. "However, my keen sense of strategy tells me that the centaurs and goblins will need to run interference with the humans until you deal with Taynor."

Ashel stepped away from the dragons as the group sectioned off instinctively. The centaurs and goblins began deep conversations about how they would slow the attack in the Rock Clouds. The dragons faced each other in silence.

"Someone has to kill him," Kodoran finally said.

"Hiro is The One," Milah said. "Doesn't that mean he should fight him?"

"Shouldn't The One be Rakgar?" Mitashio finished.

Hiro shook his head. "I'm not The One," he said.

Mitashio's eyes popped open. "But that's what Visi said!"

"She said what you needed to hear," Hiro said.

Milah threw up a claw and rolled his head to the sky. "Then what are we doing this for?" he exclaimed.

Kodoran stepped forward, glaring at Milah. "You're doing this to fulfill your own prophecy," he said.

Hiro remembered and said, "your ambition and talents will be utterly wasted, unless you listen to your betters. In this case…"

All eyes fell on Kodoran, who grinned.

Both brown brothers groaned at the same time.

"Does that mean you're going to fight him?" Milah asked.

Hiro shook his head. "No one of us would ever beat him."

Kodoran whispered, "Not alone."

19

HASTY APPEARANCE

"What is this?!" Anna yelled as she burst into Philip's tent. "You're attacking tomorrow? As in, in a few hours, tomorrow?"

Philip tumbled from his pallet bed at the outburst. He hadn't been sleeping, but he'd hoped to at least get a few hours of quiet rest before going into battle against dragons.

"I'm sorry, Sire," a captain ran in with a glowing cube, averting his eyes from the princess.

For good reason. Anna had come into the room with a simple fine robe thrown hastily over her shoulders and only a brilliant green cloth wrapped around her body under it. Philip had a hard time looking at her with so much skin showing, but the shock of her unexpected appearance distracted him.

"You're alive?" he shouted back.

Tierni ran in – fully clothed, thank Shurta. "I tried to stop her, Sire," she said, carrying a bundle of what Philip hoped was Anna's missing clothing. But when she looked at Philip, she averted her eyes as well. He realized he was only wearing his undergarments and no shirt, so he quickly pulled a blanket off the bed to cover himself.

Willing the attention back on Anna's sudden appearance, he said, "Where have you been?"

"Never mind that now," she said, pushing away Tierni's attempts to clothe her and probably responding to Philip's question as well.

"What's going on in—!" Torgon yelled before being cut off at the sight of Anna and Philip. Instead, he turned to Tierni. "What am I missing?"

"The question is, what are *they* missing?" she mumbled.

"I thought you were dead!" Philip said. He couldn't help staring at Anna in awe. How did she keep surviving dragon attacks? "I was going to use your name as a battle cry for the men when we attack."

"In the morning?" she bit.

"At first light," he said. "But, how—"

"Why?" she asked. "Why at first light? Can't you delay it?"

His shoulders dropped. "Don't you think I've tried? The faeries have given me no other choice." He hated to admit it, especially in front of Tierni. He felt helpless. A weak and useless king, his helplessness on display as much as his body right now. She would never respect him.

"There's always a choice, Philip," Anna said.

He slowly trained his eyes on hers. He saw hope in her face. And kindness. She knew his difficulty. Somehow she knew the torment he'd been suffering.

She stepped toward him and grabbed his hands. He remembered the clammy feel of her cool hands at her wedding. She had been terrified and miserable and he thought it had been his fault. Her hands now were warm and gentle, despite her haste and seeming anger. She cared for him. She wanted to help him, he knew. "You must lead the battle and make yourself seen – by everyone," she said. "Get to a platform."

"Are you mad?" Torgon shouted. "It's bad enough the faeries are forcing our men to use them. He could fall or be snatched by a dragon. It's too dangerous!"

"Philip," Anna said, ignoring the general's response. Her voice softened. He could see it in her eyes. She did care. He could tell she knew more than she was revealing, but he realized that she must have a good reason for holding it back, because she definitely had fear and concern for her brother in her eyes. "You must trust me. If you want this war to end, you must be seen by the dragons."

"If this war ends and we're still alive," Torgon said, "the faeries will kill us. All of us in this tent, will be the first to die. Then they'll either seize control of the kingdoms or kill the rest of the humans."

"Don't you mean if the war ends before the dragons die?" Tierni said.

Torgon shook his head. "No, I mean *when* it ends, however it ends. The faeries want complete control."

"Please, Philip," Anna squeezed his hands tighter. "Trust me."

He couldn't think. He hadn't slept properly in days. He couldn't eat. The faeries forced him in directions he didn't want to go and couldn't see any way out of. Now, finally, someone was cracking the unopenable door the slightest bit. He didn't know if he could trust her completely, but in that moment, he knew he had to take the chance.

He nodded.

"I'll see you there safely," a rough voice joined them. A small gray man with blood red hair appeared at the wall of the tent.

Everyone jumped at the apparition. Torgon reached for his sword, but the sheath was empty. The captain dropped the glowing cube, the only light in the tent, and leveled his staff at the small stranger. The little man reached out and touched the tip of the staff. Immediately, the captain yelled in pain and buckled at the knees.

"Svorgh!" Anna yelped.

With the captain incapacitated, the gray man looked up at Anna. "You kept your word," he said. "I will keep mine. I'll see you in the morning, young king," he said over his shoulder as he walked out the tent door. Before he passed through the flap, he disappeared.

Anna reached out and grabbed Philip's wrist again. "Trust me," she said quickly. Then she turned and ran out the door as well.

Tierni ran out behind her, calling to Anna. The captain stood and excused himself on shaky legs. Torgon stood staring with his mouth hanging open at the tent flap where the little man had disappeared into thin air.

Philip stood in his small clothes, his blankets on the ground at his feet, staring at the door to his tent and whispered, "What just happened?"

20

HORRIFIC CONFRONTATION

As the sky became a deep indigo, a large group of dragons, led by a pure black dragon, flew from the centaur camp to the Inner Mountain. Many of the dragons who had watched and listened to the plans of Hiro and his group followed, but hadn't quite decided what to believe. They simply wanted to witness what would happen.

The group landed outside the lair. There were so many that Hiro held them back from going inside.

At the mouth of the cavern, Hiro bellowed into it, "TAYNOR FEIRA RAKGAR!"

He didn't know what he expected, but he prepared for some kind of outburst or anger. Instead, they were met with silence.

Hiro glanced to the others surrounding him. Kodoran shrugged. Milah shook his head.

Kodoran stepped in front of Hiro. "TAYNOR FEIRA RAKGAR, I CHALLENGE YOU!" he screamed into the pitch.

Silence.

Mitashio whispered, "Maybe he ran."

Hiro glared into the cavern, "Then he concedes."

"I concede nothing," the Traitor formerly Rakgar purred from the dark.

The many dragons stepped back as the massive gray dragon appeared from the darkness. Any anger, hatred or rage within him was covered by a calm, even serene, demeanor. "You call me 'traitor' yet you challenge me as Rakgar. Unless you offer proof of my treachery, I am still Rakgar." He growled. Then, searching the eyes around him, he whispered, "Who challenges me?"

In answer, Kodoran launched himself at Taynor. He went straight for the throat. Rakgar roared and batted him away, but Kodoran slipped away from the claw that was almost the size of his entire body.

Hiro and the others watched as the two fought. Kodoran, faster and smaller, slipped in to scratch and bite, while Rakgar swatted and kicked at the nuisance.

"He's quick," Milah said to Hiro. "Better than I expected."

"Don't watch Kodoran," Hiro said. "We should be learning."

Milah nodded and settled into an anticipatory silence.

The fight between the massive and diminutive dragons lasted much longer than anyone expected. The small brown dragon darted away from the enormous claws, biting and scratching every angle he could reach. A couple of times, Rakgar caught the smaller dragon with a claw or a tail, slamming Kodoran to the ground or against the side of the mountain. But Kodoran always jumped up, slower each time, but rise he did.

Kodoran began drawing blood early. He ripped scales from the behemoth dragon. He didn't attack the body, but the legs and neck. As stars overhead began to wink over the Inner Mountain, the little dragon grew in the sight of every other dragon present as the left front leg of Rakgar trembled with missing scales and gushing ash onto the stones.

Unfortunately, Rakgar connected once with his claws to Kodoran's back and a second time raking his rear claws across Kodoran's shoulder. He threw Kodoran into a tree, breaking the tree under him. Hiro wasn't sure if Kodoran didn't get up as quickly because he was tangled in the branches or because his strength waned. When he finally returned to his feet, however, Hiro watched the young dragon's claws falter on the rocks. His tail was cut, his wings bore pin pricks that seeped light, a clawful of the spikes running along his spine had been broken off. He was missing scales and bleeding from one gouge in his shoulder and one in his leg, but he walked toward Rakgar.

"Kodoran," Hiro said, low, "you can concede."

He could only shake his head in response.

"'Kodoran'?" Rakgar scoffed. "How in Khurta's name can you be a commander?"

Kodoran looked up. "I lead by example," he said, right before he jumped, slid under the larger dragon's belly and raked his claws along the soft side by the legs.

Rakgar roared at the pain. Kodoran had sliced next to both left legs. As the bigger dragon's legs buckled to that side, Kodoran rolled out from under him. Rakgar saw the dragon rolling and kicked him with one right leg into the boulders on the mountain behind him.

Both dragons lay still for a moment. All the others held their breath until Rakgar began to rise. He walked over to Kodoran and lifted his claw to end him.

"I concede," Kodoran said softly, but decisive.

Everyone could see the pain Kodoran was in. Hiro could see the rage in Rakgar's eye. And the temptation. Kodoran had done serious damage to the older and larger dragon. Hiro knew the small dragon might be an equal adversary one day, given some growth and training. And Hiro knew that if Rakgar struck him down now, he would kill a rival, but confirm his own status as a murderer. He would be swarmed and killed for the crime. Releasing the smaller dragon would ensure his life, at least for the time being.

Slowly Rakgar lowered his claw, but as he opened his maw to sound the three roars pronouncing his name and title of Rakgar, another voice sounded.

"I challenge you!"

All eyes turned to Milah.

Rakgar bared his fangs. "You?" he growled. "You, who were once my counselor, challenge me?"

Milah crouched. "I challenge a blood and ash traitor."

Rakgar nodded. "So be it."

21

UNRESTRAINED

"Well, I've lost her again."

Philip could almost sense Tierni before he heard her. He turned to see her with Hilde and a handful of Black Sabers in her wake. All dressed in their black uniforms and black armor, they were a terrifying sight, even for the most accomplished swordsman.

Philip knew he'd taken too long enjoying the mesmerizing sight of Tierni when she said, "Anna – Philip, I've lost Anna again."

Philip couldn't help but chuckle. "Now you see what I've had to deal with," he answered.

"Did you ask her maid where she went?" Torgon said, half-heartedly. He had, after all, been tried by Anna's disappearances alongside Philip for the same amount of time.

"Yes," Tierni answered with a bite in her voice that she reserved just for her brother. "I think she's lost her mind. She only said, 'You'll see her' and 'My job is done'. Strange girl."

"Weren't you and she friends in the laundry?" Torgon asked as they all strode toward the horses' corral.

"Yes," Tierni said, stealing a glance at Philip, "but she's changed since she's been in Anna's service. The two are constantly speaking in whispers, counseling at all hours of the night, and she doesn't even seem to do any work anymore. Every time I try to speak to her, her mind is somewhere else entirely and sometimes she'll scamper off in the middle of a sentence."

"That still doesn't mean you…wait—" Torgon stopped as he and Philip began to mount their horses for the ride out to the platforms. "Where are you going?" he asked his sister.

Tierni stopped in the middle of mounting her own horse. "Where do you think?" she answered. When Torgon looked ready to argue, she cut him off with one finger. "Anna's gone. We have no one to protect here. We will accompany the king because he is likely to be the first person made aware of her discovery."

"But," Torgon started, then lowered his voice and glanced around, "what about Mother?"

"Don't worry," Tierni said. She jumped onto her horse, arranged herself with her reins and began to trot away. At the last second, she yelled over her shoulder, "She's already there!"

Philip shifted to stare at Torgon. "Your mother?" he said, low so no one else would hear. "You're going to allow your mother to be at the front line of a war with dragons?"

Torgon, who had been staring after Tierni, spun on Philip. "Have you ever tried to keep a woman in my family from doing something?" He didn't even bother to keep his voice down. "I don't recommend it, as it could be more dangerous than *any* battle with dragons!" He swung up onto his horse and, waving a hand after Tierni, he yelled at Philip, "And *that's* what you have to look forward to!"

22

MORTALITY

The sky lightened to a pale purple as the two beasts threw themselves at each other. Hiro skirted the fight, circling around to the injured Kodoran. Mitashio kept his eyes locked on the fight, unblinking.

When he got to his side, Hiro crouched next to Kodoran. "Can you walk?" he asked.

The little dragon shook his head. Hiro turned to Mitashio, next to them. "He needs flarote," Hiro told him.

With a quick dip of his chin, Mitashio ran to the entrance of the cavern and slipped inside. Hiro's eyes moved to Rakgar as he fought, but Rakgar watched Mitashio run inside. Then his eyes met Hiro's and fell on Kodoran. He bared his fangs, but the distraction was enough for Milah to reach up for Rakgar's shoulder. The mighty dragon bellowed in pain and returned his attention to the fight.

Soon, much sooner than Kodoran had lasted, Milah conceded. Again, Rakgar left his challenger on the verge of death. As he started anew to roar in victory, Hiro stood, but Mitashio appeared and roared, "I challenge you!"

Dropping the flarote at Hiro's feet, Mitashio threw himself into the fight. Kodoran's wounds slowed and he was able to right himself. Hiro ground his teeth watching their would-be leader tearing down dragon after dragon mercilessly. Dragons who Hiro had thought to be his own enemies were now following his lead. Dragons who he thought would follow him, he realized he would follow instead. He couldn't let these dragons die or suffer more.

"What's going on?" a dragon from the crowd asked Kodoran from behind.

"We need your help," Kodoran answered. He placed his nose against the other dragon.

"He's a traitor?" the dragon said. "How? Why?"

"I can't give you the rest," Kodoran said with a flit of his eyes to Hiro. "But show others. It must be known."

The dragon ran off with the memory. Hiro assumed it was the memory of himself telling Kodoran of Rakgar's treachery.

Hiro ran into Rakgar's lair. They needed more flarote. Kodoran followed him.

"Gather all of it," Kodoran told him. "Hopefully others will join us – we may have to use all of it."

The two dragons limped outside the cave with heaps of flarote in their claws. They piled it by Milah, trusting he and his brother to protect and give it to those who need it.

When Mitashio conceded to Rakgar, Kodoran threw himself into the fight again.

"You did well," Milah said as he fed his brother flarote.

"Lasted longer than you," Mitashio whispered.

"Did not," Milah scoffed.

Milah took another turn against Rakgar when Kodoran was thrown into a large pine and didn't emerge from the branches. Everyone heard his strangled cry of concession before Rakgar could stagger over to him.

"He's wearing down," Mitashio said, seeing his brother get up to fight again.

As they watched, Tog came to sit next to Mitashio on the other side, away from Hiro. "Is it true?" he asked Mitashio. "Did Rakgar really betray us?"

Mitashio grunted. "Do you really think I'd risk my life like this if I didn't believe it?"

"You mean, believe *him*," Tog said, flicking one eye to Hiro.

Mitashio sighed. "I never thought it possible, but yes," he said., "Though you've abandoned your friend, I believe him."

Hiro chanced a look at Tog. Mitashio didn't see the look on Tog's face. Hiro could see the pain sear through him. He knew Tog was remembering Visi's words; words telling him that he would abandon his friend in their greatest hour of need.

"I concede!" Milah yelled before Rakgar could swipe at him again.

"It's my turn," Hiro growled.

"No!" Kodoran limped toward them. "We can do more, Hiro. You have to save your strength to take him down. The rest of us will continue until we can't take more flarote."

Tog's eyes widened as they took turns and the battle continued. He watched Kodoran go back in to fight the enormous enemy. His eyes flitted between Hiro, Rakgar and whoever happened to be Rakgar's challenger at the moment.

When Kodoran, Milah and Mitashio could finally take no more, Hiro thought his time had come. The others were broken, cut and bleeding ash onto the ground even with the help of flarote to heal them. Rakgar waned, but still stood strong. He seemed to have the strength of ten dragons. Rakgar roared twice after his last bout with Mitashio and the anger in Hiro burned brighter. Hiro didn't know if he could beat him, but he knew he would die trying. As he opened his mouth to shout his provocation, Tog roared first.

"I challenge you!"

Hiro watched dumbfounded as his best friend, until recently the only dragon to know his secrets, stepped between himself and Rakgar.

Rakgar growled and bared his teeth. Though he was prepared to continue the fight, Hiro could tell he must have tired from the constant challenges. He wanted to be done with this as much as Hiro and the others, but he was willing to attempt taking down as many as necessary before ending the confrontation.

Tog turned to Hiro. "I'm sorry, Hiro. I shouldn't have…I'm sorry. For everything."

"How noble," Rakgar sneered, then lifted his claw while he wasn't looking and batted Tog, knocking him into the side of the mountain. Tog stood, but slowly. They fought as more dragons from the ruck gathered around them. Surneen, Tog's mate, growled as Rakgar swiped a massive claw across Tog's ribs. Tog roared at the gashes along his side. But Surneen stood straighter when Tog added a large slash of claw marks across Rakgar's neck.

Rakgar eventually stopped swatting at the smaller, younger dragon and waited for his challenger to come to him. When he did, Rakgar would simply anticipate which way Tog was going, then rake his claws across him. Where Rakgar had tried to bite and attack Kodoran and the brothers previously, now he waited for Tog to make the first move. Tog's energy seeped quickly.

As Hiro watched them fight, his belly burned in anger toward Rakgar. Now he knew that this massive dragon who had always watched over Hiro and Tog had turned on them long ago. Tog had been shocked and appalled at the revelation of his heart breaking for Anna, but that was understandable. Tog felt betrayed by the secret. He had probably gone back to his cave to sulk and felt terrible ever since.

"I concede," Tog finally called out before Rakgar could strike him down. The crowd of dragons surrounding the fight heaved a sigh. Surneen ran to Tog's side, ignoring Hiro's cry.

"I CHALLENGE YOU, TAYNOR FEIRA RAKGAR!" he cried. He wanted to make sure every dragon heard it.

"How dare you try to name me Taynor. If any dragon here is traitor, it is you!" Rakgar rumbled. "To think you know better than me. To think you know the answers to questions you have yet to ask. How dare you challenge me?"

Hiro didn't wait. He ran at the massive dragon, feigning toward the throat and waiting for the coming strike. When it happened, he spun away from the claw and clamped his jaws around the limb. As he continued this form of attack, feigning and spinning, he knew his strength would soon exhaust like the others.

He began attacking the legs. He had seen Kodoran's attacks on the legs force the leader to move away or falter for pain. While Hiro was able to threaten the massive dragon with similar swipes, eventually he realized Hiro's purpose. Rakgar used his tail and claws to strike at Hiro when he went low toward the legs. In this way, he landed many painful strikes, often using his claws to slam Hiro into the unforgiving mountain floor.

After the third of these strikes, Hiro struggled to stand. His left front leg felt broken, causing much more agony than when Shampy had drained it of marrow. He couldn't extend his wings with the pain slicing through them. An icy cold spread across his neck, back and shoulder. A stiff ache swelled in his eye. Joints trembled as they pressed against the ground when he tried to stand. Hiro could feel his fire slipping away as if a strong wind blew across it. Rakgar lifted a claw over Hiro.

"I challenge you!" Kodoran yelled from behind Rakgar.

Rakgar stilled his claw but didn't look away from Hiro. "You can't challenge until the current challenge has relinquished," he muttered. Hiro could hear the weariness in his voice.

"Hiro," Milah crouched near Hiro, but kept an eye on Rakgar. "Hiro, you must concede."

"No," Hiro whispered, "he must die for his crimes."

"He will die," Milah whispered. "After all, we know Kodoran will be Rakgar, don't we?"

Rakgar, claw dangling over Hiro, blinked. His claw dropped onto Hiro, pinning him to the ground, but he snaked his head around to look at Kodoran. Rakgar opened his mouth to bare his fangs at Kodoran, then turned to Hiro again.

Rakgar threw his teeth toward Hiro's neck, but before they could connect and end him, Hiro yelled, "I concede!"

Milah huffed a sigh of relief as Rakgar was forced to stepped off Hiro. He slowly turned toward Kodoran.

Hiro shook from the icy pain. Milah shoved a flarote bulb into his mouth as Rakgar and Kodoran began another fight. Once the flarote fire burned through him, dulling the pain, Hiro tucked his legs under him to sit on the ground and wash his wounds with fire.

"I'll just have to repeat my challenge," he said to Milah.

Milah nodded. "Kodoran believes the rest of us only have one more chance. I can already feel the flarote burning too bright."

"Are any others willing to help?"

Milah shook his head. "They're all waiting to see what happens," he said.

Hiro turned to watch Kodoran. He still flew around the giant dragon, slipping around his defenses and past his giant claws. When one strike would knock him down, he would get back up and slip away once more.

"He's like a leppi," Milah whispered while they watched Kodoran fight Rakgar. "Small, but able to incapacitate a much larger creature."

Startled to hear such praise for Kodoran, Hiro turned to Milah in shock.

"Oh, snap it," he said when he saw the look on Hiro's face. "If you ever tell him I said that, I'll break off your horns."

Hiro grinned after him as Milah ran to take the fight from Kodoran.

Hiro limped over to Mitashio, who rolled his previously injured shoulder, testing it, and Tog, who lay on the stones, tentatively stretching his hind legs. They watched in silence as Rakgar fought Milah.

Hiro noticed that dragons from all over the Rock Clouds gathered around them. Not just the ones who heard the news from the centaur camps, but all the rest who had been told to gather too. He knew they were running out of time.

Milah switched to Kodoran's tactics. He slipped in and out of Rakgar's reach, scratching and biting. He slid under the massive dragon's belly and tore at his legs again. At one point, Milah launched himself onto Rakgar's back. Hiro could see the flarote burning energy into Milah's movements.

Emboldened by Milah's fiery burst of energy, Hiro shouted, "Finish it, Milah!"

Milah threw himself into the air, flipped over Rakgar's outstretched claws and landed with his claws digging into Rakgar's neck and shoulder. With a grin, Milah bit into Rakgar's shoulder. Roaring, Rakgar shrugged his shoulder – rather than jerk back as another dragon might have – and lifted his claw under Milah, effectively plunging the smaller dragon into his jaws. With a single snap of the massive maw on Milah's neck, the young brown dragon disappeared into a pile of ash and ember.

23

INCREDIBLE

"You're going where?" Kradik shouted. He floated on wing next to Philip on his horse.

"To a platform," Philip said. He couldn't have imagined saying that to Kradik before last night, but now he barked his answer with confidence. He knew he could trust Anna and it felt better than ever having not trusted her.

"You should be in your tent," Kradik ordered, "commanding men from nowhere near the front line. I will assist you in communication as I always have."

"No," Philip said, "I will lead my men into battle. They deserve to see me go before them, facing the dragons with them. It's the right thing to do. It's the noble thing."

"And if the dragons kill you?" Kradik sneered. "You have no heir … perhaps I will rule in your stead."

"You're not a human," Philip said, not letting the threat move him. He kept his horse steady on. "Unfortunately, Torgon will be forced to rule if the worst should happen."

"Which is why," Torgon said from astride the horse next to him, "I'm going along to make sure the worst doesn't happen."

Both young men grinned at each other, then at the faerie. Philip could have sworn he heard the faerieman's teeth grind.

They had ridden for some time, having woken and dressed before dawn. Finally, they approached the platforms as the light of the sun fully topped the edge of the world. Philip hadn't slept and couldn't eat, but he hadn't felt more clear-headed since Kradik had arrived in his kingdom.

Philip hadn't been able to escape the notice of many people as he mounted his horse that morning. Torgon had placed General Tommak in charge of Maelin and his claw of men. They all walked directly behind the king and Torgon. However, General Riddig, an associate of Lord Dieko – and constant condescending thorn in Philip's side – had decided to not only accompany the king, but bring along Murzod as well. Philip couldn't refuse. While in the Great Northern Mountain he had insisted on having Murzod by his side at the Rock Clouds. At the time, it was an excuse to end production on the dragon poison, now he must suffer the consequences. Unfortunately, Riddig and Murzod also brought an entire claw of men with them. Philip couldn't be certain he could trust Riddig's men. Tierni, Hilde and a dozen Black Sabers brought up the rear, by Tierni's choice. The entire party dismounted in front of the middle of five platforms.

"I won't do it," Kradik barked. "I won't lift your platform."

Philip and Torgon shared a glance. Philip didn't know how the platform would work without the help of a faerie. The faerie council was spread thin as it was and several more shaman had been called upon to help raise the platforms. Only two other faeries hovered nearby and after a glance from Kradik, they settled on the ground with their hands folded in front of them.

"I'll do it, Your Majesty."

Philip turned to see Travaith, the king's majishun, walking up behind them in his sweeping blue robes with a determined grin spread over his face.

Philip turned back to Kradik. "It seems we won't be needing your service anyway."

As the faerie began to puff out his chest, waiting for a chance to bellow, Murzod slapped his gloves together. "Don't worry, Your Majesty," Murzod nodded toward the faeries, "I'll deal with him." He ushered the faeries away from the group and began speaking to them in low tones.

Although not entirely comfortable with the situation, Philip turned back to beam at Travaith. "Pleased to have your help," he said to the royal majishun.

Torgon sidled in close to Philip and Travaith. In a low voice, he asked, "Are you sure you have the power for this, Travaith?"

The old majishun stood up tall but kept his voice low too. "I couldn't save either of your parents, Your

Majesty. I haven't done nearly as much with my majikal training as I would have liked. I will do this, even if it's the last thing I ever do."

Torgon glanced at the seething faeries and muttered, "It might be."

"Nonsense," Philip said to the majishun, hoping to buoy his spirits. "You have always served the royal family with nobility. I am and will continue to be proud to have you by my side."

Travaith mumbled his thanks as the entire party tramped onto the platform.

"No!" Kradik shoved past Murzod, yelling. "I won't allow you to do this. You jeopardize everything we've worked for!"

Philip placed his hand on the bright blue gem on the pommel of his sword. "You mean war," he said. The months of being bullied by the faeries bubbled to the surface as Philip felt his face flare. "You've been working toward war. I only jeopardize that by seeking peace."

"Threaten to hurt him."

Philip heard the words in his head. He had been trained from a tender age to hide shock or surprise, or any reaction at all, really. He searched the area quickly with his eyes and saw no one else reacting to the sound. Waiting to see whose words he'd heard, he watched Kradik for a response.

"There can be no peace," Kradik hissed. "Between us or the dragons."

"Threaten to hurt him," came the words to Philip's mind again.

Philip's mind immediately went back to the invisible presence from the previous night's interruptions. He remembered that the small man had promised to see Philip safely to the platforms this morning. The man must have more powers than Philip knew of. Power to be invisible? Power to speak to Philip in his mind? Power to…?

"You're not the only one with power, Kradik," Philip said awkwardly. It didn't sound natural or confident by any means, but he managed to get it out.

Kradik grunted. "You dare…"

"Touch his arm," the voice in Philip's head said. Svorgh, is that what Anna had called the little man? Philip could definitely hear the same lilt as that he'd heard in the voice last night. He reached out and brushed three fingers against the faerie's arm. He didn't touch his skin.

Immediately, Kradik yelled. He threw his head back as his knees gave way and he fell to the ground, panting.

Without waiting for anyone else to react, and to hide his own shock, Philip spun on his heel and bounded onto the platform.

24

LAST OFFENSIVE

"NOOOOOOOOOOO!" Mitashio screamed in rage, running toward Rakgar.

Rakgar grinned at the grief in Mitashio's shout and opened his mouth to roar. Kodoran and Tog both dove at Mitashio, pinning him to the ground. "I chall—!"

Kodoran clamped his claws around Mitashio's snout before he could finish the call to challenge. Looking up at Hiro, Kodoran shook his head. "He can't fight now," he said. "He isn't thinking straight. He'll get himself killed."

Mitashio wriggled and shook under the claws and bodies of his friends. Tears seeped from his eyes. Burning fluid leaked from his nose and corners of his mouth as he tried to breathe fire and roar.

"It's up to you now, Hiro," Tog said. "You have to kill him."

Hiro turned to challenge Rakgar again, but the massive dragon stood over him.

"Yes, Hiro," he sneered. "It's up to you." Without another word, Rakgar slammed his claw onto the pile of flarote. Then he picked up one of the few pieces outside the squashed mess and threw it into his mouth.

He turned to smile at Hiro. "You wouldn't want to tempt fate, now would you?" he said, then he turned and spewed fire onto the pile of flarote mush.

Hiro could only watch in shock as Rakgar turned the little pile into black slime, then backed away.

"Hurry, Hiro," Kodoran said, "before the flarote can take effect."

He nodded Hiro toward Rakgar, Mitashio limp and shaking in the two dragons' grasp. Tog shook his head. "It's too late, Hiro," Tog countered. "He'll kill you."

Hiro felt the fire flare in his belly as he watched Rakgar tromp over the embers of Milah. "Then he'll kill me," he whispered.

As the sky brightened into an orange glow, in the distance, beyond Rakgar's hulking mass, Hiro watched wooden platforms filled with humans lift into the Rock Clouds.

25

IRREGULAR AMBUSH

Once all the platforms were filled, including the platform baring the royal party, Philip nodded to Torgon and Torgon nodded to Travaith. Travaith stood on the ground nearby. He said he would be steadier and thus stronger with the ground's stability underneath him. The older majishun closed his eyes and bowed his head. He began chanting inaudibly and slowly lifted his hands.

After a moment, the platform shook. Everyone kept their footing as the heavy base shook free of the earth and lifted smoothly into the air. The other Noble platforms also lifted in turn.

As the wooden transports glid into the sky, Philip heard the voice in his head again. *"Keep your hand on the pommel of your sword and only think the words you want me to hear."*

"Who are you?" he said in his mind. He struggled to keep his lips from moving.

194

"I am King Svorgh of the Goblins," he answered. *"I am the one you saw last night. I'm here to help you."*

"How do I know that?" Philip asked. *"How are we communicating?"*

"We are speaking to each other through a blue dragon stone embedded in your sword's hilt," Svorgh answered. *"If you release it, I won't be able to hear your thoughts or speak to you without others hearing us."*

Careful not to draw attention as they continued moving upward, Philip glanced down at the pommel his hand rested on. It glowed with a soft blue light.

"And the first matter?" he asked the supposed king in his head.

"You will know I am here to help you by two admissions," Svorgh said. *"First, I am the one who pained the faerie. They need to know that you are strong. If not you, then your allies. For now, it was necessary for you to take the credit.*

"Second," Svorgh continued, *"I followed the man who pulled Kradik aside after he was injured. The man is one of yours, but it seems they are previously familiar with working together. He told Kradik he was going to try to kill you by pushing you off the platform. The man told the faerie to kill the majishun on the ground and he would toss you from the height so it looked like an accident, or even better, like it was the majishun's fault. Unfortunately, they both seemed amenable to the idea."*

Philip couldn't keep his eyes from widening but he continued to stare straight ahead. *"What should I do?"*

"I would advise you to hold on."

Philip searched around him. With his height, he could see most of the people on his platform and the other platforms surrounding him as well. He worried about those on the platform with him, but his gaze also wandered to the other transports. He had put all these men and women in harm's way. He had agreed to place the lives of everyone in the hands of the faeries. At any moment, the faeries might decide to turn on them and drop all these people to their deaths. *"The others,"* he asked the voice in his head. *"Can you save them?"*

"I'll do all I can."

Philip watched the platforms around him floating higher in the sky. The people on the other Noble platforms watched Philip as they lifted together. He saw platforms far to the north and south rising into the sky at the same time. He could even see specks rising on the horizon to the west on the far side of the Inner Mountain.

As the king's platform lifted, the sun shining from behind lit an odd scene on the mountain in front of them. Dozens, possibly hundreds of dragons sat with their backs to the humans floating by. Roars echoed from the mountainside. A commotion centered in front of a large opening in the Inner Mountain. Most of the dragons faced the Inner Mountain and watched the chaotic happening before them, their attention turned away from the beings on the platforms.

"What are they doing?" Philip whispered.

A few dragons at the back of the gathering noticed the intruders. Some lifted casually into the air to fly away. Many others shifted at the interruption but kept their gazes away from the oncoming humans.

"Is this what we've come to?" Torgon asked from Philip's side. "Attacking animals while they ignore us?"

Suddenly, a deafening roar made Philip flinch and turn. Everyone on the platform scanned the skies to find dozens of dragons of all different shapes, sizes, colors and configurations flying toward them on all sides.

26

TENDER MEMORIES

"Go!" Hiro barked at Kodoran. Without another word, Kodoran spoke low in Mitashio's ear. Kodoran ran away to launch into the sky. Tog allowed the mourning dragon to slowly rise.

With a glance at Rakgar, Mitashio growled low. "Kill him, Hiro." The two nodded to each other and most of the rest of the dragons flew off to face the humans.

"I challenge you," Hiro said, keeping his voice low. The embattled leader of the ruck didn't move as Hiro flew into his face.

Just as he raked his claws across Rakgar's snout, Hiro heard a scream of protest behind him.

"Hiro, no!" The early morning sun sparkled on Visi's white scales as she flew above them. Hiro only registered her presence for a moment before Rakgar struck back. He was thrown into a boulder, knocking the air out of his lungs.

"Hiro," Visi said as she landed beside him, "you don't understand."

"I do," Hiro said. He threw himself at Rakgar again. He slipped under a claw to scratch at the healing wounds Kodoran and Milah had carved into his leg joints, reopening them.

Rakgar roared, recoiling his leg before pushing Hiro away with it. Visi ran to him as Hiro landed against another rock. At least this time the push didn't have enough force to harm him…much.

"You can't let him kill you!" Visi yelled. The sound of the battle raging around them muffled her words as Rakgar ran at Hiro. Hiro dove out of the way and Visi did too. He couldn't be sure, but it seemed as if Rakgar had tried to run into both of them.

"You're not The One!" Visi yelled past Rakgar to Hiro.

Rakgar looked at Visi then back at Hiro. He spun further than necessary and knocked Visi away with his tail. "Don't interfere, witch!" he roared.

Hiro jumped at Rakgar, latching onto his neck with his claws. The biggest risk he had taken, the mighty gray dragon clawed at Hiro while Hiro bit into his neck.

Rakgar ripped Hiro away from his neck. Hiro ignored the gouges in his sides from Rakgar's claws as he spat the chunk of scales and flesh that turned to ash on the rocks.

Visi ran to him again. "Hiro," she whispered urgently, watching Rakgar from the corners of her eyes, "my memories."

Hiro decided to risk it. It would only take a moment and he had dealt a heavy blow to Rakgar. He moved his nose to hers.

The view was disorienting. Hiro's perspective hovered high above the cavern of Rakgar's lair. He looked down upon two dragons, one large and gray — the Rakgar Hiro had always known — the other smaller and brown, with dark gray patches and two tails.

"The others won't understand," the smaller brown dragon said. "I need you to be Freeg."

"I will always be your friend," the large gray dragon said. Horns and barbels spread from his head and neck, down his shoulders, spine and tail. This was a memory from the time when the Rakgar Hiro had always known was only called Freeg, friend to the former Rakgar. Hiro knew the large gray dragon as Rakgar feira Freeg.

"As you always have been," said the former Rakgar, the smaller brown dan Hiro observed in the familiar lair below. "But we must find a human to befriend. If one of us befriends a human, we can create a bridge between our species."

Freeg nodded. "You can't do it. You have other duties here as Rakgar."

"The others would also see me as a traitor," the brown dan said.

"I might scare off any humans," Freeg suggested. "I might be too imposing for the job."

"Just be a friend," the brown dan answered. "The humans are capable of understanding more than anyone realizes."

Freeg nodded again. "And we might just break the curse while we're at it."

Hiro's eyes widened when the memory ended. He turned to Rakgar in time to dodge a strike of his claws.

"You believe," Hiro muttered, the shock of the memory sapping his anger and strength to fight. "At least, you did once."

Rakgar roared in response and lunged at Hiro. Hiro didn't dodge this time. He allowed Rakgar to tackle him. He wrapped his body around the much larger one. Reaching his head around, he couldn't reach Rakgar's neck so he bit into his shoulder. Rakgar bellowed and ripped Hiro off of him again.

Hiro used his wings to slow his trajectory and lessen the impact of his body on the rocky mountainside. When he looked up, Visi stood before him. Without a word, she pushed her snout in front of his.

Hiro was in a forest meadow. It was familiar. A grassy ridge to one side of the meadow hid the scene of a beautiful human woman walking through it. He thought it was Anna from the way her golden hair sparkled in the sun. But when she turned at a sound in the forest, he saw her face was slightly different. Hiro, watching through Visi's eyes from behind a tangle of trees, saw the woman walk toward the sound in the trees. Then he recognized her. He had seen this woman as an apparition from the World of Souls, almost a year ago.

"Is someone there?" she asked the shades.

"Yes," came a reply.

"Who are you?"

"A friend."

"If you're a friend, then come out and let me see you."

"I can't," the low, deep voice answered. "You'll fear me."

She straightened. "I won't," she said with a set jaw.

"Do you promise?" the voice said across the space. "Swear you won't run? Or scream?"

"I give you my word," she answered. "I'm Queen Annette of the Noble Kingdom, formerly of the Courageous Kingdom. I don't fear you or anyone."

The trees rustled again. This time, a massive gray dragon emerged into the sunlight of the meadow. Annette's eyes widened, but she didn't move. She didn't flinch or take a step away.

"You spoke," she whispered.

"I did," Freeg said as he walked toward her.

Annette smiled. "Somehow, that makes you even less frightening."

27

YIELDING STABILITY

"Brace yourselves!" Philip yelled as the dragons flew at them. "Ready weapons!"

He pulled his own bow from his back and began to string it. When he looked up again, he had placed a black-tipped arrow.

The original plan was to lift the platforms from the surface and set them against some of the larger floating rocks, the ones with trees and foliage for cover. Then the men and women would dismount and the faeries would guide the platforms back to the ground to load the next wave of warriors.

The platforms to Philip's sides glid forward under a wave of buffs from the dragons. People were almost immediately knocked down or burned, but the platforms gradually positioned themselves and bumped against their targeted floating mountain.

However, the platform Philip stood on halted its progress. The soldiers' armor and weaponry rattled as the platform shook in mid-air. It rocked back and forth as the riders attempted to steady themselves.

"Hold on!" Philip shouted, echoing the advice from the invisible man. "Swords!"

Philip heard the repeated *swish* and *thunk, thunk, thunk* as everyone with a sword, saber or staff plunged them into the wood at their feet. As Philip's fingers wrapped his hilt, the surface under him dropped away from his feet.

28

GUILT

Rakgar growled, aware of the humans around them on the mountain and holding back his speech. He batted Visi to the side. As Visi tumbled into the onlooking dragons, Rakgar turned to Hiro. He swiped at Hiro, but Hiro dodged, shifting to simply avoid the enormous claws. Hiro realized the larger dragon was getting careless, he wasn't waiting for the attack. Something was distracting him. Rakgar continued to claw at the air, so Hiro slipped underneath his mass and raked at his belly again. Flying back out again, he bit into the gray dragon's tail. Hard. He felt bone crunch in his teeth and knew he would get a response. He let go and ran out of reach as Rakgar roared in pain and swiped at the spot where he expected Hiro to be.

Hiro skittered away, but stopped at Visi's side. This time, he placed his nose in front of hers.

He was back in the meadow, watching from the same spot, but an entirely different season.

The massive gray dragon tip-taloned toward the human woman, Queen Annette, in the sunny meadow while she admired some flowers. He kept his body low to the ground, as if that would help his cover, but he was so large even the towering trees could barely hide him. He crept up to her with a cautious grin on his lips. At least his claws sunk into soft earth and muffled the sound of his steps.

"I know you're there, Freeg." The woman didn't turn at first. A smile lit her face and she spun on her heel to face the mighty gray dragon, her golden hair flying as if it might help her take flight.

He narrowed his eyes at her. "I was as silent as death. How did you know I was there?"

She narrowed her green eyes in return. "After all these visits, I can sense you," she said with a grin.

"Well, then." He gave up all pretenses of stealth and kromped into the clearing. "I saw your flag," he said as he curled into a comfortable position on the forest floor with the grassy ridge to his left. The meadow, the location chosen to meet the queen for its seclusion, was the same place he, Hiro, had also used to meet with Anna.

Freeg's eyes met Annette's. Her grin faded and he noticed redness around her eyes. He lifted his head to face her. "What's wrong?"

"I saw the faerie shaman you told me about. Shampy." She swallowed hard but couldn't keep her chin from quivering slightly. She placed one delicate hand on her bulging belly. Without warning she launched herself at the dragon and wrapped her arms around what she could reach of his neck. "Freeg," she cried into his scales, "she said it will be a girl!"

Although taken aback by the suddenness of her contact, he seemed anything but repulsed by it. He picked up one claw and attempted to stroke her silken hair while also pulling her in tighter to the embrace. His claws were so large that he simply covered her, unable to show the tenderness he felt. "It is an honor to bear a female, Annette. I, myself, would be proud to ever have a daughter." Hiro knew Annette's reaction would confuse Freeg. Female dragons were providers. Although the genders were thought equal, the dames were known to often be fiercer and craftier than the dans. Hiro knew from his experiences with Anna that human thoughts about the genders weren't always the same.

She pulled back from him long enough to look into his onyx eye. "I might be proud if—" she cut herself off sharply.

He released her. They stared into each other's eyes, lost in thought that Visi could only imagine. Thoughts that Hiro assumed were the same ones he had experienced himself. 'What is he doing?' 'What might be?' 'How could this happen?' Hiro could practically hear the questions as they tumbled between the two beings before him.

"You are the only male to ever be kind to me," she said, as she broke the connection to curl into the crook of his shoulder and lay her head against him. "That is the world my daughter will grow up in. Human men do not treat their females as equals. Perhaps in the Allegiant Kingdom, but not here. My husband will force my daughter to marry someone she does not love for the sake of an alliance, as my own father did. And worse," her voice cracked as a fresh flood of tears suddenly fell from her eyes, "he will probably want to try to get a male heir."

Freeg froze. Hiro knew what was happening. He could see it in the dragon's eye.

Freeg's eyes popped open wide, as Annette continued her tirade against the king. "I don't hate him, Freeg. He simply has no idea. He was forced into our marriage just like me, but I still can't forgive him...or myself." Freeg choked back a small cough, but she didn't notice. "I hate the monster growing inside me. It doesn't come from love. I don't know what it comes from."

Freeg tried to swallow. "Annette..." he coughed.

"My father said I would grow to love him, but I can't!" She ranted, unaware of the struggles of the dragon next to her. "I wish I could fly away with..." She turned to see Freeg choking. "What's wrong? Are you well?"

The dragon gave one last cough and a gray teardrop-shaped gem slid from his mouth. He scooped it up in his claw. His heart had broken for the woman Annette. The smoky gem glittered against his scales. Silently, he offered her his heart.

"Is that what I think it is?" she whispered. Hiro assumed over the course of time and their growing relationship Freeg must have explained many things about dragons to the woman. He must have told her how a dan's heart only breaks once, for one dame...or woman.

"Yes," he confirmed. "If you accept it, I am yours...forever." That meant Annette could control Freeg if she wished. Hiro thought of the implications. She could compel him to do anything. He could resist, but learning how took time and practice. Hiro could only imagine what Annette might ask him to do.

She scooped the heart out of Freeg's claw. It was big enough that she had to use both arms to hold it. She knelt in front of the dragon and wrapped her arms around the heart, hugging it against her chest. Tears flowed down her pink cheeks.

Hiro watched deep emotions rage inside her. She shook her head, squeezed her eyes shut for a moment and looked back up at Freeg. "I..." she started, but she couldn't finish. She searched her surroundings in quiet desperation, unable to meet Freeg's eye any longer. "This..." she tried inspecting the heart in her arms, but, again, she couldn't put words to the war inside her.

Finally, with Freeg watching patiently, her face scrunched together and a sob tore from her throat. "Freeg," she cried, "end this!"

Leaves ceased their rustle. Birds stopped in mid-sky. Kiket chirps silenced. The cool summer breeze held still. Flames wrapped around Annette while Hiro watched helplessly. For a moment he thought she might survive. A look of peace came over her and she gazed up at the large dragon who had been her friend. She threw back her head victoriously to the sky as his flames immersed her. Flames tinged with gray, a symbol of his love for her. Her body shriveled in an instant. A moment later, her blackened body fell.

When Freeg finally closed his maw, his grief spilled forth in a roar. When it stopped, he heard his anguish echoed in the scream coming from a man at the top of the ridge. The man sat regally on a bejeweled stallion. Although fifteen dragon lengths away, Hiro heard his accusation with the perfect clarity of a dragon's ears. "What have you done?" the king whispered as he stared at the charred remains of his wife below. He lifted his eyes suddenly to lock them with the dragon's. "What have you DONE?!" He bellowed in a rage!

Hiro realized what the man, King Paudie, would have seen as he heard more men top the rise on their steeds. The next man to appear, a man Hiro himself remembered killing in the forest to save Tog, yelled to more companions, "Kill that monster! He's killed the queen!"

Horses thundered from the other side of the ridge, following the second man. The men howled their defiance. Freeg readied for flight, opening and pumping his wings. Before he flew, the draft from his wings shifted the ash from the remains of Annette. A shimmer caught Freeg's eye and was reflected in Hiro's. From something on the ground amidst the smoking ember remains of the woman. Under the *smoldering ash and soot sat a bright green teardrop-shaped gem twice the size of the heart she had been given. With the cavalry bearing down on him, Freeg snatched the egg and vaulted into the sky.*

Hiro blinked several times. He stared at Visi. He didn't see Rakgar throw himself at the pair.

Instead of attacking only Hiro, Rakgar gouged a claw into each of them, tearing them apart. Hiro flew and spread his wings again to slow himself. He watched as Visi rolled away from Rakgar, three deep holes visible in her belly and chest.

Hiro roared. He knew Rakgar was trying to keep him from discovering the whole truth. He dove toward Rakgar, landing on his head. He clawed at the massive, lion-like dragon. With all the horns surrounding the head and neck, Hiro couldn't latch on properly. He tried to dig his claws into anything, but only accomplished scratching Rakgar's face as he shook him free.

Hiro landed close to Visi. Scrambling to her side, he watched as Rakgar lifted a claw to stomp him.

"Hiro," Visi whispered, as Hiro rolled away from the deadly strike. "This is not your fight to win. Be mindful who wields you and learn to understand why they do."

With those words, Hiro knew he had to get what memories he could from her. He remembered his own father's dying words. He had to know more. He rolled next to her after another strike landed and pressed his nose to hers.

29

HATCHLING

Watching from the shadows of an unknown corner of the cave, Hiro could see the enormous and intimidating gray dragon known as Freeg alight on the lip of the Rakgar's lair. Clutched in his gray claw was an oversized, green, teardrop-shaped egg. The empty cavern echoed with the sound of Freeg's talons clacking on the floor as he landed.

Once inside, he held perfectly still. Only his eyes moved as he peered into the darkened corners of the cavern. Visi, as usual, had chosen the perfect hiding spot. Hiro, from her viewpoint, watched as the gray dragon relaxed slightly, assuming he was alone. Hiro saw Freeg place the brilliant green egg in the deep shadows against the far wall, out of sight.

With the egg tucked away, Freeg calmly turned to the sound of another dragon approaching.

"Freeg!" The brown dan Rakgar in this vision was much smaller than Freeg. And no matter one's station in life, having a friend that dwarfed other dragons had its advantages. "I can't tell you

how happy I am to see you return, my friend. I need an ally right now." Freeg didn't respond but watched as Rakgar crossed the cave, flicking his tails in obvious anxiety. "I have sown the seeds, but they weren't well-received." Rakgar shook his head. "Mordok practically challenges me with his every word. I'm sure he plans to do it openly soon." Rakgar turned pleading eyes to Freeg.

"I'll deal with Mordok," Freeg said quietly, but didn't meet Rakgar's imploring gaze.

Rakgar sighed, "Thank you, my friend." He resumed his pacing across the floor. "The other dragons resist any notion of interactions with the humans. They're set in their silence. If our plan is to succeed, we need the human." He stopped his pacing, glanced either direction, then asked in a whisper. "How goes your association with the woman? Would she be willing to come here? Will she help us?"

Freeg growled low. "She is dead."

Rakgar's shoulders dropped and his head hung. "No." Looking back up at Freeg, he asked, "We don't have the luxury of time to befriend another human. What happened?"

Freeg couldn't meet the Rakgar's questioning eyes. Although his size protected the egg tucked into the wall behind him, his eyes instinctively flickered toward it. Before he could cover his mistake, Rakgar caught a glimpse of the gem-like egg.

"What is that?" His eyes grew twice their normal size. "Is that what I think it is?" He took a step toward the egg, but Freeg growled and blocked his path.

"It's not your concern," Freeg growled.

"But the woman is," Rakgar said. "Our plan can't possibly proceed without—"

"Your plan," Freeg emphasized, "was folly to begin. Humans are the monsters."

"My plan? Monsters?" Rakgar stepped away as Freeg advanced on him. "But you agreed from the start— we planned this together—"

"I supported my Rakgar," he said, but glanced at the entrance as three dans stepped into the cavern with a dusty brown dragon in the lead. Freeg turned back to Rakgar. "But no longer."

"I must speak with Rakgar," the brown dragon at the entrance said.

"You'll wait your turn, Mordok," Freeg snapped at him as he continued his advance on the cowering leader.

"Freeg," Rakgar whispered, "don't do this."

"You have betrayed the dragons with your notion of befriending humans! I challenge you, Rakgar, for your name and position!" Freeg's words echoed through the cave and around the stunned observers. Even Mordok glanced questioningly at his companions.

Rakgar shook his head, but his eyes traveled back to the egg. He closed his eyes and shook his head. "Is it even possible...?"

Freeg launched himself at the leader to stem further words, slashing at his head with his front claws. "Will you fight for your position?"

"It wasn't your fault!" Rakgar cried as he scurried out of Freeg's reach before his talons could fully get hold. "I don't want to fight you, Freeg."

"Then you concede?" he roared in return.

Rakgar shook his head. "You know I can't do that," he whispered.

Freeg settled back into an attacking crouch. "Then you will die."

Rakgar mirrored his attack position. "I will fight for the ideals you once believed in."

The two dragons shot toward each other, claws and tails lashing in every direction. As large as it was the cavern might have had plenty of room to maneuver, but Freeg forced their path outside to prevent the egg from being discovered by anyone else present. Hiro assumed Visi knew Freeg would do this and thus positioned herself where she needed to be. With the four witnesses behind them, the challenging dans rolled outside the cavern in a mass of fire and fury.

Visi emerged from her hiding spot, listening to Rakgar's occasional exclamations to Freeg outside. He appealed with, "It's not your fault!" over and over again. But when he tried explaining his position with, "We believed that—" or "The humans aren't—" he was quickly shut down by Freeg's gigantic claws.

Hiro knew instinctively what Visi would do. He knew the challenge would distract the observers from anything she might do. The only problem would be getting away from Rakgar's lair without the enormous gray dragon seeing her. Hiro ran to the egg and, scooping it into her white claws, both Visi and Hiro felt the weight of the fully-grown being inside.

As she pulled it into her clutches, a vision she had seen many moons ago returned to her mind. Hiro's vision flickered with the added memory. The broken shards of the green egg lay on the cavern floor. A small green dragon stared up at Freeg, but was immediately struck down. Visi knew this hatchling's only chance of survival was for the egg to be taken far away.

Because the egg was fully mature, it was much larger than the partial heart it started as. Had it been that small, Visi could have easily smuggled it out of the cave. But large as it was, she tucked it partially under one wing and holding it with a claw, she limped out of the opening.

The two dans continued to fight, advancing lower down the mountain as Visi slowly crawled up the incline. She knew Rakgar wouldn't last long against Freeg. She prayed he would last long enough for her to disappear. She listened to the roaring and clashing of the dragons below without turning her head to watch. Although wanting to see what the other dragons were doing, Hiro knew she would lose her nerve if she saw Freeg's immense frame.

Freeg was the largest of all the dragons. Seeing him grow so large, everyone wondered why the gods had blessed him with such an advantage over all the others. Hiro especially questioned their choice now.

Rakgar had relied on Freeg's intimidation for many years. They were friends before Rakgar won his position. In fact, he had only won the position because of Freeg's subtle hints to the previous Rakdar. Everyone wondered why Freeg had turned on Rakgar at the time, now Hiro realized that Visi had known all along.

Stepping lightly through the few pine trees from her perspective, Hiro saw her refuge ahead. A rushing waterfall. If she could slip into its waters, her white body would be hidden. She could watch from the waters until the challenge ended.

Hiro could feel the misty spray bouncing off the rocks when the decision was made. A mighty bellowing roar up the mountain told Visi the challenge had been decided. At any moment the new Rakgar would look up into the trees. Pushing off the ground with her back legs she jumped under the falling waters as another triumphant bellow sounded below. She looked down at the bright green egg in her arms from an alcove under the falls as the third and final bellow announced the death of the former Rakgar and a new Rakgar taking his place.

Visi sat quietly for a moment, waiting. More memories flickered as Visi remembered visions in her crystal ball. Freeg had noticed her during the fight, but he didn't know why she was there. She peered out of the veil of water … just as the enormous gray dragon's eyes moved past her hiding place.

A tear in Visi's eye blurred her vision and, in turn, Hiro's. The roaring water around them turned dark and cold, like the cave walls the new Rakgar stared at now. He looked at the empty shadow the egg had occupied. He turned to glare out the entrance of the cave. Blood dripped from his fangs. As he narrowed his eyes, the gash on his jaw wrinkled and released another great crimson drop. But his anger subsided as Mordok and his friends entered the cave. Rakgar knew the egg was lost to him. He couldn't do anything about the loss – or his grief.

Visi's and Hiro's vision returned to the spray of water around her. She would hide the hatchling for as long as needed— seven years, as Hiro remembered it. She would be forced to go to the new Rakgar and acknowledge his ascension, but first she would see the egg to safety. When Freeg ambled into his new lair as Rakgar for the first time, the ancient white dragon came out from under the falls. The bright green egg clutched tightly in her two front claws, she lifted into the sky toward her home at the top of the Inner Mountain.

Blink.

"Where is it?" the enormous gray Rakgar rumbled at Hiro through Visi's memory. He kept his voice low so as not to be heard outside the cavern.

"Safe," Visi answered.

"Give it back," he rumbled again, "or I'll have you and it killed."

"It?"

"It's a monster."

"You're the monster," she spat back. "She's a hatchling child."

Rakgar bared his fangs. "I could kill you now, then find her and kill her as well."

"But you won't," Visi didn't flinch a muscle. *"Because that would make you a murderer. Plus, she's being cared for. They know what to do if I don't return. You would never find her again."*

"You don't know that for sure."

"I know you would spend your weary life searching," she said. *"And that might be better than the alternative. So, yes, I'm willing to die."*

Rakgar grumbled a moment in thought, then turned. "Give me your wyrd. Your wyrd that you will never tell anyone of her parentage."

"She's your daughter. I cannot hide that fact."

Rakgar struck the stone with his claw. "Her OTHER parentage. And I will not hunt you."

Visi glared at him. "I give you my wyrd… If you will extend the same to her." Rakgar growled but Visi pressed on. "When she is old enough, she will need to be introduced to the ruck. Extend her the same chance at a normal life and both our lives will be yours."

Hiro's vision cleared just as another claw came down. He rolled away, but he was flagging. He watched Rakgar. He wasn't tracking Hiro's movements as quickly as he had, but he followed him and lifted a claw.

This is not my fight to win, he remembered. He gazed past Rakgar to the dragons and humans. Platforms were depositing humans on some of the floating mountains. The humans loaded and shot arrows at the dragons as the dragons attempted to land on the rock mountains in front of them. Arrows bounced off the hard scales in all directions. Dragons landed and swiped humans down with their claws. As Hiro watched, a purple and blue dame in flight tried to grab a human from mid-air. As she reached out, the human shot an arrow into her belly and she dissolved instantly to embers.

Hiro couldn't even roar at the sight. His heart ached. He had to help them. He had to stop this slaughter.

Looking up at Rakgar, Hiro wanted to keep fighting, but he caught sight of a flash of bright green.

Priya hovered behind the monstrous leader.

Be mindful who wields you, Visi had said.

"I concede," Hiro shouted before Rakgar's claw could land on him again. He tried to catch his breath as the traitor dragon set his claw down next to him.

"I do not," Priya said from behind. "I challenge you!" she yelled as she flew onto Rakgar's back.

She clawed at his wings as he attempted to dislodge her. Finally, he dropped to the ground and rolled. But Priya jumped before he could harm her. As he rolled onto his back, she flapped in the air a moment, then dropped on his belly to claw and bite at the soft joints underneath.

Priya was even more adept than Kodoran. She slipped into cracks in Rakgar's defenses that even Hiro didn't see before she was in and back out again. As she flew in, scratched or bit and flew out again, Hiro imagined that she and Visi had trained to the point of a semi-coordinated attack, knowing Rakgar's every move.

As much as he wanted to watch Priya and jump in if she needed him, he heard Visi nearby.

"Hiro," she whispered. The few hits she'd taken had made her weaker than he'd ever seen her.

He crawled to her. Prying his eyes away from Priya, he placed his nose in front of hers.

Hiro stared down at the large green dragon egg. The light caught the many facets of the polished emerald-like gem. Being many times the size of a dragon's heart, Hiro guessed it was ready to hatch. Visi must have known the egg would hatch soon and he felt the strong emotion of anticipation through the memory. Finally, the egg shook. It rocked back and forth, gradually gaining momentum. It swung and shook then rattled across the floor until it rolled against a large, jutting rock.

Normally, a dragon hatchling would scratch at the egg from the inside and eventually use their strong claws to gain their escape. This egg crashed noisily into the rock and the pointed top of the teardrop shape cracked and broke. The rounded bottom rolled away from the shattered top and Hiro caught sight of the bright green color inside. When the egg finally stopped its movement around the cave floor the cracked bottom faced Hiro's field of view.

Visi slowly moved around to peer into the hollow of the egg where the hatchling rested. Hiro saw bright green wings pull back against the body as the creature emerged. But he caught his breath as a chubby pink face ringed with bright golden hair smiled up at him, with the trace of a shining green tail on her leg.

When Hiro's vision cleared, he saw Rakgar's claw flying toward him. Thinking the mad dragon had abandoned the fight with Priya to attack Hiro again, Hiro rolled. But the claw didn't land on Hiro. With a deafening crunch, Rakgar stomped on Visi. Many dragons roared as Visi howled beneath his claw. As the dragons encroached on him, he held up another claw.

"She gave me her wyrd!" he told the onlooking crowd. "I claim the right!"

Hiro couldn't move his eyes from Visi. She hadn't turned to ash so he knew the impact hadn't killed her immediately. Her head and eyes lay still as stone, but she lifted a claw toward Hiro. Despite the danger around them, Hiro crawled over the rock to her. Gently, he placed his nose against hers.

"But I don't want to go," a small human girl of perhaps ten years old stood in a dank cave surrounded by an odd assortment of cloth and herbs. Visi's cave. She wore a simple white cloth wrapped around her body and her golden hair spilled over her bare shoulders.

"I know," Visi said from Hiro's point of view, "and it will be dangerous."

"Then I shouldn't go at all!" the girl said. "Why can't I stay here and continue training with you? We can dispatch the old worm later. Together."

Visi shook her head. "I'm afraid not," she said. "While you've been training with Sar, I've been crystal gazing. You will meet friends in the ruck. Good friends. They will help you and they are instrumental to your survival."

"I can help myself survive," the girl said, punching her fists on her hips. "Don't forget, I'm still a dragon."

"As am I, and as are they," Visi said kindly. "I will visit often because we will need to make many plans together. If we are patient and smart, you'll have your chance to end your father, but you will need the strength of your friends' help. Don't worry," she purred, "you will kill him soon, little one."

30

TREMBLING CONFLICT

The platform lifted, shifted, tilted and dropped. Philip could only imagine what Kradik might be doing to Travaith on the ground. He searched the eyes of the people around him. Tierni held onto her saber, stuck fast to the wood. Maelin and Thaddeus, closer to the platform floor as they clung to their staffs, attempted to stabilize anyone within reach nearby. Tommak's sword stood abandoned. With blood dripping from his fingers, he clung to Hilde and her saber.

Torgon used his belt knife as an extra hold to shuffle to the side of the platform. He leaned over the edge and his face collapsed. When he finally pried his eyes apart, they found Philip's. He shook his head. Travaith was dead.

"Sire!" Murzod yelled as the platform continued to shake. He wrenched his sword free and stumbled toward Philip.

Philip knew he couldn't trust the man. Hoping the bucking platform would cover his actions, he tried to step back but ran into someone or something behind him.

"Yes," Riddig yelled while attempting to cling to his own sword, "protect the king! His majishun is trying to kill him!"

Philip shook his head again as Murzod advanced. He tried to keep his hand on his sword as the floor beneath him continued to shake.

Murzod reached him and took hold of his wrists. "Allow me to help you, Sire," he whispered.

Philip felt Murzod attempting to pull his wrists away from the hilt of the sword. When Murzod realized that Philip's larger, younger and stronger hands wouldn't budge, he shifted. The shorter man put one arm around Philip's shoulders, the other on his top hand.

"Don't let go, Your Majesty!" Murzod shouted over the noise of fighting and yelling going on around them every time the platform tilted or dropped. All the while, the older man tried to pry Philip's hand away from his only hand hold.

Finally, the treasonous man succeeded in pulling one of Philip's hands free. As Philip reached for the sword again, Murzod grabbed it with his own hand, stopping him.

Torgon used his sword and belt knife to work his way back to Philip's side but he was too slow. Murzod had worked his way around to Philip's front side. Once in place, he effectively concealed his actions as he blocked Philip's free hand from swinging at him. He put both of his hands over Philip's tight attachment to his sword and began prying the fingers away.

Philip wanted to thump the man in the back or head, but it seemed every time he tried, the platform lurched and rendered the blow either harmless or off-target. Finally, he couldn't hold onto his sword any longer. His fingers were torn free and Philip fell flat to the floor of the platform.

The platform tilted, sliding Philip toward the middle of it, then dropped from under him only to slam upward into him again, knocking the wind from his lungs. It tilted again, sliding him toward an edge, but a sword blade blocked his way. He rolled away from it only to bump into the legs of one of the guards. With so many bodies rolling and tumbling, Philip couldn't be sure who to trust and who to avoid. One guard, intentionally or not, fell over and kicked the king hard in the shoulder. Had the platform been pitched otherwise in the air, the kick might have landed on his head.

Another guard yelled for his king and lunged for Philip, but Maelin intercepted him. Not able to anchor himself, Maelin tried to grab the guard around the shoulders, but the guard shoved Maelin back as the platform swung wild, spinning the two away from each other.

Someone caught Maelin before he could catapult off the platform, but another guard, seemingly prompted by Riddig or Murzod, pointed at them, yelling, "They're trying to kill the king!"

Philip and Torgon knew better, but a fight broke out all the same and everyone got tangled up in it. The two factions of men on the platform fought against each other:

Tommak, Torgon and Maelin's claw against Riddig, Murzod and his guards.

Tierni and the Black Saber took neither side, deciding instead to keep anyone they could reach from falling over the edge; although Tierni seemed to train a careful eye on the fight. The two claws fought each other under impossible conditions, with the ground underneath them quaking as if trying to shake them all free of it. In the back of Philip's mind, he thought the scene might be rather humorous to watch, seeing as most of the blows and kicks didn't find a mark. The attempts only served to further destabilize and hinder any footing or safety. Many of the men fell either into the swords that were stuck into the platform or into each other, with only a lucky blow landing here and there, and harming the attacker more often than the attacked.

Philip found himself flat on the floor of the platform while men around him fought and tumbled into him, and the women watched judiciously while clinging to sabers or each other to keep from falling. Then Murzod advanced. His bow long since lost, Philip pulled his boot knife. "Don't—!" he yelled, but was silenced by another lurch and drop.

Murzod, holding to a sword, stomped a foot onto Philip's hand. "Oh, I'm so sorry, Your Majesty," he said quietly enough that not many would hear the words dripping with spiteful sarcasm. He bent to pick up the knife, placing the other hand on Philip's shoulder and giving him a shove.

Philip slid in synchronization with the tilt of the platform. He swung around, looking for a handhold, but only swords surrounded him, like some vicious, unforgiving forest of blades. He rolled to his back just as his feet slipped over the edge of the platform. He rolled again, onto his stomach, and his legs flew over the side. At the last moment, the platform tilted again, and Philip caught himself by his arms near the edge, grabbing at anything to find a hold on the solid floor.

While he struggled, he watched Murzod and Torgon look first at each other, then at Philip. They both scrambled, legs and bodies swaying, to get to Philip. Murzod was the closer.

The vicious man fell to the floor of the platform. He grabbed Philip's arm and pulled it away from what little hold the younger man retained.

Philip tried to yell over the noise, but Murzod grinned. As he slowly pushed Philip over the edge, he whispered, "You'll never demote me again."

Hearing a yell from behind him, Philip watched a blade project from Murzod's chest. The older man continued to grin, pushing Philip toward the edge. But slowly his grip slackened, as did his face. Confusion overtook him as he inspected his chest. The blade twisted as they watched. Finally, Murzod's face drained of emotion, then color, then life. With a final shove, Torgon pushed the traitor over the side.

"NO!" Riddig came bounding through the chaos on the platform. As it tilted, he fell and slid directly into the king and his royal general.

Both younger men slipped over the edge.

31

TRANSFORMATION

Her father. The girl. Priya. Her parentage, Hiro thought. It all hit him at once. His eyes searched out Priya's.

Her eyes were locked on his. With a slight nod, Priya faced Rakgar. Rakgar raised a threatening claw. In a blink, Anna stood in front of Rakgar. She was wrapped in a brilliant green cloth, the exact color of her scales, her hair blowing around her like a golden halo. Hiro immediately remembered the vision he'd had of Anna standing before Rakgar as he lifted a claw in rage.

But the claw didn't fall. Hiro saw the blood dripping across Rakgar's face from Hiro's attempt to claw at his head. Rakgar's claw stilled, then slowly lowered as he said, "Annette?"

"No," Anna said, her eyes locked on Rakgar. "My name is Priyanna. I am the daughter of King Paudie of the Noble Kingdom, Queen Annette of the Courageous

Kingdom, and the dragon known as Freeg of the Rock Cloud Ruck."

The dragons surrounding them were as still as stone. Hiro couldn't imagine what, if anything, the humans could see and were thinking.

"You're a monster," Rakgar growled.

"No," she shook her head. "You're the monster. You killed her. You killed Annette and you've never forgiven yourself for it…nor her for desiring it."

Rakgar threw his head back and roared. Not a roar of triumph, but a roar filled with anger for himself and the pain of losing Annette. The bellowing roar overpowered the noise of the scuffles around them. Priyanna was right, he had never forgiven himself for the death of Annette. His hatred for himself had merely shifted to include every dragon. In his eyes, they all deserved to die.

Before the painful roar could subside, Priyanna changed back into a dragon and shot toward the exposed neck of her father. She latched her strong jaws onto his neck where Hiro had weakened it. Rakgar's cries gurgled to a stop. He clawed at the small dragon attached to his neck, but the strength of his mighty arm diminished. He fell toward the ground, still scratching at his daughter, but his head hit the ground as a pile of embers and ash.

Priyanna flew down to land next to Hiro, but she didn't look at him. Her eyes locked with Visi's. As Hiro watched, Visi smiled at Priyanna, then dissolved in a cloud of ash and ember.

Hiro tried to connect to Priyanna's gaze, but she kept her eyes on Visi's remains and bowed her head.

Hiro, however, heard the sounds of the battle around them. Scanning the skies, he saw ice blue and purple dragons diving and attacking the humans on the platforms as they reached into the Rock Clouds. He saw green and blue dragons the color of crystal-clear waters from the Island Ruck far north. They slithered through the sky around the humans like water that burned all that touched it. As he watched, one of the silky teal dragons flew toward a human and opened her mouth to unleash her fire. The human shot a poisoned arrow directly down her throat and she evaporated into ash around him.

Without glancing back at her, Hiro growled. "Priyanna, we have to stop Kodoran!"

"Kodoran?" she said. "Who has been named the commander?"

"Kodoran feira Prakyndar," Hiro answered. "I named him."

Priyanna nodded. "Well named," she said, "but I have a different name in mind for him."

Hiro searched the fight surrounding them. "We don't have time to discuss it," he said. "Sound your roars of triumph here and perhaps we'll get the attention of most of them out there."

Priyanna nodded. She flew a little higher to perch above the main cavern where Rakgar had resided. Opening her maw, she sounded three ear-splitting roars to declare her victory and pronounce herself the new Rakdar of the Rock Cloud Ruck.

Several dragons turned their heads at the sound, but the message to return to the Inner Mountain was drowned in the fighting. Some of them stopped to listen, but many of them either didn't hear the call or were overwhelmed with the effort of trying to defend themselves and others. Luckily, Kodoran feira Prakyndar heard the call and went.

"What do we do now?" Kodoran asked as he landed next to Hiro. "Taynor feira Rakgar is dead, but the fighting has already begun. Dragons are dying!"

"We have to stop the fighting," Hiro said as he watched a sleek, teal-colored dame with only back legs and gills burst into embers in mid-air.

"How?" Kodoran shot back as Tog and Mitashio landed next to him.

"Priyanna," Hiro said to her, "you and Visi have had all of this planned from the start."

"Priyanna?" Kodoran asked.

Hiro leaned over and passed the memories from Visi to Kodoran, then to Tog, then to Mitashio.

"Visi knew everything," Mitashio whispered. Hiro could only imagine he was thinking of his brother's death.

"Yes," Kodoran said to Priyanna. "What do we do? You must know!"

Priyanna shook her head as she watched a dark blue-gray dragon dive at another platform lifting into the air. The men on it were all knocked to the ground hundreds of dragon lengths below, but as he picked himself up another human already stationed on one of the floating mountains shot a poisoned arrow at him. Ember tumbled to the surface of the platform before he could lift into the air.

"You don't understand," she said. "There are too many variables now. Too many possible outcomes. We couldn't discern anything after the victory over my father. We couldn't even be certain of that!" She looked to the small brown dragon. "You have to lead us now, Kodoran."

Kodoran feira Prakyndar puffed up a little. "Bring everyone in," he said. "Get them back to the Inner Mountain, call them in from the outer Rock Clouds," he said. "But not to Rakgar's lair. We can't let them pin us in. We'll have to go higher. Try to get out of reach of the humans and their arrows."

"Tog," Kodoran continued, nodding to the dragons indicated as he spoke, "go to the dragons on the west; Priyanna, go north. Hiro go east and Mitashio go south."

"Where are you going?!" Hiro yelled as he watched the small brown leader run and leap into the air.

"To the centaurs," he called over his shoulders.

As they flew in different directions, Kodoran roared and dragons below him heard and followed him. Hiro knew most of them were used to following him when they worked with the centaurs. Whenever a head would turn in his direction, Hiro would swoop in, pass the memory with the information to return to the Inner Mountain, and move on.

As the others did the same, Hiro watched dragons withdraw only a few at a time to head to the Inner Mountain. Perhaps it might seem like they were organizing, but he knew that wouldn't matter much longer.

Searching for more fighting dragons to call in, Hiro stopped his gaze at one of the platforms. It hovered at a point most of the way into the Rock Clouds, but it shook violently. He couldn't tell if the humans on the platform were holding on for their lives or fighting amongst themselves. One figure, with a golden circlet on his head, dangled over the edge.

There he was, King Philip, clinging to the edge of the platform. Hiro watched as one human stabbed another through the heart and flung the dead man over the edge. As the human then helped King Philip, a third man attacked them both, pushing them into a free fall.

32

REVOLUTION

Philip felt his fingers slip from the surface of the platform. In a brief moment of serenity, he hoped Anna could be found to serve the kingdom in his stead. He worried that seeing their king fall, the warriors might lose their nerve at the beginning of the battle. Then he worried they might get even more angry at seeing their king die, and rush into the battle with fresh rage. He couldn't decide if he would wish to see them stop or press on. Either way, the faeries had won.

Suddenly, his body jerked from the middle. His head almost hit his toes as he folded in half around something large and scaly. He sucked air back into his lungs after it had been so forcefully expelled and touched the thing around him. It seemed to be a dragon claw. In fear, he looked up.

The black dragon.

The image of the black dragon flinging him and his body smashing against the side of the mountain popped into his head. He started to struggle against the claw, then realized that it wasn't squeezing him the way he expected it would. He certainly wasn't uncomfortable, and no talons dug into him.

His attention was caught seeing Torgon in another of the dragon's claws. He wasn't struggling, but he didn't look necessarily happy about his life being saved in this manner either. When Torgon looked up and saw Philip, he yelled, "You see? It's always the black one!"

The dragon, holding the men in his claws, coasted toward the ground. The men on the ground had arrows nocked but seemed afraid to fire for fear of hitting the king or general. As they neared the ground, Philip wondered if the dragon would plant his claws first and land on top of him and Torgon, or throw them into the crowd. Both would be deadly.

Suddenly, the dragon reversed his body position and instead of diving, he pushed his back legs forward. He spread his massive wings and pumped them against the force of the surface to slow his descent. The heavy draft from the dragon's wings knocked many of the men to the ground, including, to Philip's pleasure, Kradik and the other faeries.

The faeries righted themselves in time to halt the one platform still loaded with humans that was freefalling toward the earth. At the same time, several centaurs pounded through the humans on the ground, knocking them aside and heading straight for the center of the action. The platform settled on the ground next to them. The guards and Black Saber dashed off it with swords drawn, pointing at the dragon that held the king in his claws. More centaurs thundered into the center of the group, led by a brown female with her sword drawn. A second, brown dragon flew overhead, but circled a little farther off as the centaurs rumbled into the waiting humans. Everyone converged as the black dragon gently set Philip and Torgon on the ground.

"Stop!" yelled Philip as the humans began to aim their weapons at the dragon. He didn't know why he was stopping them. Other than – maybe – out of gratefulness to the beast? Hadn't that Hamees man said this dragon was tamed? What if the centaurs had tamed him? Then why would the black dragon want to rescue humans, but the centaurs want to attack? Whatever the motives or training, this dragon had just saved his life and that of his closest aide. Two lives that might have been lost if a handful of humans had their say.

As Philip ordered everyone to stop, the black dragon spun his back on the humans and spread his wings in front of them, roaring at the centaurs to make them stop as well. The brown dragon hovered overhead.

"What are you doing?" Torgon said from Philip's side.

Philip hadn't noticed Torgon standing shoulder-to-shoulder with him between the humans and the dragon.

"Hold your fire!" Philip called to the men and women surrounding them. To Torgon he muttered, "I don't know. What are you doing?"

"This dragon may be the most backwards, deranged animal in all of Avonoa," Torgon said, "but it just saved my life." The young friends shared a glance, but Torgon's face wrinkled like he'd been asked to eat dung.

Philip studied the people around him. The humans lowered their weapons. The few faeries stood watching. As he turned, he saw the centaurs still pointing their weapons at Maelin and his men. The men in Maelin's claw hadn't lifted their weapons and so, stood defenseless. That was probably the only reason they were still alive.

The black dragon growled low and bared his fangs at the centaurs. It inched in front of the centaurs' drawn swords and arrows.

"They killed Vikal!" the centaur leader screamed. Tears made her large eyes glow and her face burned in anger. Even as she screamed her sword point held steady in Maelin's face. In the back of Philip's mind, he acknowledged the control she possessed, besides the fact that her words were clearly directed at the dragon.

"You're right!" Philip called to her, without thinking. She spun the sword point at him, but he already knew what he had to do. Defenseless and at her mercy, he held up his hands. "You're right," he said again in a milder tone. "The killing needs to stop. For everyone."

"What are you doing?" Kradik hissed.

"Ending what never should have started," Philip said without taking his eyes from the centaur. He stepped toward her. "I'm calling a cease-fire," he said. "Torgon."

Beside him, Torgon turned to the men who had been waiting on the ground. "Cease fire!" he said. "Send the call." Philip noted a hint of hesitation in his tone, or was it anger? Several guards ran off to relay the message.

"This has to end," Philip said to the centaur.

Overhead, the smaller brown dragon drifted lightly to the ground. The centaurs standing around and behind the female shifted aside to allow the dragon to land. The brown dragon quietly crept up behind the centaur to bump his nose gently against her flank.

With pure rage in her eyes, the centaur glared at the black dragon a moment, then burst with a guttural scream. She lifted the sword over her head and thrust it into the ground at Maelin's foot. The sword sank almost to the hilt.

Glaring at Philip, she hissed, "You're a fool for ever allowing it to happen." Her eyes shot to the faeries, then the dragon, before she spun and the group of centaurs galloped away behind her. Once they were gone, both dragons glanced around, jumped high into the air and flew away without looking back.

Philip knew the female centaur was right. He was a fool. He had let this war between the species go on for far too long. What had he expected would happen? He knew people would die. He knew dragons would die. He thought he could deal with the human losses to be rid of the beasts. The human kingdoms of Avonoa hadn't seen such war in decades. This was wrong and he'd known it all along, but he'd been too weak and scared to do anything about it.

"She's right," he said searching the faces of the men around him. "I *am* a fool." They stared at him with blank eyes until he turned to the faeries. "I'm a fool for ever having listened to you!" he yelled at Kradik.

"On the contrary," Kradik said, his voice low. "You're a fool for not believing in my promises."

He spread his hands and lifted into the air, mumbling at first before his voice grew louder. The song issuing from his lips sounded beautiful and alluring. Then the other faeries joined in. But as Philip watched, all the faeries – one at a time or in groups – lifted into the air, singing distinctly sinister words.

Philip didn't know enough faerie language to understand what they said, but he didn't have to wait long to find out. Everywhere, guards began falling to the ground. Men fell from the Rock Clouds. Platforms crashed to the ground. The men on the platforms bounced, unconscious, atop the platforms. The men underneath them were crushed. Horses fell unconscious, crushing unconscious men and women who had stood next to them. Every human guard surrounding the royal group fell to the ground, lifeless.

33

AUTHORITY AND ACCORD

Once the young king had called a cease fire, Hiro and Kodoran fled back to the Inner Mountain. As they flew past the new Rakdar's lair, further up the mountain Hiro could see very few dragons flying amidst the Rock Clouds. Some, he knew, were dans protecting hatchlings. A few dames hovered beyond the reach of the humans' arrows. Hiro knew that, slowly over time, no more humans would arrive in the Rock Clouds to assist them or deliver more arrows.

He and Kodoran feira Prakyndar landed in the center of hundreds of dragons. The Rakdars and Rakgar of the other rucks stood snarling at Priyanna, the new Rakdar of the Rock Cloud Ruck.

"You want us to *WHAT*!!??" The Ice Ruck's Rakdar roared the last word. She shook her feathery purple mane in disgust, but kept her eyes on Priyanna.

"The humans need to know that dragons have the gift of speech and intelligence," she said.

"What you're suggesting is sacrilege!" Maggoran spoke from the Ice Rakdar's side.

"Blasphemy!" someone yelled from behind them. A few roars and bouts of flame lit the air.

"No," Hiro said as he stepped into the center. "The faeries taught us to think that, and only for their selfish purposes. Now they've turned on us.

"The faeries," he continued, "want to kill dragons because they think it's the only way to end their curse."

"Their curse is their problem," the Desert Rakgar said.

"Until they started killing dragons," the Island Rakdar said.

As she said it, the sound of an eerie song drifted to them on the wind. The entire group searched the skies for the new threat. They watched as some of the human men fell from the mountains, and those that didn't fall buckled to the ground beneath them. The platforms plummeted from the skies. Faeries could be seen as far as a dragon could fly, lifting into the air and singing.

"The faeries are turning on the humans," Hiro whispered.

"Why?" Kodoran asked.

"Because Philip called a cease fire," Hiro answered. As the last words left his tongue, Hiro's vision swam. His eyes threatened to close and his legs began to buckle. He shook it off and stood up.

"Hiro," Priyanna said, "are you alright?"

Hiro straightened and focused on her. "They're doing something to the humans." He didn't know how he knew it, but the faeries were attacking the humans somehow and he knew whatever they were doing must also be affecting him.

"It must be something we didn't see," Priyanna said, thinking of Visi. She blinked and looked toward the Noble Kingdom. "Philip," she said. "We have to get to him. We have to explain—"

"Silence!" the Ice Rakdar hissed, cutting her off. Her eyes dug into Priyanna like Ashel's sword that was probably still plunged into the earth. "You have no say here, *human*!"

The memory of Priya changing into Anna and announcing who she was must have spread through the rucks faster than any dragon poison could take effect. Once dragons returned from the Rock Clouds, the story began to spread. The entire story was passed from memory to memory. In moments, every dragon on the Inner Mountain knew the truth.

Priyanna roared, setting back with her haunches raised. "I am the Rakdar of this ruck," she growled back.

"You're just a human in dragon scales," the Ice Rakdar hissed again. She maintained her standing position. She obviously didn't plan to fight. Her attitude projected that it was beneath her to even notice the green dragon's stance. "You have no right to speak for a ruck. You're not fully dragon."

"I agree with the Ice Rakdar!" The Rakdar from the Island Ruck stepped forward. She and her warriors crawled forward fluidly, every movement like water trickling over stone. The Island Rakdar was a shade of blue and green mixed with spots of deep blue across her back like raindrops.

The Island Rakdar faced Priyanna. "Our islands haven't taught our hatchlings to fear humans like the other rucks do, simply because we haven't the need," she said. "We could easily agree with you to speak with the humans and find peace, but that order cannot come from one who isn't fully dragon."

"Yes," the Ice Rakdar nodded firmly. "You, being only part dragon, have no say in the matter. I don't recognize your authority as Rakdar of the Rock Cloud Ruck."

Hiro looked to the Desert Rakgar with pleading in his eyes, but the mighty brown dragon only shook his head. "They're right," he said, his voice as low and soothing as his temperament, "I'm afraid I would agree that only a dragon can lead a dragon ruck."

"Don't you see?" Kodoran barked. "She's The One! She's meant to unite the humans and dragons!"

"That's a myth," the Island Rakdar hissed.

"A scary story for hatchlings," the Ice Rakdar echoed the sentiment.

"Unite in ways unimaginable," Hiro muttered. He met Priya's eye. "She's The One. She united humans and dragons in a way none of us could imagine. She was the first to be part dragon and part human. And she wields my heart." He finished and earned a smile from Priyanna.

"But she does *not* wield *us*," the Ice Rakdar said.

"Let me get this right," Kodoran said, stepping into the mix. "You all agree that speaking to the humans is…" he tilted his head at the Ice Rakdar, "…inevitable, if nothing else?" The group around him nodded. The Ice Rakdar looked at the others and eventually shrugged her shoulder.

"Ok," Kodoran continued, "but the order, or suggestion, to extend ourselves in peace to the humans, you will vehemently deny unless it comes from one who is only and fully dragon?"

The others looked uncomfortable but said nothing.

"Then I have a solution," Priyanna said. "But first, I have to get to my brother."

34

DEADLY INTIMIDATION

"No," Philip mumbled. "What are you doing?"

Torgon ran to one of the guards and felt the man's neck. He dropped his head momentarily but turned back to Philip. "He's alive," he said. "Hopefully they all are."

"For now," Kradik called. He floated down to them on humming wings, allowing the other faeries to continue the spellcasting around him.

"Why?" Philip called up to him.

Kradik drifted slowly to the ground. He calmly lowered his hood. The eerie grin on his face made worse by his transparent skin, he walked in a wide circle around Philip and Torgon to stand among the fallen men. "I live up to my promises, *King*," he hissed at Philip.

Philip's breath caught in his throat as Kradik bent to pick up a sword. His smug grin widened as he held the sword over one of the guards. Philip felt the blood drain from his face as the faerie knocked aside the man's helmet to gently press the blade into his throat.

"No!" Torgon yelled.

"I'll kill them all," Kradik hissed. "Rest assured, they won't feel any pain."

Philip reached a hand out to Torgon without taking his eyes from Kradik. He could feel his royal general shaking but didn't know if it might be from fear or anger.

"Torgon," Philip said, ignoring the tremor in his voice, "we have to continue the fight."

Torgon's jaw clenched as he ground his teeth. He stood beside Philip, but said nothing. "We'll do as you say," Philip muttered to Kradik, allowing his voice to crack. He didn't care. He couldn't allow his people, the entire kingdom and all the other kingdoms, to die. Helpless. Both he and his people. Helpless.

"No," a voice came from behind them. Philip didn't realize that Maelin and his men hadn't fallen to the faeries' spell. "Your Majesty, you can't do it."

"We don't have a choice," Philip said, keeping his eyes on Kradik.

"There's always a choice," Maelin and Torgon said at the same time.

The familiar words echoed in Philip's mind. The same words that Torgon had said long ago. The same words that Anna repeated only a few hours ago. The same words that his own father and General Bragon told him his entire childhood.

"Please, Sire," Maelin insisted. The other men in his claw came to stand beside him.

"How are you all still awake?" Torgon asked.

"Um…" the little man with the spectacles cleared his throat. "We didn't take the faeries' potion for speed."

"The potion," Torgon breathed. "That's how you did this? You used the potion to…"

"Render humans as incompetent as they have already proven themselves to be," Kradik nodded at the body beneath him, the blade still pressed against the man's throat.

Philip shook his head. "That doesn't change anything," he said. "I made the choice to allow the men to use the potion. I must make the choice to allow them to live."

"They will only live if they can defeat the dragons," Torgon said.

Philip finally tore his eyes from Kradik to turn them on his best friend. "I've done this, Torgon, I've set this in motion. Me. He'll kill them," he nodded toward Kradik. "Right now. In front of us. I can't…"

"Sire," another man from Maelin's group said, "all these men would die for you if they knew you truly believed your choice to be the right thing to do."

Philip's hands shook. A chill ran down his spine. "Only to be killed by a dragon when they wake up? Possibly by the same dragon that I just ordered them to put down their weapons for? Allow them to die for *one* dragon?" he whispered.

"A dragon," Maelin said, "that saved my life."

"And yours," Torgon said to him.

Philip met Torgon's eye. Torgon dipped his chin, remembering the fall. The black dragon had saved his life. Then Philip had saved the dragon's life by not allowing the men to shoot it. If Philip ordered all the dragons' lives saved, he would lose all the lives of his people. Save the black dragon, or fight all the dragons and save the humans? What was the right thing to do?

Philip's breath came ragged and sharp down his throat. His head pounded to the sound of his own heartbeat. A human heartbeat. This choice could end tens of thousands of lives. He knew he couldn't continue the path the faeries had set for him. His ears buzzed. He couldn't feel his fingers.

He pulled in a breath that felt like knives going down his throat. He ignored the tears that leaked from his eyes. "I won't," he said, but his voice stopped in his throat. He swallowed and forced it out louder. "I won't do what you ask," he whispered. "I won't kill the dragons."

Kradik's smile faltered. His swift nod acknowledged the expected refusal. With a flick of his wrist, he slid the blade across the unconscious guard's throat.

Philip sucked in a breath but paused. He stared at the man on the ground. Kradik had to look twice as all those gathered stared at the man under him. No blood spilled. His throat remained whole. The man breathed evenly, as if sleeping peacefully.

"Wait!" yelled Philip as Kradik lifted the sword to plunge it into the man's neck. The sword bounced away before it touched the man's skin.

Kradik threw the sword to the ground. He sank to the ground beside the man and reached for his head. His hand bounced off an invisible barrier before he could make contact. Finally, with a grimace, Kradik looked up, but not at Philip or his men. He scanned the surroundings, and baring his teeth, he screamed, "Where are you, demon?!"

Philip watched, confused. But Torgon kept his wits.

"Lieutenant," Torgon growled, motioning to Maelin, "arm your men."

Maelin and the men in his claw scurried to recover their weapons and their senses. Philip did the same, arming himself with a nearby bow and quiver. In the back of his mind, he thought of the little gray invisible man and wondered if he'd had anything to do with the shift of power and protection of the unconscious men.

"Shoot them down!" Torgon yelled, pointing his sword at the faeries still chanting the sleeping song. A couple of the men took aim and fired. A couple threw daggers. The few faeries around them dodged in the air and continued singing, though the song quivered.

Philip lifted his bow. He watched as the other men shot. Knowing which way the faeries would dodge, he anticipated and fired seconds after the first. He stuck one faerie in the leg and another in the shoulder before the singing stopped and all the others zipped away toward the faeries in the north.

Seeing them flee, Kradik flew up in the air. "Don't you see, young king," he said as he drifted on the breeze, "the potion is already in them. We have the power to—"

Before he could finish his threat, a streak of black came at him from the sky.

35

CURSE

The black dragon tackled Kradik to the ground, while two other dragons, a brown and a green, hovered over them. When they stopped tumbling, the dragon stood atop the faerie. Philip assumed the beast would bite his head off or maul him. Instead, he held his claw on the faerie's chest, pinning him to the ground. The dragon bared his fangs and pressed.

"Do it!" Kradik yelled. "End it!"

The dragon stopped. He blinked and pulled his maw away from the faerie.

"I am."

Philip then broke every rule he'd ever been taught. He didn't contain his emotion. He didn't contain his shock. He stood staring at the black dragon, his mouth agape. "Who...?" he breathed.

The dragon snaked his head around to look Philip in the eye. "I did," he said.

Philip felt the blood drain from his face. His eyes searched the faces of the men around him and saw the same shock reflected. He felt cold and his hands got clammy like they did every time he saw Tierni. "You can speak?" he muttered.

"Yes," the dragon said. Pushing off the faerie, who gave a satisfying groan, the black dragon approached him. "And we don't want this war any more than you do."

"Hold your fire!" Philip called, reminding the men to stay their weapons as the other dragons landed. The men who were conscious repeated the order as the other men and beasts around them were roused. The faeries had ceased their song, restoring, at least momentarily, the Noble army.

Torgon ignored the order, leveling his sword at the dragon's throat. "How can we believe any of this?!" Philip wondered at his friend's sanity as he yelled up at the beast. "You have plagued our kingdom for nearly a year, you and your kind. You've killed hundreds of us. How do we know this isn't another trick? How can we trust you?"

The dragon sighed. Philip looked into the dragon's eye and in an instant the dragon was no longer in front of them, but a man stood in his place. This man was as tall or taller than Philip himself and couldn't have been more than twenty years old. His skin was soft and brown, his hair was black and a black cloth was wrapped around his waist. Philip saw the tattoo of a black tail wrapping down his leg to his ankle.

Maelin, recognizing the man, took a step forward. "Owyn," he said.

"My name," he said with momentary hesitation, "is Hirowyn. Hiro as a dragon. Owyn as a human."

Torgon shook his head. His sword hadn't moved. "You're a criminal."

"No, sir," Maelin pushed past the other men. "He's not."

Torgon didn't blink. "He insulted the Princess."

"That was no crime," Maelin insisted.

"But he threatened her life too."

"That's my fault," the green dragon stepped forward this time.

"You," Philip breathed, staring at the green dragon, "you're the one who kidnapped Anna."

"No," she shook her head and a moment later Anna stood in her place. "I *am* Anna. Priyanna. Priya as a dragon. Anna as a human."

"Anna?" Philip muttered, baffled by this conversation and what was taking place before him.

"Yes, Philip," she said, stepping toward him. She was once again dressed only in a green cloth that wrapped around her chest, waist and the top of her legs. Her yellow hair tumbled over her bare shoulders. But her nakedness didn't influence Philip, still befuddled. He glanced at the green dragon tail tattoo wrapping around her ankle, which he hadn't noticed last night. The rest of his mind reeled over the many new revelations.

"I allowed Owyn to threaten me so he could escape," she told Torgon and Maelin. "It was actually my idea."

"This changes nothing for us," Kradik, who still sat in the dirt, growled from under the brown dragon's gaze. The faerie ripped off one of his gloves. "It does nothing!" he yelled, shaking his hand at them.

"Actually," Anna said calmly, looking down at the faerie, "it does."

"Visi and I discovered early on," she said, "that the curse would end if the leader of the dragons spoke to the leader of the humans." Turning to Philip, she stated, "Your Majesty, I'm Rakdar, the leader of the Rock Cloud dragon ruck."

As everyone watched, Kradik's skin fogged with a soft blue glow. By the time he pulled his other glove off, everyone could see the opaque glow of lavender covering his skin. He shook his head while staring at his hands. "I don't understand."

Everyone, even the dragons, jumped when a little gray man popped into existence, saying, "I'll explain."

36

SIFTING ALLIES

Philip immediately sent out written orders for a cease-fire. Runners were sent to every kingdom with orders to cease hostilities and a request for the kings and queens to attend a meeting. Before the end of the day, horses with each of the kingdoms' representatives galloped into the Noble camp, to the tent of King Philip.

"What have the faeries said?" Queen Sarador of the Allegiant Queendom asked Philip from her seat next to her daughter and soon-to-be queen, Samat. The two women were intimidating not only for their beauty, but they wore divided skirts and armor much like the Black Saber's. Philip knew they also hid weapons in those skirts.

"They only said that they must convene," Torgon answered, "like we are."

"Ours left as well," Sarador answered. "Once the message came, they fled without a word." The other kingdoms indicated the same abandonment happened in all five kingdoms' camps. "Has no one heard from them since?" Sarador asked.

Philip had gotten as much new information as he could handle before leaving the dragons and centaurs that morning. After he sent the messages and began preparations to receive the delegates from the other kingdoms, he and Torgon spent the day attempting to put together the pieces of what they'd learned. They requested Svorgh attend the meeting to answer further questions. His daughter, Shvika, stood behind him, looking wholly the warrior with a sharp face and suspicious eyes. Philip also insisted Maelin join them with the rest of his claw nearby.

The rest of the group was made up of kings and generals from all the kingdoms. All of Philip's generals attended as well as several more from every kingdom. Most of them stood quietly behind their rulers, except two of Torodov's generals and Philip's own General Riddig. Riddig stood off to the side of the group, glaring at Philip and Torgon.

Philip spent a good amount of time trying to convince the other royals that the dragons could speak, and that two of them, including his own sister, were humans as well as dragons. Torgon, Maelin and Svorgh were there to corroborate the details. Indeed, the very existence of Svorgh, and a previously unknown race of intelligent beings, convinced the royals more than anything that shocking things were more than possible in the world around them.

"Well," King Torodov of the Courageous Kingdom said. "Has the faerie council convened? What are they deliberating? Are they furious? Are they placated? What are we to assume?"

"We are to assume," Philip said, "that the faeries no longer influence the human race."

"But the war," King Theodor of the Honorable Kingdom said, "the war was their doing. Their idea."

"They nearly killed every human," Riddig sneered from behind. "If we make a decision they don't like, won't they just follow through on that threat?"

"My people," Svorgh said, "are ready and willing to assist."

"Can you protect everyone?" Riddig asked.

Svorgh dropped his eyes.

Philip shook his head. "I don't know about the rest of you, but I prefer the willing ally to the forced." He inspected the eyes around him. He had set up their chairs in a circle in his large tent so they all faced each other and could openly discuss…well, everything. "The centaurs are allies with the dragons, and the dragons have requested peace and hopefully an alliance with the humans as well."

"Don't forget the goblins," Svorgh spoke from his seat in the circle. "We are allied with the dragons and centaurs. We would also be allies of the humans, if you see fit."

Riddig grunted. "And you, master…goblin, or whatever you are."

"King!" Philip and Torgon said together, but Torgon deferred to Philip.

"He is a *king*, Riddig," Philip said, purposefully excluding the man's title, "and you will address him as such."

Riddig pursed his lips but continued. "*King* Svorgh, then," he said, "what do you offer the Noble Kingdom and ask from us?"

Svorgh shrugged. "Our people have many things to offer," he said. He tapped his circlet. "We mine gems of great power that we can offer in trade to the humans, centaurs, dragons—"

"—and faeries?" Riddig interrupted.

Svorgh stared him down. "To all who wish to benefit from our alliance."

"You shocked Kradik," Torgon said from Philip's side.

Svorgh nodded. "We can do many things. Including producing a gateway to the location where the dragons have indicated they will meet with us tomorrow."

"We wouldn't have to use the platforms?" Sarador asked. Svorgh shook his head and a noticeable sigh of relief was heard throughout the group.

"To get into the Rock Clouds?" Torodov asked.

"Yes," Svorgh nodded. "The gateway would also be permanent. It takes a good deal of energy to create such a connection. It will not come down easily."

"It would give us an escape," Theodor said. "If the dragons or centaurs turned on us, we could get away."

Svorgh nodded. "But you didn't let me answer the rest of the general's question," he said. "He asked me what we have to offer, but also what we ask in return." He searched the eyes around him.

"What do you ask?" Sarador said.

Svorgh searched every eye before answering. "We ask that the Five Swords be redistributed."

The room stiffened as one. "What are you talking about?" Philip muttered.

"I'm talking," Svorgh said, "of the fact that there cannot be a balance of power in Avonoa if one race has the five most powerful weapons."

The room sat in silence. Finally, Riddig stepped forward. "You can't ask that," he hissed. "You can't ask us to give up our only advantage."

"Your advantage," Svorgh said, "is in your numbers. The swords were meant to bring about peace for the humans and they have served their purpose. Now the swords are meant to bring peace between all the races of Avonoa. And it must be done willingly."

"Mine was stolen," Sarador said suddenly. All eyes turned to her. She nodded toward Philip. "Before your coronation. I have been trying to find it, but…"

"Allegiance is easily changed," Svorgh said. "Not to worry, I know where the sword is."

Philip sat up. His eyes wandered to the only silent man in the room. "King Grisivere," he said, "you don't have an opinion on the matter? As king of the Just Kingdom, you are the Avonoan expert on justice."

Grisivere lifted his gaze from the floor to stare at Svorgh. "You took it," he said. "Didn't you?"

Svorgh crossed his arms. "It was my right," he answered.

Grisivere nodded. "He's right," he said to Philip and the rest of the room. "It's the only way to ensure justice."

As the nobles and royals around the room nodded and agreed in silence, Riddig stepped forward again. "This is a mistake," he growled, "and I'll have no part of it." He stormed from the tent. Philip wasn't sad to see him go and didn't send anyone after him.

257

37

THE KRUSIBLE

Philip, Torgon, Tierni, Tommak, Hilde, Maelin and several other generals and guards rode up the edge of the Inner Mountain. Amidst a plethora of large boulders, Svorgh sat on a smaller one, his daughter, Shvika, tenderly rubbing his back.

Philip still wasn't sure what he thought of the man. He claimed to be a king, yet he did the things a staff guard would do. Relaying messages, doing majik — he didn't even wear fine clothes or emblems of his station. Although the circlet around his head held many more gems than the other goblins' circlets he'd seen, the man didn't seem to put himself above anyone else. It reminded Philip of the young woman who had volunteered to be The Voice and brought him a message he needed that could have ended her life. Hadn't she said that King Theodor listened to all his people equally? Philip dwelled on his own virtues as a king while Shvika spoke gently in her father's ear. As the group arrived, Svorgh slowly lifted his head. The little gray man's skin had a green tinge, with green lines under his eyes and across his forehead.

Worried for the little man, Philip asked, "Are you alright, Your Majesty?"

Svorgh gave slow, somber nods. Shvika looked up at the dismounting party. "My father told you last night that it takes a tremendous amount of energy to create a gateway. He's been working several hours, but it is done."

After dismounting and closer inspection, Philip could see the king's hands shaking and sweat dripping down his back. "Why didn't you have another perform the majik?" he asked.

Shvika shook her head. "It is required that only the king perform such powerful majik. Fear not, he will recover soon."

As she turned her attention back to her father, Philip searched their surroundings. Between the largest of the boulders a large black archway yawned at them. Wide enough and tall enough for two fully grown dragons to enter side-by-side, he was almost certain this was the gateway the goblins promised.

The ground at the bottom of the gateway seemed to drop away. It didn't fade into darkness gradually the way a natural cave might appear to do, it just…ended. The top and sides appeared much as a natural cave might, with a simple, wide opening cut into the rock and side of the mountain. But, perhaps because of how the morning sun struck at the correct angle, the bottom of it seemed to quickly drop away into nothingness inside the opening.

While Philip and the Noble party waited, the royal parties and armies of the other four kingdoms of Avonoa arrived. King Svorgh began to look better and gained the energy to stand, but Philip saw his knees shaking.

"Is this the gateway?" King Theodor asked upon his arrival.

Svorgh and Shvika affirmed that it was.

"Is it safe?" Queen Sarador asked.

"More so than traveling by dragon," Shvika confirmed.

Before Philip could move, Torgon strode forward. Without hesitation, he thrust his hand into the consuming darkness. His hand and part of his arm disappeared at the threshold as if they had been sliced off with a sharp sword.

A few in the large groups of humans gasped. Torgon stood for a moment before withdrawing his hand and arm from the opening, apparently testing how it felt to move through the gateway, when the thundering of hooves rumbled toward them.

Dozens of centaurs galloped up the incline toward the hesitant humans. Most of them wore swords and knives around their waists. Several had a bow slung over their backs. The female who had threatened Maelin was in the lead. She stopped long enough to take in the view of humans around her.

Philip was struck by the beauty of her large eyes and flowing black hair. But admiration turned to concern when he saw the weathered bracer on her arm. She was a seasoned archer. She might even have been the one leading the attacks on the humans. Philip stiffened at the sight.

Her eyes fell on Torgon, standing in front of the dark opening, then shifted to Svorgh and Shvika. "Is this it?" she asked, indicating the gateway.

Shvika nodded.

The warrior centaur female turned to look back at two male centaurs. One wore a leather band around his head like a circlet. The other wore a bright silver sword slung on his back. The female nodded to the male with the sword. The sworded centaur nodded to the circleted centaur, then the nods reversed course. When the female received confirmation, she yelled, "Go!" and the herd moved forward as one. Without the briefest hesitation, the centaurs thundered through the threshold as if they were being chased by a dragon.

Torgon dodged out of the way but stayed near the opening until they were gone. When he nodded at Philip, all the humans gathered there moved forward. Torgon stepped in front of Philip.

"Shouldn't the king go first?" Philip said low so only Torgon would hear.

"Shouldn't the royal general protect his king?" Torgon muttered back.

"Do I get a choice?" Philip asked.

"When it comes to your safety," Torgon answered, "absolutely not."

When Philip stepped through the opening, he tried not to watch his front foot disappear. He thought he might lose his nerve if he saw it detach. He shut his eyelids in a blink that was probably longer than absolutely necessary, but he didn't close his eyes. Definitely not. After the briefest sensation of falling, he blinked again in the morning sun.

Torgon walked ahead of him, carefully taking stock of the people and beasts surrounding them. They soon arrived in something Hirowyn had called the Krusible. He'd said it was a secluded and safe place to meet. Philip looked past the jagged edges of the Krusible to see the tops of some of the floating mountains around them. He thought they must be very high in the Rock Clouds, but the smooth bowl-like impression of the Krusible was still attached to the Inner Mountain. Philip had noticed a large protrusion from the Inner Mountain above them, and now he realized he was setting foot amidst the clouds within the dragon ruck's homes.

Philip was wary of meeting on the dragons' territory, but Hirowyn had said he could bring as many people as he wanted, with all of their weaponry. They would not be asked to surrender their armaments and would be guaranteed safety. After all, the dragons' weapons could not be surrendered. The only thing Hirowyn requested is that the humans not bring the poisoned arrows.

When Torgon stopped, Philip stood next to him.

Tierni stood on Torgon's other side; Hilde and Tommak were behind her. Along with Maelin's claw 3-4, a general from an outlying district named Arrys and several of his guards and several Black Saber women all stood behind them. Philip's hand rested on the Noble Sword at his hip. It might be the last time he possessed it.

While the rest of the kingdoms' representatives followed them out of the gateway into the Krusible, Philip focused on the scene in front of him. His breath caught for a moment. It was unimaginable.

Seven dragons sat waiting in the smooth bowl shaped out of the mountainside. Although the morning was cool, Philip's palms began to sweat as he walked toward the large dragons. In front of the dragons stood Owyn and Anna, being in their human forms. Anna donned the same green cloth as she had worn the previous day. Owyn wore his black cloth, although he hadn't bothered to wrap it around his upper body as Anna had; she had skillfully wrapped it around her shoulders as well.

The centaurs who had barreled through the gateway ahead of them now stood next to the dragons. Thankfully, their weapons stayed sheathed. Philip's heart beat a triple-time rhythm in his chest.

Coming through the gateway last, Svorgh and Shvika joined a few dozen goblins on the opposite side of the dragons from the centaurs. Many of them wore sashes across their chests with brightly colored designs or writing across them. They gathered in groups of five or six, unified by the same color sash lettering, and sported a wide variety of hair colors and designs. Their clothing also ranged widely in colors as well as style. Some had etched blue lines across their grey skin. Most, if not all, wore circlets on their heads – some with only a few gems, some with several. None contained as many gems as Svorgh's.

Philip's stomach lurched when he thought of the majikal powers those gems contained. His instinct to question and suspect peaked. Should he even be here? Should he instead have listened to Riddig and not trusted the dragons? Should he trust this small man who had the ability to disappear in the blink of an eye? Should he trust a man who was a criminal in his own kingdom? Could he trust Anna? He turned to Torgon questioningly. Torgon, catching Philip's eye, gave him a slight nod before Philip set his jaw and turned his attention to the would-be black dragon.

"King Philip," Owyn said. "Thank you for coming here. Do you know if the faeries accepted the invitation as well?"

Philip shook his head and turned to the other kings and queens of the five kingdoms. He saw that they were all looking at him for confirmation. "We haven't spoken to the faeries or the faerie council since yesterday."

As he said it, Owyn was the first to look up. After a moment, Philip heard the unmistakable hum of faerie wings in flight. Turning, they watched as several faeries flew over the rough edge of the Krusible.

With their hoods thrown back and hands and feet bare, everyone could see their softly opaque skin. In different shades of purples, blues and greens with a pearlescent sheen, their appearance was beautiful to behold. They had even changed their clothes. Philip remembered stories of faeries dressed in creamy whites and silvers like the ones before them now. These were the beautiful faeries of old. They alighted just past the lip of the bowl and walked, almost gliding, toward them.

Humans at the back made way for the faeries to come up the middle to the front. As the band neared Philip, he noticed two in the back. One wasn't a faerie at all, but Riddig, draped in one of the old brown faerie cloaks and supported by a slender, silver-haired faeriewoman.

The faeriewoman unceremoniously dumped Riddig at Philip's feet then moved back behind the other faeries. The older general's face was marked by a black eye and a cut lip. He was pale, with deep purple circles under his eyes. He didn't bother to raise himself in front of his king.

"What happened to him?" Philip asked, while Tommak stepped forward to inspect the general.

"He came to us last night," Qialla answered from the front of the group. Philip had never imagined the bitter old faerie could be so beautiful. His pale purple skin shimmered in the sunlight and brilliant silver hair framed his face. Even his voice had become more melodious than Philip thought possible.

"He wanted you dead," Qialla continued. "He and his nephew, Murzod, have been plotting and scheming for several months. I'm ashamed to say that I was party to these plots and will submit myself to your disciplinary actions. He has been punished by our system of justice and we turn him over to you for yours."

Philip couldn't speak. He stared at Riddig. He knew the man was arrogant, rude and often vile. But treason? His nephew, Murzod, had indeed tried to kill Philip on the platform, so he couldn't deny the plausibility of his uncle agreeing to it. But to hear it said out loud. It stung. Philip glanced at the royals around him. They all watched to see what his reaction would be. Then his eyes wandered to Anna.

"He knew Dieko," he whispered to her across the gathering.

Anna stepped forward. "Yes," she said, "they were plotting against you. Dieko discovered your ruse to find a loyal noble. They decided together that he would marry me and they would dispatch you and he would be king. It's the only reason he married me."

"You…?"

"Yes," she nodded, "yes, I killed Dieko."

Philip's breathing became ragged when he realized he might have to try his own sister – she being part dragon – for murder. He pointed at Riddig and cast his eyes to his side, looking for Tommak. "Get him out of here," he said, straining to keep his voice steady. "He'll have a fair trial when we return to Kingstor Noble."

He looked into Qialla's face. The serene features were so peaceful, as if nothing in the world could upset him. His countenance calmed Philip. "We'll discuss your involvement later," he said. Qialla dipped his head and moved away.

Finally, gaining control of himself with a deep breath, he met Anna's eyes. "How many?" he asked. "How many humans have you killed?"

She hesitated a moment. "As a human, or as a dragon?"

Philip couldn't stop his teeth from grinding. "You." He spat.

Before she could answer, Torgon pointed his sword at Owyn. "You killed my father. How many humans have you killed?"

Owyn shook his head. "Too many to count," he admitted.

"But he saved human lives too," Maelin said from behind.

"Well, I keep a list," the female centaur said, folding her arms over her chest. "And if it's a contest, I'm up to 394 dead humans. Do I have six volunteers so I can even it out?"

Angry murmurs grew among the humans as Torgon stared her down, but the centaur with the leather band around his head spoke loudest.

"This is no laughing matter, Ashel," he said.

"Joss is right," the centaur with the shining silver sword said to her. Philip noted the sword and wondered if he recognized it. "You shouldn't take this subject lightly. None of us should."

"I'm not," Ashel snapped. "But how many dragons and centaurs and even goblins were hurt or killed in all of this? There has been death and betrayal on all sides."

Her voice cracked on the last word. Her angry eyes blinked and she turned away from the other centaurs. She trotted toward the dragons and leaned against a small brown dragon with two rows of spikes running along his spine, keeping her eyes lowered and her arms wrapped around herself.

"For the second time, she's right," Philip said, finding his voice. His words earned a glance from the intimidating centaur female. "There has been death and betrayal on all sides. Blaming won't help it. We need to own our misdeeds."

Torgon grunted at his side, so Philip turned an eye on him. "You know your father would say the same."

"He would," Tierni reaffirmed Torgon.

"But," Owyn said, "the humans were only acting according to the information you had. It is the fault of the dragons for not speaking up sooner."

Several of the dragons hissed. One dragon muttered loud enough for all to hear, "So says the blood and ash traitor." At those words, the other dragons growled amongst themselves.

The small brown dragon snapped, "Unimaginable, you worm," he said. "Not treacherous. Priya is The One. Not Hiro."

At that point, the dragons began arguing among themselves. The centaurs jumped in as well. Ashel defended the little brown dragon. The humans began muttering – not arguing, but thoroughly confused as to the accusations. The goblins sat quietly watching.

Philip saw Svorgh watching the entrance of the gateway he had created. His daughter tried to say something, but he held up his hand to her.

Unsure of what he was watching for, Philip followed the eyes of the minute king just in time to see a small, hunched faerie come bounding through the gateway opening.

"Oh, spit!" she cried. "Have I missed it?"

Her long, straggly gray hair hung sparsely, and her purple skin was darkening in spots. One side of her head was shaved and an iridescent snake tattoo swirled around her ear and down her neck and arm. She bounced into the Krusible, but Philip couldn't make out if she was jumping on her own or if something that supported her bumped her along. She finally landed on the ground and scurried forward as fast as her knobby knees and hunched back could carry her.

"He's not the traitor!" she yelled. "Freeg did it and the faeries are murderers!" She cackled at no one in particular. Then she turned aside and muttered, "It is NOT animal cruelty, you thankless creature!"

Svorgh nodded. Owyn looked at the old faeriewoman as if she were crazy, which she very well seemed to Philip.

"Shampy?" Owyn said. "What are you doing here?"

"Shurta's tangles!" she cursed. "Did you think Visi was the only one that knew these things?" She spun around and pointed to Svorgh. "Yes, Svorgh, I knew about you too. If my kangaroo would listen to me, I would've been here sooner."

"No one invited you here, Shaman," Qialla said, stepping forward.

"Of course not!" Shampy threw her hands in the air. The only cloth she wore wrapped around her body came dangerously close to exposing more than those around her wanted to see. "You don't want me here because I know, that you know, that I know everything you know…and more."

A perplexed silence followed.

Finally, Philip brushed aside the confusion, intimidation, fear and anger.

"What do you know?!" he yelled. "Everything. From the beginning."

"Oh, big, little king," she hummed. "We could be here for a year."

"The short version, then!" Torgon called.

"The short version, he says …" Shampy clapped her hands and reached behind herself. Philip feared she might push aside the tiny covering she wore. Instead, she directed a clawed hand at the stone behind her. It liquified until it shaped itself into a large mound. The little faeriewoman opened her wings and flew to the top of it where everyone could see her, then opened her mouth to pronounce:

"The faeries made the dragons speak,
a choice they wouldn't share.
They made a spell no word be said,
no faerie ever dare.
The centaurs disagreed of course
and so they ran away.
A prophecy came from the pain,
The One to come someday.
The faeries' curse turned ugly soon,
await The One to come.
Darkness took their hearts
as well as they hid from the sun.
Then Freeg fell in with sweet Annette,
but she don't love him too.
From her death and with his heart
they made a baby coo.
The One was born with golden hair
and dragon scales of green.
But she would hide from all beside
the father she had seen.
Once Freeg now leader of his ruck,

he did betray them all.
The faeries and dragon Taynor
did plot and plan with gall.
They tricked the young king Philip
into taking all the blame,
as humans hunted dragons
and with poison in their aim.
But Visi knew all ins and outs
with Shampy she did plan.
Create did we a dragon
with the heart of a tall man.
With these we played like little pawns
and made sure they would meet.
Because all things befell on them
as their two hearts did beat.
They must to kill the traitor
but first to take a throne,
before they speak to humans
and a new world they could hone."

Silence echoed through the Krusible until Shampy held up her hands and yelled, "Now clap!"

A smattering of polite applause followed as the old faerie flew down from her perch. The stone melted back into the mountain floor when she landed.

"The faeries lied to me," Philip mumbled as the clapping ceased. "It felt wrong, but I didn't...I couldn't..." his voice trailed off as guilt swept over him.

"It's not your fault." Hearing this, Philip looked up into the eyes of the tall man, Owyn. "No one blames you," he said.

"No," Svorgh said from across the Krusible. "No one blames the humans. It's the faeries who are without honor."

He stood and walked to the middle of the gathering. Shampy hadn't stepped aside. Instead, she stood in the middle of everyone, appearing to whittle away with nothing in her hands, watching Svorgh.

"The centaurs," he indicated the group, "are and have been loyal to their allies to their core."

The centaur removed the sparkling silver sword from his back. Philip realized it was the Silver Sword of Allegiance. Stealing a glance at Queen Sarador, he saw the sharp woman purse her lips at the centaurs, but she said nothing.

"They have," Svorgh continued, "by their very actions, claimed the highest allegiance in Avonoa. As have the goblins claimed in the Just."

Svorgh pulled the small sword from his side and it grew into the long Black Sword of Justice. Torgon's and Philip's heads snapped to Grisivere.

King Grisivere stood tall. "The sword cannot be stolen," he said. "It can only be claimed by the Just."

Philip and Torgon shared a glance.

"As for the other swords …" Svorgh continued. He indicated each and the humans still in possession of them removed them from their sides as Svorgh approached.

He first approached Torodov. Torodov shot Philip a questioning look. Philip nodded – he couldn't go back on his word now. Besides, Svorgh could easily take the sword;

better to hand it over willingly. Torodov relinquished the Gold Sword of Courage to Svorgh.

Although this sword, as well as the others, was easily double the length of his height, the small king handled them deftly. Taking the Gold Sword of Courage, Svorgh walked it over to Philip.

"I believe," he said, "King Philip has, at such a tender age, shown that he has the courage to face adversity. He is the only one capable of leading the human race into a world with four other races who have more power and majik than himself and his kind. He will lead with courage into this bold new existence."

He handed the sword to Philip, who accepted it. Switching the gold sword to his left hand, Philip pulled the Blue Sword of Nobility from his sheath.

"I shouldn't have two swords in my care," he said.

Svorgh shook his head in agreement and took the blue sword. As the sword moved away from him, Philip felt an equality settle on everyone around him. He realized that the faeries were no more honorable than bullies and he felt bolstered by the fact that he had withstood them. He looked around at the kings and queens around him and knew they were all equal with the guards and servants behind them.

Tierni smiled at him and he knew there was no difference between her and Queen Sarador besides a title. He knew nothing would stop them from being together.

Svorgh walked the blue sword to Owyn, but the tall man held out a hand to stop him. "Dragons have no need for swords, customs or titles," he said.

"And they don't need shiny things either!" Shampy yelled. Cocking her head as if speaking to someone next to her, she mumbled, "That was a myth created from Freeg and Annette too."

"Dragons are the most noble creatures in Avonoa," Svorgh said to Owyn, ignoring Shampy. "That is why only dragons can claim the Noble Sword. You don't believe nobility to mean you're above anyone in status or better than anyone else, but you strive to better yourselves."

Owyn tentatively received the sword.

"Perhaps the faeries should strive to better themselves," Ashel grumbled.

"Perhaps," Svorgh said as he walked away from Hirowyn. "But the faeries' virtues would eventually lead them to believe they are better than others and start all these problems again."

"Perhaps," said a faerie Philip knew he had met but couldn't quite put a name to her, "we shouldn't receive any sword. We created them. We would only corrupt their value."

"On the contrary," Svorgh stopped in front of Theodor. Again, the older king looked to Philip for approval before handing the red sword to the goblin king.

Svorgh brought the sword to stand before the faerie council. "The other four swords will go to the races of Avonoa who already embody the traits of those swords. But this," he said, handing the Red Sword of Honor up to the faerie woman, "goes to the race who most needs to cultivate its honor."

The faerie shook her head. "I cannot swear that every faerie will live up to the expectations of owning this sword."

"Nor can any other race," Svorgh said, indicating the others in attendance. "There will always be exceptions. There will always be certain variants. The power of a sword works on those closest to it and those willing to succumb to its effects. It will guide leaders and influence the lives of the people. That understanding of its power is all that is required."

The faerie dipped her head, accepting the sword. "We have already decided, as a council," she said, "that the faerie race will diminish. We must focus on curing the diseases of our own hearts before we thrust our judgment on others again."

They turned to leave, but a shout rang out.

"Wait!" It was Ashel. She stood up tall, pointing to the faeries. "Don't they need to pay for their crimes? They started a war and tried to wipe out an entire species of intelligent creatures all for the sake of their own vanity! Centaurs and dragons have died!" After a nudge from the brown dragon, she waved a hand and added, "And humans."

In a singularly unique reaction, the faeries turned and bowed their heads at the accusations. They said nothing.

"And you killed them," Sarador spoke up. "You and your centaurs destroyed our supply caravans and our people. Your hands are no cleaner than theirs."

As everyone began to speak and accuse each other at once, Svorgh raised his hands to quiet them, but the taller beings yelled over his head. Instead, Shampy flew up over the crowd. Clapping her hands together, a force swept over the gathering, knocking everyone, even dragons, back a step.

"By Shurta's tangles," the old faeriewoman cursed again, "get control of yourselves! Everyone has a share of the blame. We just have to find the beginning."

She drifted down to stand next to Svorgh again, who nodded to her. Or did he wink at her? Philip wasn't sure so he begged himself to forget it.

"It started when the faeries came to Kingstor Noble," Torgon said. "They told us that the dragons were going to kill everyone."

"So," Philip jumped in, "they insisted we kill the dragons first."

Owyn shook his head. "But we don't blame you for—"

"Well, I do!" Torgon shouted.

Philip searched his best friend's face. Torgon's eyes brimmed. His face flushed with color and a vein stood out on his neck. He had to wonder how long his best friend had been holding onto this pain and anger and never shown it. Philip counted himself a dismal friend for not having seen it and helped him sooner.

He stepped closer and tried to speak with him, but Torgon shoved his king and friend aside. "No," he said, pointing at Owyn. "You, the black dragon, killed my mother's husband. He led the guards into the mountains to ambush you. When he captured one of you, you killed him and all his men."

"We couldn't let them live," a larger gray dragon said.

"Yes, Tog," Owyn said, "we could have."

"You removed his head," Torgon said. Torgon's eyes were bright red. Somehow he held back the tears, but his entire face seemed to turn deeper and deeper red. He might burst into flames himself. "I had to grieve with my mother and watch my best friend grieve over his father at the same time."

Owyn nodded. "Then that's where it started, so let it end here. Your father killed my father, so I killed him. I give you my life in compensation."

Anna tried to stop him, but Owyn stepped away from her toward Torgon. "My life is yours in amends."

"No," Torgon shook his head. "You didn't take my spouse."

He turned. Philip hadn't realized the number of servants who had accompanied the guards and generals into the Rock Clouds and the Krusible. They parted and from behind walked a short, older, graying woman. Her face held the sternness of Tierni's and the laugh lines of Torgon's. She wore a simple blue dress and a black apron. Embroidered on the bottom hem of the apron was a small blue sword.

She didn't dip her head once while walking forward to meet Owyn in the middle of the gathering. As soon as she was within arm's reach of Owyn, he opened his mouth to speak, but she swung her arm at him. His face lurched sideways from the slap, with a loud CRACK echoing through the Krusible.

Definitely Tierni's mother, Philip thought.

When Owyn's vision cleared and he swung his head back to face her, the woman pointed a finger at him. "A man didn't kill my Bragon," she said.

Instantly, the man changed into a black dragon. He prostrated himself in front of her.

Standing over the humble yet mighty dragon, she slowly brought her hand forward and gently placed it on his head. "I forgive you," she said, "as long as you spend the rest of your life protecting that which you took. I constrain you to protect the lives of humans the rest of your days."

The huge black beast looked up at her from the ground. "I give you my wyrd. My life is yours if I break it."

As the dragon changed back into a human again and agreed to her terms, Philip leaned over to Torgon. "You do realize that that dragon might have just killed her if he'd really wanted to," he whispered.

Torgon nodded as the two embraced and everyone around them cheered. "Yes," he answered, "but then he would have had to deal with the wrath of Tierni." He met Philip's eye, who forced an expressionless look. "And, by Khurta's claws, he wouldn't have stood a chance."

38

COMPLICATION

Everyone in the Krusible agreed that the rest of the day be spent in mourning. The centaurs asked that they be allowed to bring their dead to the Krusible for the proper burning rites. The dragons extended the same opportunity to the humans and goblins. The goblins hadn't sustained any losses, but they agreed with the inclusion of all.

Ashel admitted to killing many human men. After returning to the surface and placing Vikal's body on one of the platforms, she helped stack the human remains. The bodies, enough for five platforms, were lifted into the air by Hiro and several more dragons and brought to the Krusible.

While many dragons removed bodies of the fallen after proper rites were conducted, groups of huntresses left to hunt. The young ones were fed elsewhere, but some of the huntresses brought back several lydik and giant two-headed scorrand. The centaurs insisted on feasting with their new allies, as was their custom. The humans assembled some of their own cooks and chefs. The woman who had forgiven Hirowyn earlier for her husband's death – who was, as Hiro learned, Torgon and Tierni's mother – cooked and shared food with goblins, centaurs and dragons alike. With a splash of mint here and there, even the dragons enjoyed the feast. Now the five intelligent races of Avonoa ate and talked together around a massive fire in the middle of the Krusible.

As the evening wore on, Owyn surveyed the scene. Several groups consisting of most of the five races of Avonoa sat and talked and laughed and mourned together. The humans wanted to learn more about the dragons. Everyone was curious about the goblins, and the goblins were amenable to divulging their secrets and joining the world once more. Most of the faeries didn't partake in the sharing and the mourning because they'd suffered no losses. A few hung around to converse and learn, but before long most either returned to their own camp or had already set out for home.

The centaurs took to an alliance with the humans quite easily, especially considering the prior bloodshed. The alliance may have been possible only with the assistance of the Allegiant Sword. But with the sword's aid, once allied, always allied.

At one point during the course of the day, Owyn found Jarek and the Hamees men among those from the Noble Kingdom. They were there to help gather bodies and see to the proper rites, but they had no desire to participate in the social gathering, citing that they had not participated in the war and felt they would be an intrusion on the mourning. However, they accepted a ride from the dragons to speed them home sooner the next morning, and stayed on the surface in the Noble camp for the night..

While returning from the Hamees, Owyn passed Adair's circle of friends who were interrogating a few goblins and stopped to talk.

Adair, the first man to befriend Owyn, sat with his own claw of men from the army where, to raucous laughter, he relayed how Owyn first started out as a man.

"Chinkle!" Adair laughed. "He said he had to chinkle!"

The entire group laughed and Owyn could only shake his head, remembering those first few days. "Blame Anna," he finally answered. "She's the one I heard it from and I had no idea what was happening to me!"

He laughed as he walked away from the group to rejoin Anna. They sat in a large circle of different species with Philip, Torgon, Tierni, Ashel, Joss, Rylan, Kodoran, Tog, Surneen, Mitashio and the men from Owyn's claw. Owyn's claw consisted of Maelin, the leader and lieutenant; Koris, Adair's brother-in-law; Thaddeus, the second largest man in the claw; Brandell and Taka, the two men as close as brothers and as mischievous as children; Nolan, the former nobleman; Tua and Darwick, the quieter, kind men and Addil, the brilliant, small man that saved the group from trouble most often. These men were the most comfortable with Owyn and had the most questions for him about his species change. The king trusted them all and enjoyed their company.

Ashel, still grieving over the loss of Vikal, lounged against Kodoran's side in melancholy. Occasionally she would throw out a question or flash a small grin. Whenever she got too quiet for his comfort, Kodoran would whisper to her and she would smile again.

"Why are you so good with a sword if you've never trained with one?" Koris asked. They had been peppering Owyn with questions for a while.

"My dragon senses," Owyn answered, "allowed me to see better and react faster."

"Yeah," Addil said, "what about those senses? I've heard dragons have better hearing, smell, sight, touch, all of them! Are your senses better than a normal human's?"

"Yes," Owyn nodded. He glanced at Tog, who widened the one eye watching him. "For the most part. I have increased hearing and smell, and sight…during the daytime."

"And at night?" Addil said. "I suppose a dragon can see better at night. Or do you use your other senses at night?"

"Actually," Owyn watched Tog, waiting for his consensus. When he finally looked back at him, the gray dragon nodded at Owyn to continue. "I have never had very good night vision."

"That was Visi's doing," Anna said. "She had to bless you as a child with an enchantment so your heart would break and turn you into a human. But she said it might have some side effects."

"Really?" Kodoran said. "I've always wondered. You never acted like you were superior that way, but I thought you were just humble."

"Well," Owyn continued, "I had to hone my other senses because of the poor night vision. So I have better-than-average senses of smell and hearing."

"Like, how much better?" Koris asked.

"Well, I could hear you snore at night!" Owyn answered.

"Really?" Brandell said. "You could hear Koris over your own snoring? That must be outstanding hearing!"

Everyone laughed and Anna poked him. "I told you dragons snore!"

Owyn shook his head. "Alright," he said. "The human snoring was tolerable. Much more than their smell."

"Our smell?" Tua shook his head. "I smell like daisies!"

"Daisies?" Owyn laughed. "I could follow you across all of Avonoa, just by your odor. And it certainly wouldn't lead me to any daisies!"

After the laughter died down, Torgon spoke. "The time in the rocks," he said, almost whispering. "After you destroyed our halfway point for the arrows. Why didn't you kill me and my men? You could've. By the sounds of it, you should've. There were only a few of us and we weren't armed with much. You must have heard us and followed us by our scent. What made you leave us alone?"

The others waited while Owyn thought. "I smelled Anna," he finally said, "–or, Priyanna. I thought I was following her. I thought you had taken her, but her scent tracked away from yours and so I followed it. I didn't want to hurt you."

"How many times could you have saved us all this trouble," Philip murmured, "if you had only spoken to us in your dragon form."

"Not many," Anna said. She sat next to Owyn on the ground but leaned against a log someone had brought up for the humans to rest on. "Visi had many, many years to delve into possible futures. While it isn't possible to see everything, she knew the general path we would take to get us to this point. We wouldn't have this peace without her foresight and guidance."

"Or the faeries' pride," Torgon mumbled.

Talking amongst the group quieted. Everyone wanted to hear the faeries' side of the story, but it would have to wait for another day. Before leaving, the faeries claimed that they needed to hold many trials yet and plan the appropriate punishments. But many in the Krusible group shared the belief that the sword of honor would keep the faeries from getting involved in other races' affairs unless they were specifically called upon.

"Don't be too hard on us," Shampy came floating over. She had been buzzing around the fire offering majik, company and answers to many, mostly the goblins. Svorgh didn't seem to mind her presence, but Shvika couldn't stand the crazy old witch. "Don't forget, the centaurs weren't under the same spell. They could have told the humans about the dragons whenever they wanted."

As the crazy shaman flew away, cursing a red flower under her breath, Ashel glared after her. "How dare she," the centaur began to complain.

"She's right, though," Joss said, stopping Ashel's rage from flaring. "I believe the centaurs didn't say anything at first because they agreed that the humans couldn't handle it. Then, being former faeries, a hint of fear of the curse still had an effect on us. More recently, we enjoyed seeing the curse backfire on the faeries. There's been so much hatred between us for so long, it will be a struggle to gain any trust. For both sides."

"Which reminds me," Keeahrspi said, popping into existence in front of Rylan.

"You're not supposed to do that anymore," Rylan said, swatting away the goblin like shooing a fly.

"Do what?" the little gray man said, stumbling away from the centaur with a cup of ale in his hand.

"Be invisible," Anna said.

Keeahrspi squinted at her. "Was I inbisivle?"

Everyone laughed. Even Ashel cracked another smile.

"There you are!" Shvika shouted, running to Keeahrspi's side. She pulled the cup from his hand and threw his arm over her shoulder. "I think you've had enough for tonight."

She swung him away from the group, but he jerked his arm away and turned back. "I was aksing a questiosh," he said.

Pointing at Anna, he said, "Do you get both swords now?"

"That's not our affair," Shvika scolded, pulling him over her shoulder again. As he fought her off, she threw him over her back. Despite their difference in size, she handled him with ease. She apologized to the group and promised not to let him bother them again.

Once they were gone, Philip turned to Anna. "He's right, you know," he said. "Aren't you the leader of the dragons now? It hardly seems fair that you have access to both the Noble Sword and the Courageous Sword."

Anna shook her head. "I'm not Rakdar," she said, drawing everyone's attention. "I've conceded the name to one greater than I."

Everyone followed her eyes as they landed on the small brown dragon next to Ashel, who nodded to Anna in return.

"No," Mitashio grumbled. "No, no, no! Milah is probably throwing a fit in the World of Souls right now. No. It's not possible. I won't acquiesce to this. No."

"Oh, come on," Rakgar feira Kodoran feira Prakyndar said to him. "Milah liked me! He wouldn't say so, but I know he did. I'll be a good Rakgar and he would agree. I'll be better than Taynor, no doubt. And Milah would agree with that too."

"He admired you," Owyn said, remembering Milah's last words to him. "He told me so. He also said he would tear off my horns if I told anyone he did, but I think that danger is in the past."

Rakgar grinned. Mitashio grumbled, but laid back down, shaking his head.

"I'll still need counselors," Rakgar said to him. "I'll need someone who can tell me when I'm making a bad decision. Someone who can be brutally honest. Someone who won't hold back."

"Oh," Mitashio said, "I'll do that no matter what."

Ashel threw her arm around Rakgar's shoulder. "I knew dragons were smarter than they looked." She grinned up at him and their eyes held each other's a moment.

Suddenly, Rakgar's eyes popped open. "Uh," he breathed, but instead of speaking he choked back a small cough. His eyes searched out Owyn and Tog. "I have to go," he said, jumping from his position next to Ashel.

"What?" she said. "Why?"

"I just—" he said, and coughed again. "I just have to go. I'll be back." Cough. "I'll come back as soon as I can." Cough. "I promise, I'll—" Cough, cough.

Without another word, Rakgar flew away.

"What's wrong with him?" Ashel asked the group.

"He's fine," Owyn said, stifling a smile.

"Yeah," Tog offered, not bothering to hide his own smile. "I'm guessing he'll come back feeling better than ever."

Owyn and Tog shared a smile and a nod.

"More secrets?" Philip said. "I thought we were past those."

Owyn shook his head. "This is someone else's secret and it's best left alone."

"At least," Tog said, "until the owner is willing to share."

"Like you?" Philip whispered to the ground. When he lifted his eyes, he looked at Anna. "Are you willing to share any of your secrets?"

Anna lifted her chin. "Anything," she said.

"Then start at the beginning," he said.

Anna nodded. "I am the daughter of King Paudie and Queen Annette," she began.

"We know that part," Torgon said.

"But you don't know the rest," Owyn told them.

Anna continued. "The dragon Freeg fell in love with Annette and his heart broke for her. Married and pregnant with the king's child, she was miserable about her circumstances and told Freeg to end her life. Because she was holding Freeg's heart when she begged it of him, he was under her control and he had no choice but to comply with her plea. And so, unable to control himself, Freeg burned her to death with his fire. But dying in his fire as she held his heart, the heart transformed into an egg with a child inside, created from both the woman and the dragon. However, Visi predicted Freeg's grief and knew he would kill me. So she spirited the egg away to her lair at the top of the Inner Mountain." She stopped to take a pause as everyone stayed rapt with attention.

"I was born as a human from a dragon egg. I've been able to change between the two species my entire life. Visi raised me on the Inner Mountain and taught me how to control when I changed. Then when I was old enough and she deemed me prepared enough, she took me back to my dragon father, by then Rakgar feira Freeg, and introduced me to the ruck. But she had always told me he would try to kill me, so I lived in constant fear of him." Her eyes drifted to Owyn. "Except when I was with my friends.

"As I grew," she continued, "Visi had me trained as a noble."

"With Sar?" Philip said. "Or is Sar not real?"

"Yes, Sar was real," Anna's gazed shifted. "Visi taught me to tell as much truth as I could, especially to you." She looked directly at Philip, indicating he knew more than he realized.

"You were raised in the mountains," he said.

"The Rock Cloud mountains, not Torthoth like I said, but yes," she replied. "Although, I spent a good deal of time in the Torthoths, training with Sar, hunting…"

"Did you kill her?" Philip asked.

Anna couldn't meet his eyes. After a moment, she answered. "She would have ruined everything. I saw it for myself. The faeries would still be cursed. Most of the dragons would have died. The Noble Kingdom would be decimated, and the faeries would go on a rampage through the other human kingdoms. I only ever did what I had to do to prevent that outcome."

Owyn gently placed a hand on her shoulder as they all took a moment to mourn Sar.

After the silence, Torgon cleared his throat. "What about your sword training?" he asked, changing the grim subject. "I've seen your work. You fight like my father."

Anna grinned. "That's because he trained me."

Torgon's mouth fell open, but Anna shook her head. "Not like that. We watched in Visi's crystal ball the two of you practicing. Day after day, I mimicked you the best I could. I could never be your equal, but I was trained by the same man."

"That's a match I would pay to see," Brandell muttered at the edge of the fire.

"Where did you always disappear to?" Philip asked.

"I wouldn't mind knowing that one myself," Tog said.

Torgon and Owyn nodded emphatically.

"It varied," Anna said, chuckling. "When I disappeared from the castle, I was usually meeting with Visi or Hiro. Visi and I had to plan many things, but recently I left with Hiro when you all thought he had kidnapped me."

"Quite the struggle, I'll say," Owyn added.

"Or when I went to him for help with the wraith," Anna said.

"I knew it was a wraith," Addil smacked Darwick on the arm. "I told everyone, I…" he trailed off at the stares.

"So," Tog said, training one of his toggling eyes on Anna. "Whenever you disappeared from the Rock Clouds, were you in the Noble Kingdom?"

"Yes, and no," she said. "Over the past year that is only partially where I've been. Owyn, I told you I had been busy as well, remember? Well, I'd been visiting the other rucks, begging for their help and warning them of the dangers to come."

"The only reason they showed up," Surneen said from beside Tog.

Anna nodded. "I knew when and where to meet them. I had a rough guesstimate of what I could or should say. Even up to while you were fighting my father. I had to time everything perfectly."

"You have been busy," Owyn said admiringly. As she nodded, he thought back to the time in his dragon cave when she told him she was seeking allies. "Wait a second," he said when a thought occurred to him. "You yelled at me!"

Anna scrunched her eyebrows. "Which time?"

"In the cave," he said. "My cave. You yelled at me for loving a human! For loving you!"

"Ah," she answered, looking abashed.

"You did," Tog said. "Prak and I heard it. Sorry,… I mean, Rakgar."

"Yes, well," Anna hemmed. Her face grew pinker and her skin warmed. "You have to understand that Visi trained me well to think of myself as two very different beings."

"So, you were jealous?" Ashel asked.

"Of yourself?" Owyn added.

Anna shrugged. "In my defense, I knew that if you had fallen in love with me as a dragon, things would have gone a lot easier. I did *try* to get your heart to break for me as a dragon. But you always have to do things the hard way."

As the laughter drifted away, a different centaur trotted up to the group, someone no one had seen before nor recognized. While the other centaurs usually wore some kinds of weapons, leather adornments or decorations in their hair, he wore nothing. No decorations in his short, scruffy, brown hair. No weapons, armor or anything else strapped around his brown horse belly or brown human chest. The only thing he possessed was carried in one hand and turned just enough for the others not to see it.

Not quite as tall as her, he stepped beside Ashel. Ashel, clearly not recognizing him, stepped away hesitantly. He looked at her reaction, watched the others in the group for a moment, glanced down, then in a familiar, nasally voice said, "Well, I suppose this is yours."

He held out a small, smoky brown gem in the shape of a teardrop toward Ashel.

Ashel stared at the heart a moment, then met the centaur's eyes. "Prak?" she whispered.

After a moment of quiet contemplation, Ashel reached out and scooped the heart out of Prak's hand. She smiled and threw her arms around him again.

"Mitashio!" Prak said over Ashel's shoulder. "It would seem you might be Rakgar after all."

"Oh, spit," Owyn muttered. "It's contagious."

THE END

The next series by H.R.B. Collotzi...

PEOPLE OF THE STORM

Note to Readers!

I hope you are enjoying the adventure in Avonoa as much as I enjoyed creating it! Although I love to write and create these stories, being an independent author is hard. I don't have teams of people ghost-writing, editing, formatting and marketing for me. I do it all on my own, so my only support comes from readers like you! Thank you for supporting me and my craft.

Another way you can support a lowly indie author like myself is to leave me a review. Feel free to use the link above to let others know how much you enjoyed the story and you can pick up the next book at the same time! Enjoy the adventure!!

You can also sign up for my newsletter to be the first to hear about sales, signing events and new books! Sign up at avonoa.com, hrbcollotzi.com, or peopleofthestorm.com.

Or follow me on social media…
Facebook @hrbcollotzi
Instagram @hrbcolloti

PEOPLE OF THE STORM

In despair since losing her mother, will superhuman powers embolden her to fight the darkness?

Ella is trying to survive her depressing life by avoiding her life-of-the-freakin'-party aunt and cousin. She never imagined that finally submitting to one of her cousin's stupid outings could almost get her killed…or worse.

When Ella wakes in the hospital able to read minds, she prays that's the worst of it. But it turns out there's a whole obscure world of powered people like her, and they're intent on dragging her into their little underground war.

Now with dangerous people after her, she has to decide if there's anything in this life worth dying for…or possibly, worth fighting for.

Melt into a world of magical realism with the first in a duology of young adult urban fantasy novels by HRB Collotzi, The People of the Storm.

www.ingramcontent.com/pod-product-compliance
Lightning Source LLC
Chambersburg PA
CBHW030122010826
48973CB00002B/373